THE LOST BARINOV DRAGON

Brothers of Ash and Fire - Book 4

LAUREN SMITH

PROLOGUE

Excerpt from Barrow's Journal – My Year with Dragons

There are four types of skills that dragons can be born with or develop as they age. The first is the battle dragon, a dragon suited to fight and defend in territorial disputes. The second is the hoarding dragon, who is a guardian for the valuable gemstones and treasures that dragon families collect. The third is the family patriarch or matriarch. This dragon ensures the survival of the line of dragons by arranging matings, overseeing the running of territories, and protecting the interests of all dragons in their family. The last type of dragon is the questing dragon, a dragon so rare that only one in every two or three hundred years is born. This dragon quests for dragon heart stones, the gemstones that possess the ability to hold a dragon's soul and keep it safe, a mission so sacred that many questing dragons die at the claws of their enemies in their search for these stones.

. . .

SWITZERLAND, 1292 AD

Vasili Barinov dug his claws into the craggy rocks and ice as he scaled the mountainside. Despite the thick protection of his dragon scales, the cold temperature still sent a shudder through him.

Cannot stop . . . The thought pounded inside his head like a steady drum, over and over. He was close. He was certain.

How much farther, my heart? The thought came to him in a steady, clear feminine voice. His mate, Marina, was a little way below him, carefully following the path he forged, placing her clawed feet where his had been.

It's close, my love, very close, he answered through their mate bond. Not all dragon shifters had such a strong mental connection to their mates, but he and Marina were intensely bonded. They had grown up as children together and had known their whole lives that they were mates. That was even rarer. To find a true mate was not an easy thing; some lived thousands of years and never did.

Vasili's front left foot slipped, and he snarled, steam huffing from his long snout as he caught himself from falling.

Careful! Marina cautioned him.

He didn't reply but focused harder on the ascent. Every few steps he would pause, take the cold air deep into his cavernous lungs, and close his eyes. Only then did he hear the hum, the magic of the dragon heart stone. The stones were almost gone from the world now, many destroyed, others lost beyond recovery.

Vasili's purpose was to find and protect such stones, as well as the dragon souls contained within them. In the event that a human should become a dragon's mate, the stone could bond the human with a dragon soul inside. Such a thing was crucial for the survival of his race. When a dragon died, its mate would quickly follow. And since human lives were so brief and fragile, the dragon's life would be cut short.

He had lost one of his sister this way, when her human mate had fought and died in battle. Vasili had vowed never again to let anyone in his family die from the "mate grief" of having a mortal mate.

I sense it too, Vasili, Marina said in excitement.

He huffed and began to climb again. They were almost there. The hum became a murmur of voices. The dragon souls were singing; there was more than one soul inside the stone. Incredible! His heart swelled with pure joy at the thought of such a wonderful discovery.

A cave opening appeared a few feet above, and Vasili pushed his way inside. It was far larger than he had expected. Even in his massive dragon form, there was room for Marina to climb inside behind him.

He changed into his human form just as his mate slid into the cave behind him. They possessed enough dragon magic that they could change between human and dragon form and keep the clothes they wore. Many dragons never mastered such a skill.

Vasili waited for Marina to change, and then he held out his hand to her. The raven-haired beauty beamed in excitement as he pulled her close and kissed her temple. It had been a long and dangerous journey to get here and find the stone, but they had made it. Just beyond them, nestled in the ice, was the large sapphire that had called to him in his dreams: the Heart of Sorrows. As a questing dragon, he had the ability to sense dragon heart stones, gemstones that held dragon souls within them. He'd left his home and his family to find this stone, and now here it was, within reach. It glowed, and an ethereal light made it pulse like a beating blue heart.

"There is more than one, Marina," he whispered. "More than one soul inside the stone. Can you feel it?"

Her brown eyes widened. "Oh, Vasili . . ." She brushed away tears. "So many lives will be saved with it."

They walked to the wall of ice, and he placed his human palm on its surface. He summoned his dragon side, and the fire that filled his veins now reached out from his skin, melting the ice directly into steam. Soon he was able to free the stone.

He turned to his beloved mate. "We must hurry, love. Now that we have it, we can fly back to Novgorod."

Marina kissed his cheek. He nodded and brushed away the remaining ice that still clung to the sapphire before he slipped it into a pouch on his wrist. The straps were designed to stretch with him as his dragon form took over.

"I'll go first and clear the way in case we were followed." Marina morphed back into a dark-golden dragon and crawled to the cave entrance. She kept her tail straight and her wings folded as she approached the ledge, then took a breath and leapt into the air.

He watched her take to the sky. His lips curved into a smile, but a moment later, black shapes appeared on the horizon.

Black dragons . . . The Drakors had found them. Too many of them not to be a threat. Fear for his mate's safety exploded through him as he rushed toward the edge of the cave entrance.

Marina, they've found us. Go!

His mate didn't reply. She shot up into the air, vanishing above the clouds, no doubt attempting to draw them away. She was smaller and faster, and they would assume she had the stone in her possession.

Vasili began to change, but he wasn't fast enough. He saw his mate's view in his mind.

Black shapes filled the skies. Several of the enemy dragons burst up above the clouds, barreling toward Marina. She roared, the sound fierce and as loud as an earthquake shaking an entire continent. The walls of the cave vibrated around him, and cracks in the ice formed rapidly.

Wait for me! Do not fight them alone! He shouted the thought to his mate. Marina was a fierce battle dragon, but even she was no match for ten Drakors.

A shadow flashed across the cave entrance just as Vasili slid out and dropped into the air. Dimitri Drakor, the eldest son of the Drakor family's patriarch, was just above him, careening straight for Marina's back.

Vasili took flight and rocketed upward. He sank his teeth into Dimitri's flank, but Dimitri swung his tail toward Vasili. Vasili dodged the blow, but not quite enough.

Poisoned spikes raked his side, cutting through his thick hide. He roared in rage, releasing Dimitri as he fought the wave of pain that followed.

Don't fight them, Marina. Flee! he urged his mate as he cleared more clouds.

His heart shook as he saw his mate fighting off several dragons twice her size. He swooped toward them, claws out, striking at as many as he could, but everything that happened next was a blur straight from his deepest nightmares.

His mate fell from the sky, blood misting the air around her. A black dragon roared in triumph, its teeth stained red with blood. Pain exploded through Vasili as his mate's agony became his own. He tucked his wings against his body and plunged toward the ground, chasing her falling form, desperate to catch her before she hit the ground.

She crashed against the mountainside and came to a stop on the ledge just below the cave to the dragon heart stone.

Vasili gripped the mountainside, skidding down toward Marina, bloodying his clawed feet as they slipped along jagged rock. When he reached her, her breath was slow and shallow. Her throat had been torn, and she was losing precious blood. He keened softly and nuzzled her, huffing out short breaths in dread.

My heart, he murmured to her. *Don't give up. Try to heal . . . try . . .* Marina had a unique ability to heal herself and others. The magic in her blood was strong enough to work miracles. She was the last of her bloodline, and the drakeling children they had planned to have would have held that ability too, but a terrible fear whispered that she was beyond miracles now.

I can't . . . Vasili . . . too much. Hide the stone . . . Marina's voice in his head was weak, tired. His wings rippled to flatten against his back. Above them, the other dragons circled, waiting for them to die. The stone tucked against his leg burned hotter than a dragon's fire as he snuggled closer to Marina, desperate to let her feel him beside her in her last moments. The Heart of Sorrows pulsed, like a heartbeat, beating against his hide and Marina's. He prayed that her soul would find its way inside the sapphire, to be safe, but he had never performed the transition ritual before and didn't know what to do.

He let out a keening cry as his true mate's breath slowed, and then with a soft huff she was gone. His limbs gave out beneath him, and he curled his body around hers, their blood mixing in the snow.

Let me die swiftly, he thought. There was no reason to live without her. The mate grief began to overpower him.

A sudden burning pulsed against his front leg, making him hiss in rage. He shook himself to stop whatever was causing the sensation. The bundled sapphire bounced against his scales. The dragons circling above were slowly descending.

They cannot have it. Vasili nuzzled Marina's scaled cheek one last time before he tore himself away and climbed back up into the sheltered cave. His blood stained the icy rock floor as he dragged his injured body through the cave. Her death could not be in vain. He had to protect the Heart of Sorrows from the Drakors with his last breath.

He curled up against the farthest wall. His sharp reptilian eyes studied the cave walls and the fissures in the rocks. He knew what he had to do. Vasili took a final look toward the cave entrance, raised his snout, and inhaled the cold air that blew in from the mountain. It smelled of snow and blood . . . his mate's blood. The one blessing of dying from mate grief was that he would not have to live long in a world without her, would not have to think every day of the future that had been taken from them and the children they would never have. There would be an end, a quiet, dark, cold end to his pain. His only hope was that he would see Marina again on the other side, where the skies were endless and always under their wings.

He threw back his head and roared out all the pain and heartbreak. The mountain trembled around him, and rocks crashed down and sealed up the entrance with him inside. More rocks than any number of dragons could move, if they could even find the entrance.

Cloaked in the cold darkness, he relaxed. Dimitri Drakor and the others could not get to the stone now. He felt the pain of his wounds fade as the mate grief numbed him. At least his younger brother and his mate had three healthy, grown drakelings who could carry on the Barinov line. The Barinovs would continue to defend their land against the Drakors and protect the humans.

My time is ended.

With his last breath, the ice froze his body, and he felt

lost. The dragon heart stone's glow faded, its energy expiring. His last thought was that not all things lost *stayed* lost.

But he was glad that if he was found, he would be long gone from this mortal realm. To lose his mate, his other half, stole life itself from him. As the mountain's rumbling finally settled over the fitting tomb that served as his last resting place, the cave was silent, dark, and cold.

CHAPTER 1

Excerpt from Barrow's Journal – My Year with Dragons

There is perhaps no greater territorial dispute in all of dragondom than between the Russian Imperial dragons, the Barinov family and the Drakor family. The conflict began so many millennia ago that none seem to remember where it began, and it is unlikely to end. The greatest period of peace began when Grigori Barinov signed the renewal of a treaty I had the honor of witnessing. I believe this will lead to a golden age for dragons, or at least a time without war.

MORE THAN 700 YEARS LATER – NORTH CAROLINA

"You must always be safe. Never open the door without me, do you understand?"

The words she'd heard almost all of her life from her mother echoed in Tasha Bellamy's mind as she removed the lasagna from the oven. The kitchen was quiet; her mother was in her bedroom reading while Tasha checked on their dinner.

"Never open the door without me . . ." Tasha was twenty-one years old now, and she'd had to go to school online her entire life, even college.

Thankfully, she'd been advanced in all of her classes, and at twenty she'd graduated with a bachelor of arts in graphic design. It allowed her to work from home and take care of her mother.

The few times she'd ventured out into the world, usually to get things they couldn't have delivered to the house, Tasha had looked about her and wondered *why* it wasn't safe. What had created such fear in her mother? She didn't seem mentally unstable; it was just this single unexplainable fear of whatever was outside that door.

All of Tasha's life, the idea of safety had been a concern for her mother. And because of it, the two of them had lived a quiet life in remote locations or small towns well away from big cities. Once a year—*only* once—her father would come to see them.

Whenever the doorbell rang, she rushed to open it, despite her mother's warnings of waiting for her to be there just in case—though she never said in case of *what*. Tasha didn't care. She always seemed to know when her father was there; it was as though she could sense his presence, even through the door. So many times she'd dreamed about him, even though she knew he was far away. She would wake convinced that she had been with him while he traveled or sat alone in his office. It was like seeing him through a slightly foggy mirror. They were likely the imaginings of a child, but she hadn't cared—she'd wanted to feel connected to him, to be a part of the life that he couldn't share with her and her mother. It made her excitement to see him that much stronger when he finally came to visit.

"Tasha, my little one," he would say in that deep, rumbling voice, and she would hug him tight, never wanting to let go. Her father was a tall man, with dark hair and fathomless eyes that would have intimidated anyone except for the woman and the child who loved him.

Then, after he kissed her cheeks and hugged her tight, he would seal himself in a room alone with her mother for an hour, their whispers too muffled by the closed door to hear. Tasha would always try to eavesdrop by pressing her ear to the wood. More often than not, her father would open the door and find her standing there. He would arch one dark brow, but he never grew angry with her, never yelled. He simply placed his palm on her head, gently patting her hair, his dark eyes unreadable.

"You will listen to your mother, yes?" he always asked. "Do whatever she says?"

She would nod, and then her father would share dinner with them before leaving them with a briefcase of money and a little present just for Tasha. Small trinkets, stuffed animals, then books, then as she grew older he would leave her jewels. She had half a dozen necklaces of brilliantly colored gemstones. The stones were large and seemed almost too heavy to hang from the delicate chains they had been bound to.

"Cherish them, little one. Promise to protect them.

They are *very* valuable," her father would say about the gemstones.

"I'll keep them safe, Dad." It was important to him, and she knew that whatever it was that kept him away from them, it had to be important. She tried never to get upset that she was growing up without him in her life. That one single day a year was a day she clung to, a day she cherished.

Her time with her father always ended the same way each time. Her father would hold her close and whisper words in Russian she hadn't understood until she was older and had started learning the language. *"Be safe, be strong, be brave."* Then he would leave in the middle of the night and vanish into the darkness. All she would have left then to look forward to until his next visit were her dreams of him.

Now, as she set the lasagna on the stovetop, she stared at the calendar in the kitchen. Her gaze lost focus as she counted the days.

It had been *more* than a year since her father had last come. He'd never let so many days pass between his visits.

"Mom! Dinner's ready!" she shouted toward the back of the house.

When her mother came into the kitchen, she smiled as she saw the food. "Where you learned to cook, I'll never know. You didn't get it from me." Her mother came up to her and hugged her shoulders before she went to retrieve dishes and silverware for the table.

"You just follow a recipe. Besides, there's a lot of good videos online to walk you through it."

Tasha grew quiet a moment as she set the table with

her mother. It had been a few months since she'd dreamed of her father, and something about that bothered her. She'd never gone that long without having one of her dreams. They were silly, childish imaginings, she knew that, but she'd always clung to how *real* they felt. And the sudden halt to the dreams left her edgy in a way that made no sense.

"Mom . . ."

"Yes?" Her mother looked up at her, and Tasha had the strangest sense she was peering into a mirror of her future. Her mother was a beautiful russet-haired woman with soft brown eyes and a warm smile. Everything about her was warm and inviting and so at odds with the fears she carried about the world and the dangers in it. Tasha wanted to be like her mother, but not including her fear of the world outside.

"Dad hasn't come to see us. It's been more than a year."

Her mother froze as she placed a fork down on the table. "It . . . it's been more than a year?"

"Just by a few days, but he's never waited this long." Tasha didn't like the sudden pallor of her mother's face.

"I'm sure he has a reason . . ." Her mother resumed setting the table, but her hands trembled slightly. They'd both lost track of the days recently. Tasha had been busy designing websites for clients, and her mother was an accountant and busy working with her own clients.

"We should eat," her mother suggested.

Before they could sit down, there was a knock on the front door. Tasha and her mother both stilled.

Her mother looked relieved, but Tasha didn't sense her

father. She'd always been able to know he was there before. Now she sensed nothing.

"You see? He was just running late."

Despite her misgivings, she had to believe her mother was right. Tasha rushed to open the front door.

"Dad!" Her smile faded as she saw that the man who stood on their porch wasn't her father.

An elderly man in a funereal black suit held a closed umbrella, its silver pointed tip resting on the wooden floor of the porch. Tasha looked at the evening sky behind him. There wasn't a cloud to be seen. Did the man think it was going to rain tonight?

"Miss Bellamy, I presume? My name is Lionel Bovill. May I come in? Is your mother here?" He waited politely for her to answer his string of questions.

"Yes, come in. She's in the kitchen." Tasha stepped back and he entered, rolling a large suitcase behind him. Was the man planning to move in? The thought drifted across her mind a second before he spoke.

"Regretfully, I am here to inform you that your father has passed away. I am the attorney who was designated to be the executor of his estate."

Tasha stopped breathing. Her lungs constricted inward, squeezing out the last of her breath as she tried to process Mr. Bovill's words. Her father was dead. The dreams had stopped. Had she known somehow that he was gone? Was that even possible?

Her mother stood in the doorway to the kitchen, her eyes wide. "What?"

"Mrs. Bellamy?" The man directed the question at her mother.

"Yes?" her mother whispered.

"Very good . . ." The man cleared his throat and straightened his silver-rimmed glasses. Then he reached into his breast pocket, pulling out a letter-size envelope. "I have here the last will and testament of your husband. I apologize for the late hour of my arrival. My instructions were to come here only when it was dark out."

"How . . . ?" Her mother cleared her throat. "How did it happen?"

The man's face dipped slightly as he studied the floor. "It was a deliberate death, madam."

Her mother crumpled, and Tasha dashed over to her, catching her by the waist.

"Sit down, Mom." She pushed her mother gently into the nearest chair.

"I'm sorry for the shock this news causes. I wish there was an easier way to deliver it." Mr. Bovill removed the papers from the envelope. "I will read this brief document aloud. I've included a list of assets that have been passed to you both, as none of his other children survived."

At this, her mother's head shot up. "His sons are gone?"

Sons? She had brothers?

Had . . .

"Yes, all of his other children were killed. The extended family was killed as well. Only Miss Bellamy remains."

The man's words finally began to shatter the dazed confusion in Tasha's head.

"Killed? By whom?"

"The Barinovs," her mother said in a lifeless tone. She looked to the wizened attorney, who nodded his confirmation. "He always warned me that they would come after him. It's why he feared for our safety, Tasha."

"Who are the Barinovs?" Tasha's chest tightened with a strange pain. She couldn't breathe. There was no oxygen left in the room. She swayed and everything tilted wildly on its axis. This time it was her mother who steadied her and helped her to sit down.

The name *Barinov* echoed in her head over and over, like it was spoken through a tunnel. She knew she had heard that name in her dreams of her father, but she couldn't remember in what context.

"The Barinovs are a powerful family in Russia. They have been at war with your father's family since before you were born," her mother explained. "They are why we have been hiding all these years, why we have only been able to see him once a year. They would watch his movements, so he could only come to visit when he felt it was safe to see us."

"Dad had other children? Was he married to someone else?" Tasha was still dizzy, and a pounding headache was starting to beat against the backs of her eyes. Were these Barinovs some kind of Mafia? Her father was Russian and lived in Moscow. She had always wondered if maybe he had criminal ties. The suitcase of money he left them had always seemed shady. She'd just never let herself really think about it until now.

"He wasn't married. Those other children were from

several other women. He needed them to protect his family interests in Russia."

A bitter taste filled Tasha's mouth. Her father had slept around that much? How did that make her mother feel?

"You were special, Tasha. His only girl. He kept you away from the family and its business. He married me in secret, but I never took his name. Even that was too dangerous."

The elderly attorney cleared his throat. "I'm afraid I must finish this matter quickly. I must leave for another appointment." He then read the document in his hands, the last will and testament of her father.

The assets were many, and they all blurred together as Mr. Bovill read them.

"Naomi Bellamy is to have a trust provided for her—$19 million—and upon her death, the remaining funds will go to her child, Tasha. Tasha shall receive a trust in the amount of $970 million, as well as ownership of all properties listed in Schedule A attached to this document. She is to have an advance on her trust, to be provided in cash, of $1 million." The man tapped a finger on the suitcase. "Which I have brought you here."

Tasha stared at the suitcase, then looked on in shock as Mr. Bovill continued.

"This is your copy of the will. I will be in touch with the remaining paperwork so we may begin the transfer of real estate assets to your name. Now, I'm afraid I must take my leave."

Tasha was trembling as she accepted the paperwork from Mr. Bovill. A storm of pain was lashing against the walls of her heart as tears blurred her eyes, and she couldn't read the words of the document.

The old man opened the door and then popped open his umbrella.

"You don't need to—" Tasha began, but then she saw the rain. It was pouring from the skies in buckets. How had he known it was going to rain?

Her mother closed the door and faced Tasha.

Tasha stared at her mother, and for the first time she saw a stranger. This woman had always held secrets from her about her father, about his life, and now . . . now he was dead and she would never see him again. She would never have answers to the questions she had. Not from him.

Her hands shook, and she curled her fingers into fists to keep the flood of emotion contained.

Her mother's shoulders dropped, and she let out a sigh. "Tasha, it's time I told you about your father. It's time I told you the truth."

"What do you mean? Like how he was in the mob or something?" She'd suspected he was involved in something less than legal, given the money he was always leaving with them. Despite guessing that, she'd loved her father, loved every minute of the few precious days he'd been in her life and how he'd cared for her.

Her mother joined her on the couch and reached up to stroke her hair away from her face. "No, honey, he wasn't in the mob."

"But—"

"Just listen. Your father . . . wasn't fully human. He was a dragon."

Tasha laughed. "Mom, that's not funny. I want you to tell me the truth."

"I am." Her mother squeezed her hands hard to get her attention. "Listen to me, Tasha. Your father, Dimitri Drakor, was a dragon shifter. A supernatural being more than three thousand years old . . ."

FOUR YEARS LATER – SWITZERLAND

Tasha Bellamy stared up at the peaks of the Swiss Alps. Wetterhorn, Schreckhorn, Mönch, and Jungfrau all reached up to the skies in glorious majesty. They towered like sleepy earth gods over the town of Grindelwald. Evening began to fall, bathing the peaks in *alpenglühen*, the alpenglow where the setting sun turned the mountains pink. She had arrived two days ago to free herself of worries on the slopes. For the last four years, she had been in a strange sort of melancholy. Ever since she'd learned of her father's death, things hadn't been the same. Only now was she trying to jolt herself out of the sadness his death had caused. For the first few years after he'd died, she'd buried herself in her web design work. But now she was desperate for open skies and views of the world she'd never seen before except in books and movies.

She closed her eyes for a brief moment, taking in a deep breath of clean mountain air. Her mother had insisted she stay in the United States and see the Grand Canyon or something closer, safer. If she'd had her way, Tasha would never leave the house.

Tasha had spent her whole life being "safe," and she was done with it.

She was the daughter of Dimitri Drakor, a dragon shapeshifter. A man who had been more than three thousand years old. The sons the attorney had mentioned had been children he'd fathered by mating briefly with dragonesses, female dragon shifters, to create a stable group of dragons who could protect his territory from his enemies, especially the Barinovs.

Tasha's mother, however, was completely human. She had been Dimitri's only true romantic partner, the one he had chosen to marry in secret. So Tasha was technically half dragon. She had asked if she could change into a dragon, but her mother had shaken her head and explained that most human-dragon pairings could not produce a drakeling. Her father had sensed she had no dragon within her, and he had done all he could to protect her from the dangers of his world by keeping her and her mother safely hidden away.

Now she was out in the world traveling, seeing places she had always longed to visit and doing things she'd only ever dared to dream before. Tasha was certain that her father's enemies, the Barinovs, wouldn't come after her. She was a human female; she had no place in their world and was no threat to them. Her mother didn't believe that, but Tasha didn't care any longer. She felt she was safe, and she wasn't going to hide for the rest of her life.

Life was too short to stay inside and hide. If she was

going to die, she wanted to *live* first. After spending a month in England and then a month in France, touring the bigger cities and the countryside, she had just arrived two days ago in Switzerland to see the Alps. And it had been worth the tricky travel plans to get to her hotel and then to the mountains for skiing.

She tilted her head back, staring up at the terrifying cliff face of what the locals called "the death wall." Back in 2006, the ice caps on the mountain had melted and sent rocks and snow crashing down the mountainside, almost crushing the town of Grindelwald. The little town had escaped disaster by a hair's breadth.

The old Tasha would have trembled at the thought of skiing next to a mountain like that, but after she'd learned the truth, a lot of things held a lot less fear for her. The things that scared her now were the dragons themselves, but according to her mother they were dying out, unable to find mates or adapt to the modern world. The old magic, the magic that had helped give birth to dragons, was vanishing.

Tasha didn't know what that kind of magic was, but this world, with its Alpine glowing sunsets, was all the magic she needed.

She followed the other skiers up in the gondolas toward the slopes and held her poles tight in her hands. She'd spent the last two days on the bunny slopes with a private instructor, and he'd said she was a natural. She did like going fast, flying down the slopes. It was as close to truly flying as she imagined it could be.

Now she was ready to face the steeper hills, even a few

moguls. The ski lift dropped her off, and she saw signs for night skiing pointing toward a trail that led to the far side of the mountain. She might try that one run in the evening before it got too dark. The slopes of the Eiger were already illuminated with floodlights, and she used her poles to guide herself toward the first snow-covered slope.

She felt a strange tingling sensation at the back of her mind and paused. It felt like something had fluttered. The sensation was so faint, Tasha thought she must be imagining it, but as she turned away from the slope and stared up at the mountain, it grew stronger, like a butterfly was inside her head, batting its soft wings against the prison of her skull, trying to get free.

A moment later, the mountain groaned. The rocks around her shook like an old dog waking from sleep and shaking its body to rid itself of a dusting of snow. Her eyes drifted up in mute shock as she saw the shelf of snow far above her breaking off . . . tumbling down . . . and crashing into more snow, creating a tidal wave of deadly white froth.

Avalanche.

Everything happened so fast. People started to run and scream and kick off their skis. But all she saw was the snow barreling toward her, and it rooted her in place.

Then, everything seemed to explode around her like a fierce snowstorm rather than a deadly wave of hard snow and rock. The storm raced past her, knocking her on her back and winding her, but she was otherwise fine. Her skis slid down the slope, far out of reach. She lay on her back, feeling the snow swirling around her.

A man's voice echoed through the storm. "This way!" She lifted her head, seeking the source of it.

A shadowy figure was waving at her, but she couldn't make out any of his features. She scrambled to her feet, struggling to wade through the thick snow in her ski boots. She hurried up the slight incline where the man had stood, but he seemed to be walking away from her.

"Wait! I'm coming!" She didn't want to be left alone in this weather—such strange weather, too. Was an avalanche supposed to do that? Explode into a snowstorm? Had it even been an avalanche at all? She kept trudging through the powdery snow until it gave way to icy rock.

What the hell? She glanced about. The man she had chased after was gone, and somehow she had made it to the rocky side of the Eiger. She had gotten turned about and climbed toward the mountain when she should have been moving away from it. She turned around, but all she saw now was snow blowing in a cloud over her. If she walked away from the mountain and into that storm, she could get lost and die.

She leaned back against the rock behind her, shivering as the temperature continued to drop.

"Help!" she screamed, but her cry was swallowed by the dense snowstorm.

She closed her eyes, filled with an unexplainable anger, anger at being trapped here and dying just when she had finally started to live. This time when she screamed for help, the sound came from somewhere deep within her, a place she'd never been aware of.

The mountain rumbled, the stone behind her crumbling away so that she fell backward. Tasha barreled down a tunnel of ice and rock, banging her head and cracking her ski goggles. She landed on the ground with a hard, pained grunt. When she was finally able to sit up, she removed her gloves and tossed the broken goggles aside, then touched tentative fingertips to her forehead. She hissed in pain.

Tasha glanced around, trying to get a sense of where she had fallen. A distant light came from the hole above where she had tumbled through and reflected off the icy walls, giving her some light to see by. It was a cave inside the mountain. Spears of ice hung from the ceiling, and a faint scent that smelled wonderful teased her nose. It smelled familiar, but she couldn't place why.

"Oh my God . . ." Little clouds puffed out as she whispered in awe. She put her gloves back on before her fingers froze and got up, hobbling awkwardly in her ski boots. The click of her steps echoed all around her. The chamber was vast, and as it continued on, less light illuminated it, until it faded into an inky darkness. Her rational brain screamed at her to stay right where she was and not wander deeper into the tunnel, but some invisible force *pulled* her forward.

That tingling started up inside her head again, and something flashed across her mind: *Clouds. Cold sunlight. Fear. Pain. Falling.*

She braced a hand on the cave wall, struggling to breathe as terror and pain ripped through her.

What the hell was that? It felt as though she had been somewhere else, like she had been falling from the sky.

Tasha moved deeper into the back of the cave, but she skidded to a stop as something glowed in the dark. A soft blue hue pulsated on the ground next to a large pile of black rocks. There was no ice or snow near the glow, just rock. Her body moved of its own accord as she fell under the spell of the glow. She had to have it, had to reach out and take it into her hands and guard it. The desire was overwhelming, to the point that her mind's eye saw only one thing—the object she must have at any cost.

She stopped a few inches from the glow, removed her right glove, and bent to pick up a pouch that half hid the object giving off the light. It was a stone. As big as an apple. As she peeled away the ragged cloth, her bloody fingertips caressed the surface of the sapphire, and heat seared her flesh. She tried to drop the stone, but it had fused to her skin like superglue and continued to burn. She screamed in pain and doubled over.

Thump thump—thump thump.

Something was pounding her chest, crushing against her heart and lungs. If it didn't stop, she would die.

"H-help . . . ," she wheezed, even though no one would hear her. She was going to die, and her mother would never know what had happened to her.

Thump thump—thump thump.

A large pile of black rocks crumbled beside her, revealing something nearly as large, but not made of stone. Tasha stared at the black thing that lay against the back wall of the cave as she tried to force herself to breathe. It looked like . . .

Scales, not rocks. What she could see resembled the pointed end of a large tail, curled around a snout with a closed eye.

A dragon. She had stumbled upon a dragon. One who'd clearly died in this cave, like she was going to.

Thump thump—thump thump.

She should run, try to flee back up the tunnel she had fallen through, but as the heat of the stone seeped into her, it compelled her to move toward the dragon. She fell to her knees by the head of the dragon and placed the stone down by its throat. Too exhausted to do more, she leaned against the frozen dragon and stroked a hand down its scaled hide.

Now she was able to let go of the stone (or did it let go of her?), and she placed her bare hand on the tip of the dragon's snout, stroking it. There was something pitiful and sorrowful about it. She thought dragons were supposed to be frightening, but this beast in front of her was beautiful, tragically beautiful.

As she studied the dragon, she began to understand what the other half of her father's life had been like. It was one thing to hear her mother speak of dragons, but to see one herself? It was beyond all her fairy-tale imaginings.

The dragon was both beautiful and terrifying all at once. He looked fierce, yet his snout was elegant, and his claws and tail all painted a portrait of something ancient and noble.

"How did you end up here?" she wondered aloud.

Thump thump—thump thump.

The beating against her chest was stronger now, but it hurt far less. She breathed through the pain. It felt more important to be here with this dragon, and she focused on the creature before her instead of the pain inside her.

"Who were you?" she whispered. The dragon had to

have been there a very long time. She examined it, noting the frill that lay flat against its neck, and then a splash of dark black on the ice by its belly caught her eye. It looked like dried blood. Her mother had told her that all dragons in the world were dragon shifters, so whoever this was had been human too, after a fashion.

Thump thump—thump thump.

She put a hand to her chest, unable to stop a groan of pain. The stress of almost dying might've been enough to give her a heart attack.

Tasha examined the dragon's stomach, or at least the side of it. Deep gashes covered the beautiful black scales and the amber-colored hide of its underbelly. Something terrible had hurt this dragon, had wounded it enough to kill it.

Overcome with exhaustion, she lay back against the dragon and closed her eyes. The heavy blue stone still generated heat, and she kept her hold on it as she tried to rest long enough to think about how to find a way out of here. Her parents had wanted to keep her away from dragons, but now here she was, dying with one.

"It's just you and me, buddy." She patted the frozen body of the dragon. "You, me, and a really weird glowing stone." She tilted her head back as the cold stole over her limbs again.

Thump thump—thump thump—thump thump—thump thump.

This time, the beat came not from her own body but from behind her. Tasha's eyes flew open, and she scrambled away from the dragon as it shook. The cave walls rumbled as a great rush of warm air puffed out of the dragon's nostrils.

"Holy sh—"

Her words were cut off as the dragon's eye cracked open, its golden iris gleaming in the dark, and a vertical catlike slit widened and then shrank again.

Fear and awe ricocheted through her. The eye focused on her, and her stomach plummeted as the iciness of the cavern melted away with a fresh heat.

She knew two things for certain: she would never be the same again, and this dragon was *not* dead.

CHAPTER 2

E*xcerpt from Barrow's Journal – My Year with Dragons*

Like many creatures in the animal kingdom, dragons mate for life. There are possible true mates, which provide dragons with a bond so deep that the dragons can hear each other's thoughts, sense each other's feelings, and sometimes see what their mate can as though viewing it from their eyes. But this bond has its dangers. If one of the dragons in a true-mated pair dies, the other suffers from mate grief, an emotional response so strong that the remaining dragon dies shortly after its mate. It is the curse of dragonkind to have such a weakness.

MADELYN LEANED AGAINST THE BANISTER AT THE TOP OF the stairs in her palatial home in the wilds of Russia.

"Grigori, come put Jackson to bed!"

After four years, she was still getting used to living in

such a massive house, with crown molding on the ceilings, gilded furniture, and priceless works of art hanging on the walls. It felt like a museum at times, but a comfortable one that she could live in.

"Grigori!" she shouted again. "Your son. Bed. Now!" She knew he could hear her. She'd used her "mom" voice, with a bit of her own thunderbird voice thrown in, something she had learned could travel very, *very* far.

The door opened at the end of the hall, and Grigori stepped out. She had not realized he was so close.

"Oh, I'm sorry. I thought you were downstairs with Rurik and Mikhail." She had last seen her husband and his two younger brothers having a drink in his study. It made her heart swell to see all three of them talking together. The last few years, they'd been separated across the globe: Mikhail in England, Rurik in Michigan, and Grigori here in Russia. This was the first time in the past year that all three brothers, their wives, and now their drakelings were under one roof. It was wonderful.

Madelyn smiled as her husband sauntered up to her in his sexy way. He still wore a three-piece gray suit because he'd had virtual meetings with his offices in Moscow most of the day. It reminded her of the first time she'd met him. He'd almost stalked her like a dragon hunting its prey, and she loved being the focus of his intense interest, like she was right now.

"Jackson needs tucking in, does he?" Grigori's hands went to her hips, holding her still as he leaned in to kiss her. He inhaled her scent and groaned softly. "I never tire of your delicious smell, wife." He nuzzled her throat, and

Madelyn responded with weak-kneed desire. "It makes me want to devour you over and over."

That brought back wonderfully erotic memories of when he'd threatened to eat her because she had been a virgin . . . and the way he'd eaten her out. She'd nearly died from pleasure.

"Keep doing that and Jackson will have a sibling," she warned.

Her husband chuckled and gently bit the lobe of her ear. "Perhaps that is *exactly* what I want. Another little drakeling to run about the house." He squeezed her bottom, and she melted into his arms to deliver a much deeper kiss.

"Hmm . . . I'm not opposed to that either," Madelyn whispered. "Let's go tuck our son in, and then we can find a quiet room with a bed and work on giving him a sister."

Grigori growled in approval, his dragon rising to the surface and causing his eyes to swirl with gold.

A little boy's voice piped up from down the hall. "Eww . . ."

Madelyn and Grigori stiffened and turned to see their son standing in the doorway to his bedroom.

"Jackson." They sighed and tried not to laugh.

"Dad, will you tell me a story?" the boy asked.

Grigori scooped him up and carried him toward the child-size four-poster bed. It was a grand piece of furniture, but the grandeur was slightly offset by the brightly colored superhero sheets. Jackson adored all things superhero. Grigori grumbled all the time about how the boy should have dragon sheets since he was a dragon shifter.

Madelyn reminded Grigori that Jackson might also be a thunderbird. He'd sneezed last week and knocked his father and two uncles flat on the front lawn. If Jackson turned out to be a thunderbird like her, he would be a natural enemy of dragons (at least those who meant his family harm), and if he was able to transform, he could flap his wings and create a sonic boom that would knock any nearby dragons unconscious.

Madelyn, being the last of her kind, secretly hoped for Jackson to at least be *partly* thunderbird. She still had plenty of years to have drakelings; she just wanted *one* child to be like her. It wasn't easy knowing she was the only one of her kind left because dragons like Grigori's father had hunted her people down.

Grigori plopped Jackson into the bed and tucked him in, then sat down on the edge. Madelyn took the other side of the bed and brushed a hand over Jackson's blond hair.

"What story do you want me to read? We have . . ." Grigori reached for the top book on the stack on the nightstand. "Harry Potter? You love him." Grigori flipped through the pages, searching for a bookmarked spot to pick up where they'd last left off.

There was nothing more attractive to her than seeing her fierce, dangerous, sexy husband paging through a book about a boy wizard and gazing fondly at their son. Maybe it was time to work on another drakeling.

Jackson was four in human years, yet he had aged quicker mentally. His verbal communication skills were more like those of an eight-year-old.

"Not tonight. Tell me about the lost Barinov dragon."

Grigori laughed. "But I thought you wanted to finish *The Half-Blood Prince?*"

"I know." Jackson glanced down sheepishly, his tiny fingers playing with the bedsheets. "But the lost Barinov is my favorite story."

"Very well, but you know I'm dying to know if Harry finds Sirius Black or not." Grigori made a show of settling in, removing his suit coat and rolling up the sleeves of his white dress shirt. Madelyn noted his muscled forearms and made herself a promise that later tonight she'd drag her husband to the nearest bed and enjoy all the things those arms could do.

"Once upon a time, there were two brothers. The brothers Barinov. Vasili, the elder, and Ivan, the younger. Vasili was a questing dragon, and Ivan was a hoarding dragon, the guardian who protected their treasures. The two brothers were close, like I am with your uncles. They loved each other fiercely and always protected each other. But the day came when it was time for Vasili to hunt for a dragon heart stone called the Heart of Sorrows. It was a sapphire the size of an apple, and it was said that the stone held the souls of ancient dragons."

"Ancient dragons?" Jackson murmured in wonder, his blue eyes bright with excitement.

"Yes." Grigori chuckled. "The *most* ancient. Some of them possessed powers we do not. They were said to be able to control the elements, and some could even see the future."

"Tell me about Vasili's mate," Jackson prompted, keeping his father on track.

"Marina was a powerful battle dragon, the last in a line of ancient dragons who could control the elements. Much like your mother, she could make it rain or storm when she was upset, or even make the mountains rumble when she was angry. When she went to war against her enemies, she was almost unbeatable."

"Tell me about the mountain," Jackson said.

"She accompanied Vasili to a land far away with snow-capped mountains to find the Heart of Sorrows. They knew that if they could find the dragon heart stone, many lives would be saved. A new age of cooperation between the dragon clans might have been possible. But there were some dragons who didn't want them to succeed. It was said that a great army was sent out to stop them, but if that is true, none of them are known to have returned. She and Vasili were never seen again."

Madelyn heard the pain in Grigori's voice that he could barely hide from their son. He had been close to his uncle, as had Rurik and Mikhail and losing him had hurt all three brothers deeply.

"But Vasili is not really gone," Jackson said.

Grigori gave his son a little pat on the shoulder. "I am afraid he is. He and his mate died a long time ago."

"But he didn't die—he was *lost*," the little boy said with solemnity.

"Yes, but—" Grigori started to say.

"But he's not lost anymore, Dad. *She* found him," Jackson said.

Grigori looked toward Madelyn helplessly. Trying to

explain death to a child was not easy. Neither of them really knew what to do.

Jackson yawned. "You'll see. She'll bring him home."

"Who is she?" Madelyn asked her son. "Do you mean his mate?" A breeze rippled along her skin, but none of the windows were open.

Her son nodded.

"I'm sorry, Jack," Grigori said. "She died too."

"She did, but she came back for him," the little boy said, as though it was so easy to understand.

"Okay, I think you have had too many of Dad's stories tonight." Madelyn stroked a hand through the little boy's hair. "Now go to sleep." She kissed him, and Grigori did the same before they turned off the lights and stepped into the hallway.

"Why was he talking about Vasili's mate?" Madelyn asked.

"I don't know. Children often try to change the parts of stories they do not like. I think it's why he likes super-heroes so much. They always save the day." Grigori put an arm around Madelyn's waist as they walked down the hall, but he paused at the top of the staircase.

"When did you first tell him about Vasili?" Grigori asked her.

"Me? I haven't. I thought you had been telling him the tale for a while."

Grigori shook his head. "I never told him the story until tonight."

"Never? But he said it was his favorite. *Someone* had to

have told him." Madelyn pursed her lips in thought. "Could it have been Rurik or Mikhail?"

"Why don't we ask them?"

Madelyn nodded. She'd had a strange feeling all day, like she had perceived a shift in the wind, perhaps even the earth. Something had changed, but she did not know what, and now their son was acting strangely. It could just be the fantasies of a small child, or it could be something else. They were beings of magic, after all.

She and Grigori found his brothers still in the study, talking and sipping cognac. Rurik, the powerful battle dragon, and Mikhail, the brooding hoarding dragon, were relaxed and smiling.

Mikhail saw Grigori's and Madelyn's worried expressions first. "Brother, what is the matter?"

"Did either of you tell Jackson the story about Vasili and the Heart of Sorrows?"

Mikhail and Rurik exchanged looks and shook their heads.

That feeling of something having changed now intensified. "Then how did he know about it?" Suddenly her stomach cramped, and she bent over to clutch at her midsection as she nearly threw up.

"Madelyn!" Grigori gently helped her to a chair. The three dragon brothers gathered protectively around her.

"Grigori . . . It's like when we first met. It's like I'm near dragons . . . or sensing them."

She could not easily explain it. The first time she had been around Grigori, his being her future mate had canceled out her thunderbird's natural instinctive response to his being her enemy. But his brother Rurik had not been her mate, and the thunderbird side of her had reacted in a similar way. But she had long since ceased to see the brothers as a threat, at least on a primal level.

Grigori knelt in front of her. "Are you feeling sick?"

"It's like . . ." Madelyn was too afraid to say the words, because they sounded crazy. They did not quite make sense, even to her. "I sensed a dragon, a powerful one, maybe more than one, being born. Or coming into existence?" She closed her eyes as images flashed across her mind, the thunderbird inside trying to communicate with her.

She saw icy-cold caves and smelled the scent of dragon upon the breeze. The scent was laced with pain, grief, and death. It was a scent both old and new. She opened her eyes to stare at the three Barinov brothers.

"What once was lost has been found." She swallowed and spoke the name to make them understand. "Vasili. The lost Barinov dragon . . . has been found."

SHE'D WOKEN A SLEEPING DRAGON.

"Oh my God . . ." Tasha scrambled backward, trying to put as much distance between her and the waking dragon as possible.

This wasn't good. This was very, very bad. If he woke up, a lot of very dangerous things could happen. He could bring the entire mountain crumbling down around them or . . . he might be hungry. Did dragons eat people? She'd never thought to ask, but hopefully not. They were people too, after all—right?

But this dragon had been here God knew how long. Maybe he was like a grizzly bear waking up from hibernation, grumpy with an empty stomach. Maybe this one was vegan?

"Nice dragon . . . easy . . ." Her voice shook as she watched the dragon stretch its scaled limbs, extending black taloned claws into the rock, scraping and gouging as the beast shook its head. It reminded her of a dog that had just woken from a nap, much like the mountain had.

Its frill unfurled, and it widened its jaws, yawning. Then it released a cry of pain, its sharp shriek deafening. Tasha threw her hands up over her ears and closed her eyes. Then the sound changed, turned softer, hoarser. She opened her eyes, and her heartbeat came to a stop.

The dragon was gone. In its place lay a human man wearing slightly loose brown leather trousers. He was face-down, and his muscled form shook as he slowly rolled onto his back. Now she could see the wound more clearly along his side. It had healed and mottled into a dark scar. He breathed hard, slow, each inhalation drawing her a step closer to him until she was within two feet.

Tasha stared down at him. The man was massive, at least six foot four and broad-shouldered, every inch of him a physical manifestation of strength. He was gorgeous too. His face was a series of angles and hard lines, yet it all came together in a way that would have made the angels weep. Older scars stretched across his stomach, and there were a few more along his arms, similar to the fresh wound on his side but not so deep. His eyes were closed, his long dark lashes resting against his cheeks.

"Hey . . ." She hoped not to frighten him.

His eyes shot open, and she shrieked as he swung an arm out, sweeping it across the backs of her legs. She fell on her backside, and he leapt onto her, snarling, eyes glowing. The slitted dragon pupils were gone, and instead a pair of stormy blue eyes gazed back at her, storms cut by golden swirls. His weight nearly crushed her as he roared. The sound wasn't quite human. Blind rage was carved into his features.

"Please, I'm sorry . . ." She wasn't sure what she was apologizing for, but the pain and anger within him reached out to her. Such loss, such overpowering grief turned into fury because it had nowhere else to go.

Whatever this man—this *dragon*—had lost, it had been everything to him. She felt a need to soothe him, to calm him. She reached up and placed a tender palm on his jaw.

He flinched but did not pull away. His roar died faded and he sagged against her, then slumped over and fell on his side. He shuddered, his gaze locked on hers as they both lay on the floor of the cave. Tears began to stream down his face, but he made no sound. He simply quaked, like tectonic plates cracking apart.

"I'm sorry," she whispered and kept her palm on his cheek, hoping that her touch helped ease his pain. His tears slowed and the shuddering eased to a stop. Her heart ached as she watched this stranger in such pain. It was as though his pain hurt her too.

He spoke rough words in Russian, and she was thankful she understood him.

"Marina, my love, Marina . . . I thought you had left me." His eyes rolled back into his head as he sank into unconsciousness.

Vasili wished he were dead.

Perhaps he was and this was some private hell for dragons who allowed their mates to die but could not follow them into the next life.

That was the only explanation he could think of as he woke in the cave for the second time. His left side burned where Dimitri had slashed him, but that pain paled in comparison to the pain he'd felt drawing breath while his mate lay dead at the foot of the mountain. Touching the place where he expected to feel blood, his fingers numbly bumped into thick scar tissue, tissue that would fade over the next few hours into a thin, pale scar. His thoughts were jumbled at first, a chaotic dark swarm that left him confused. The last thing he remembered was the rockslide that had blocked his exit and kept the Drakor dragons out. At least the stone was safe.

The stone—

He struggled to sit up, ignoring the protests of his stiff body. He glanced about the dark cave and spotted the stone, glowing in the gloom.

"You're awake," a soft voice said, echoing off the walls. He turned to find a woman pressed flat against the wall farthest from him. Her body was clothed in a strange puffy black garment that covered her from the neck down to her feet. Her feet were covered by strange boots that looked as hard as armor.

"Who . . . Who are you?" he asked. His voice felt like grinding rocks, each word causing pain as they came out.

"Tasha. Tasha Bellamy." Her voice, on the other hand, caressed his ears and made his body flood with warmth.

"Tasha," he murmured. It was a good name. Her eyes were a warm shade, the color of topaz stones. Among all of the jewels he had hoarded over the years, topaz had always been his favorite. Her hair, a soft russet, hung down in damp tendrils around her face.

"Who are you?" Tasha asked. "And who is Marina?" Her Russian accent was good, but her words were hesitant, as though she wasn't used to speaking the language.

"Marina was my . . ." He halted before he said the word *mate*. This human woman would not know what that meant. "She was my wife . . . and she died."

"I'm so sorry." The woman's voice was full of compassion.

"It was not your fault," he said. "But I wish to speak no more about it."

He climbed to his feet and examined his side. It was healing, but slowly. He needed to rest and find some food. "I need sustenance."

"Sustenance?" She said the word in Russian haltingly, as though she did not understand him.

"Food," he tried again.

"Food." She nodded. She dug around in the puffy garment she wore and held something out to him.

He came toward her and took the rectangular object from her. It crinkled a little as his fingers closed around it.

"What is this?"

"Food. A protein bar," she said. "I doubt it will be enough, since I'm not sure we'll find a way out of here. The tunnel is high up and narrow, plus it's really slick and I couldn't get a decent foothold to climb out."

In another life he would have laughed, but laughter would never come to him again. Fortunately, he wasn't likely to live long enough to miss it.

"This is not food," he said, handing the strange object back to her. "And we will not die in here. I will get us out." He didn't care if he stayed in here, but if he had but a handful of days left to live, he could do some good for others, like helping this poor human out of here.

To his surprise, she then tore the shiny thing open, exposing something soft and brown beneath the reflective surface. He raised it to his nose, inhaling. It smelled like food, but it also smelled off somehow.

"Just try it," she said, slowly getting to her feet.

He peeled a bit more of the shiny wrapping away before taking a bite of the thing. It tasted like dust and grain. He swallowed, his throat dry. He did not have time for this. He needed meat and a stout beer in a large tankard. It occurred to him then that he must have fallen into a deep sleep after he was wounded. The cold, the loss of Marina, and his wounds combined had sent him into hibernation.

He handed her the food back. "You are small and female. You eat first. I can last a little longer until we get out of here. Wait here. I will return." He began to follow the source of the moonlight up a tunnel. He transformed his hands enough to claw at the ice and drag his body up several feet. The opening was large enough for them to both climb out, and the tunnel was sturdy enough to support their weight. He returned to where she waited.

"We will go now."

"Go? How? I can't climb out of here. I tried."

He sighed. "Yes, your human hands are not suited to the task." He retrieved the dragon heart stone and handed it to her. "Secure this to your body; the straps will stretch to fit you. Then put your arms around my neck. I will get us out of here."

She wrapped the stone and its pouch around her chest, then came up cautiously behind him. Normally a stranger coming up behind him would put him on alert, but there was something soothing about her, something that calmed his dragon.

Her arms curled around his neck. "Am I choking you?"

"No, little one." His human body was almost as resilient as his dragon body. He dug his clawed hands into the ice tunnel and began to climb. Tasha's legs locked around his hips, and the feel of it was good. He had to shake off the image of her sliding around to his front so she could rub her body along his and he could—

Vasili slammed the door in his mind against such thoughts. Marina was his mate . . . and she was gone. This woman, even though she did not look like Marina, strangely reminded him of her. What was a mated dragon to do when his mate was dead? He had never heard of a dragon surviving mate grief before. Some lasted a few days at most, but in the end, they always died.

The dragon inside him was a separate being, a creature all its own. What did it feel now? The grief and pain of losing Marina had been excruciating. He remembered waking, howling, attacking this woman Tasha and pinning her down. Then the grief had overwhelmed him again. He must have passed out.

Now his dragon was quiet. He could actually picture the beast in his mind quite clearly. It was still there in his head, but curled up protectively, as though it was guarding a hoard of jewels. But if it was protecting something, what was it?

He tried to coax his dragon into answering his question, but the dragon bared its teeth in warning. That was unexpected. He and his dragon had always been close, closer than most mortals who carried dragon souls within them.

The woman on his back had been silent so far during the long climb up, so Vasili spoke to her. "You know what I am, yet you are not afraid of me."

Her warm breath escaped in a soft exhalation against the back of his neck, and his dragon lifted its head, a rumbling purr of reptilian contentment escaping it. Vasili was confused more than ever by his dragon's reaction to this mortal woman.

"I know what you are. I was a little afraid at first, but then you changed into a man, and you aren't so frightening now. You are just—" She cut off whatever she had been about to say.

"I am what?" he asked.

"You are . . . well . . . this gorgeous hunk. That's also a little intimidating, but in a different way." She said the word *hunk*, and he did not understand her meaning. This seemed to confirm that Russian was not her first language.

"Hunk?" He couldn't help but wonder if he was causing her some kind of pain.

"Oh, you're probably too old to know that word. How long were you in that cave?"

They had reached the spot where she had fallen through the ice. "I am not sure. What year is it?" His head cleared the snowy tunnel entrance, and his eyes swept over the valley below.

The world as he remembered it was suddenly ripped away from him. It was night, yet the valley sparkled with an impossible amount of light. It bloomed all over on the snowy slopes just below them. The trees were on fire. His panic halted, however, when he noticed the fires weren't spreading. They were staying still in white orb shapes and not growing larger.

"It's 2022." Tasha slid off his body and dropped down into the snow beside him, her gaze slowly shifting between him and the village below.

"2022 . . ." He repeated the year, his mind numb with shock.

Tasha placed a hand on his bare shoulder. The dragon tattoo on his left pectoral moved, rippling in response to her touch.

"When did you go to sleep?" she asked.

"Time was hard to measure then . . . but it was perhaps 1292."

"What?" Tasha gasped. "But that is . . . more than seven hundred years!"

He had been around two thousand and five hundred years old. Now it was seven centuries later. He was three thousand and two hundred years old. He had imagined it had been a few months, perhaps years, but no more. He had lost centuries in a deathlike sleep. That mountain cave should have been his tomb. He struggled to breathe as the reality of it all set in and fresh panic overtook him.

"Hey . . . just breathe, okay?" She waited while he got his breathing back under control. "You never told me your name."

He stared at the village below that was full of strange lights. "I am Vasili."

Tasha pulled her hand away from him as though he had burned her. He turned and saw her eyes wide with confusion.

"Vasili?" she repeated. "I feel like I know that name. How would I know that?"

"Are you Russian?" The Barinovs were well known among the Russian people who lived near their territory, but he was a long way from his homeland.

"No, I'm American, but my father was Russian."

She bit her bottom lip in frustration, and Vasili sighed. He turned his focus back toward the village. He did not know what *American* meant. He added it to the growing list of questions he would ask her later.

"Has the world changed much in the last seven hundred years?"

"Yes. More than you will likely understand," she warned him. "The technology has advanced."

"*Technology*." He rolled the funny word over on his tongue. "What is technology, and do I need to slay it?"

"Slay it? No, technology is—oh God, how do I even explain it?" She suddenly pointed to a distant ball of the fire that did not spread. "You see that?" When he nodded, she continued. "That light is made with something called electricity."

"This is a type of fire?"

"No, not fire at all." Again, she struggled for an explanation. "You know what lightning is?"

Vasili's brows rose. "That is lightning? Your people have harnessed the weapons of the thunder god?"

"The *what* god? Never mind. No, it's not lightning. It's powered by the same . . . I mean . . . well, it just looks like it." Tasha gave up trying to explain. Her teeth started to chatter, and he realized she must be freezing. The breeze coming down the side of the mountain was far colder than the air inside the cave.

"You need to get warm," he said, and before she could argue, he scooped her up in his arms and started to carry her down the mountain. He had to face this new world—a world where lightning was harnessed—and he would need this woman to help him and his dragon find their place . . . if they could ever belong to it again. Marina would not have wanted him to die, and while his body still had breath in it, he would honor her by trying to live, trying to find new purpose in a new world.

Inside his mind, he felt his dragon look down at Tasha, and Vasili was flooded with his dragon's contentment. What did this mean? How could she soothe him so much? The answers may come with time, but he just was not sure how much time he had before the mate grief claimed him. *If* it claimed him. Until then, he would watch Tasha and learn from her.

"You don't need to carry me," she said. "I can walk."

"You can," he agreed. "But your odd shoes will only slow us down. Is it some type of foot binding? I once visited the Chinese Serpent dragons, and the humans they ruled bound the feet of women."

"They did?" Tasha's voice was filled with horror.

"Yes. Human males claimed it was beautiful and desirable for women to have small feet, but all it did was hobble the females and make them barely able to move, and even then with great pain." The Chinese dragons of his time had remained out of human affairs, but Vasili had often wondered if they had intervened, the humans might have ceased such a barbaric practice.

"History is full of men hurting women to control them. How do you treat lady dragons?" Tasha asked.

Vasili almost laughed. A harsh snort escaped him instead.

"Any male who is foolish enough to think he can control a dragoness is a dead dragon. Mates, by our definition, are equal partners. My own mate, Marina, was a battle dragon, and I was proud of her strength and ferocity."

Some of the tension in Tasha's body eased. "For an ancient man, you have some pretty modern thinking."

"Ancient? I am not old," he protested. The idea of her thinking him old bothered him.

"You're at least seven hundred years old, right?"

"About three thousand and two hundred," he reluctantly corrected.

"That is by definition *ancient*."

He growled softly. "Once a dragon hits twenty-eight years of age, they do not physically age. Not by human reckoning. We age in appearance only one year for every few thousand human years. I am a male in my prime."

"You certainly are." Tasha murmured something else, and he heard that word *hunk* again.

"What is this *hunk* word you keep saying?"

"It's, umm . . ." Tasha cleared her throat. "It means you're sexy."

"Sexy . . ." That he partially understood. *Sex* meant mating. But he was still baffled by her word choices.

"I am not mating you."

"Not sex, *sexy*. It means you're good looking. That you make women think of sex."

"You think I am attractive." He understood now, and for some reason it delighted him to know that.

As a dragon who'd had a true mate, he would not have given another female even a thought, but he was no longer mated. That bond was broken. Guilt washed over him at the realization that he wanted Tasha to find him attractive. That part of his mind found her attractive as well. That despite what he had just said, he *could* imagine mating with her.

His dragon was not bothered by this. In fact, the damned creature was practically preening over the human female's attention. It made no sense. It went against everything he knew of dragon lore. Maybe his dragon, unable to die over Marina, had a death wish. Perhaps it wished to find a true mate in this human, knowing his life would be cut short and he would perish shortly after her death, whenever that came. What were mere decades to a dragon?

Is that what you want, you daft beast? To lose another mate and die?

All the dragon in his mind did was roll its eyes and curl up in contented peace once more, its focus completely on Tasha.

With a low growl that Tasha couldn't hear, Vasili glared at the distant human village. He chose to ignore his dragon —and the unexpected temptation of the human female in his arms.

CHAPTER 3

Excerpt from Barrow's Journal – My Year
with Dragons

*Dragons have a complicated set of beliefs and their
own mythology. I have often pondered the idea of myths having
their own myths. It's a bit like thinking of the old Roman gods
worshipping their own gods. But it is true—dragons, the creatures
we humans see as myths, have legends all their own. What creatures and stories would be worthy of a dragon's mythos?*

TASHA GASPED AS A BLACK MACHINE ROARED TOWARD
them up the hill, its lights nearly blinding them. It was a
snowmobile. Vasili roared at it, the sound shaking snow off
the branches of the nearest trees. He dropped Tasha to her
feet and shoved her protectively behind him.

"Stay here. I will protect you," he vowed. "It is a *todorat*
—an evil demon that is half human and half horse. I have

never seen one, but I have heard other dragons speak of such creatures."

"A *todorat*?" Tasha had no idea what he was talking about. "Vasili, it's okay." She gripped his upper arms. *Oh my God, his muscles are like steel* . . . "It's a snowmobile. A human is riding on it. He can help us. Just be calm."

"A snow . . . mobile?" He broke down the word to examine each facet of it. He still kept her behind him and shifted whenever she tried to move to get around him.

The man on the snowmobile stopped and turned the engine off. "Hello there! Are either of you injured?" The man's English was tinged with a German accent. The medic logo on his chest and the medical cross on the side of the snowmobile indicated he was part of the search-and-rescue efforts.

Vasili stiffened as though confused; most likely he couldn't understand what the man was saying.

Pushing herself around Vasili, she stepped forward. "We aren't hurt, but we need a ride down to the village. Could you help us?"

"Of course." The man stared at Vasili's bare chest. "Are you sure he's all right?"

"He lost his clothes in the avalanche," Tasha said, hoping the man wouldn't look too deeply into that story since Vasili wore loose-fitting brown leather trousers that no one in their right mind would go skiing in.

"Climb on behind me. We're searching for anyone who got stranded during the storm," the man explained.

"Come on," she said to Vasili in Russian. "Follow me." When she pulled on his hand, he still did not move. "Trust me." His eyes were locked in dread on the snowmobile, as if waiting for it to attack them. He might still think it was a *todorat* demon horse thing.

"It's safe," she promised. "*Trust* me." She tugged on his hand again, and this time he followed her. She got on the seat behind the driver, and Vasili followed suit, his warm, hard body pressed tight to hers.

"Hold on." She reached for Vasili's hands, pulling them around her waist. He was so large that his arm easily encircled her body. He cuddled against her like one might a stuffed animal.

The medic started the engine, and Vasili went rigid. As the snowmobile moved down the mountain, they flew past trees and around the large floodlights that illuminated a clear path down the slopes for night skiing. Vasili kept his arms locked around her in a death grip, but she felt surprisingly safe. She turned her head to look back at him a few times and saw his gaze was full of wonder as they passed people skiing down toward safety beneath the bright floodlights on the slopes.

"I will keep you safe," he told her as he kept his arms tight around her.

Even though she knew they were safe, it felt nice to have him still determined to protect her. She wasn't used to having someone else looking out for her like this. Her mother had been protective, in a way, but her protection meant staying away from everything. With Vasili, it was different. He was vowing to protect her while she was out in the world and living in it. Was this what most men were like? If so, she really had missed out on dating all these years.

Tasha tended not to think about men or romance. Living as she did with her mother, she'd never been able to go on any dates. She'd stayed home and done the safe thing. But she was tired of being safe. Vasili was the opposite of safe, yet when she was with him, she felt unafraid. She felt like the person she'd wished she'd been for years, someone who knew how to *live*.

By the time they reached the boarding area for the cable car, Vasili still had a firm grip on her waist. Each time she thought about it, that strange fluttering in the back of her head started up again.

"Are you both able to get back to your resort?" the medic asked. He shot a glance over at Vasili's bare chest. "I have a light jacket for him." He retrieved a thin black rain jacket and gave it to Vasili, who took it without a word, and with a glance at Tasha, he nodded in silent thanks at the medic.

"Yes, we can get back to our hotel," she assured the man as she and Vasili climbed off the snowmobile.

He walked barefoot in the snow about half a dozen feet and then turned to glare at the snowmobile, his body tense as though he expected it to attack him.

"A horse with no face, no legs, and moves at such a pace . . . What sorcery is this?"

Tasha tried to put herself in his shoes, picturing the world around them with ancient eyes. If he didn't like the snowmobile, he was really going to hate the cable car.

She held out her hand to him again. Something inside

her stirred as he turned his gaze toward her, and it wasn't just her hormones. If all dragon shifters were like this, she could understand why her mother had fallen for her father. She didn't just feel a physical attraction to Vasili, but a magnetic pull toward him. She also couldn't ignore the fact that every time he touched her, something strange like butterflies fluttered inside her head.

I should get him to town and then get as far away from him as possible.

Yet the moment his hand grasped hers, his warm and firm grip sending delicious tingles through her body, she knew she was going to have trouble walking away from him.

"Where do we go now?" he asked her.

"Somewhere private." She noticed the other skiers who had gone out to night ski were all halting in the snow to stare at the man with bare feet who seemed immune to the freezing temperatures.

She pulled him toward the cable cars. "Okay, handsome, let's go—quickly." They lined up at the nearest base station, and Vasili stared at the slowly moving cable cars. When it was their turn and the car stopped, she showed him how to climb inside.

Vasili kept a death grip on her hand as they rode the entire way down the mountain, and he held her close to his body as he seemed to be bracing for an imminent fall and planning to use his body to protect her from the crash he expected to come. It was rather cute.

"This is no different than flying," she said, hoping to ease his concerns.

"This is *very* different from flying." He opened his eyes, staring out the windows. "When I fly, I have control over my body. I can use the wind to change direction and speed. This . . . This is death in a strange little box with glass windows."

"You know what glass is?" That surprised her.

At this Vasili chuckled, though he didn't smile. "The Romans used glass for windows. It took the rest of the world a little while to catch up. It is strange that so many cultures conquered by the Romans refused to maintain the advances they made. Aqueducts, glass, and so many other things were abandoned when the empire fell. The conquered cultures returned to their primitive lives."

"Says the man afraid of snowmobiles," she teased.

She thought for an instant that his lips twitched, but nothing more. Tasha could not help but wonder what it would take to make him smile.

He was quiet the remainder of the ride down. When they reached Grindelwald, she hailed a taxi. The last thing she wanted were odd looks on a train, given Vasili's state of undress.

A taxi pulled up in front of them. The driver rolled down his window, and Tasha gave him the address of her hotel.

"What is this?" Vasili nodded at the taxi.

"It's like the snowmobile." Tasha opened the car door.

"I see." Vasili nodded and slowly climbed inside. She joined him and reached across his body to grab his seat belt. As she pulled the belt across his chest, she breathed in the most wonderful scent. He smelled like evergreens, snow, and things that made her think of Christmas morn-ing. It inspired a pure sense of joy within her.

"Tasha?" Vasili murmured her name, and that bubble of joy inside her grew. She closed her eyes and, without think-ing, tried to get closer to the intoxicating scent. Then her cheek rubbed against warm skin where he'd left the thin rain jacket open.

She jerked back, her eyes flying open in mortification. "Oh!" She had rubbed her face against him like a cat marking its territory. That was not good. She couldn't risk becoming interested in this man, given her heritage.

"Sorry." She jerked the seat belt around and clipped it in, then moved back to her own seat and buckled up.

"You do not need to apologize," Vasili said, his tone gentle. "My kind is intimidating to yours, but we also attract you. Like sirens, we tempt mortals."

"Now you're telling me mermaids are real too?"

"Of course, sirens are very real. The merfolk and dragons have had an easy alliance for several thousand years.. . . I've been asleep a long time, so perhaps we've gone to war with the merfolk and they are all gone."

Tasha glanced at the cabdriver, relieved to see that the man didn't seem to be following their conversation or even particularly paying attention. Thank goodness for small favors. The last thing she needed was someone thinking she and Vasili were mentally unstable and calling the authorities on them.

"So mermaids are real. Don't tell me unicorns are too." She tried to laugh, but Vasili just stared at her.

"Why would they not be? The unicorns do not show

themselves in the world of men? What a terrible thing . . . to lose all but dragons. Is there any magic left at all in this world?"

Tasha rubbed at her temples. This was all too much. First she had nearly died, then she had stumbled upon a three-thousand-year-old dragon who smelled like Christmas, and now he was talking about mermaids and unicorns. "I think I need some Tylenol."

"What is Tylenol, and how do we acquire it? You look very pale." Vasili cupped her chin and turned her face to his. His touch was gentle, warming her skin, and yet it ignited a fire deep within her feminine core, making it suddenly, embarrassingly, throb to life. That didn't help her headache one bit.

"I . . . have some at the hotel. It's just a forty-five-minute drive from here. Maybe a little longer, depending on traffic."

"Hotel?" He echoed the word. "And who is *traffic*? I will not let them stop you getting to this Tylenol."

His archaic knightliness was freaking adorable. She tried to banish the blush she could feel creeping across her cheeks.

"A hotel is where I'm staying right now. It's like an inn. Traffic is when you have a bunch of cars, like this one." She patted the seat they were sitting on. "They get crowded on the roads, and that's called *traffic*."

He made a small sound of puzzlement but asked no other questions.

"So, mermaids and unicorns?" she asked, unable to deny her own curiosity.

"Yes. You really do not see unicorns anymore? You are a maiden. They should reveal themselves to you."

"A maiden?"

"An untouched woman—a virgin," he clarified. "Creatures like dragons and unicorns are drawn to them—for different reasons, of course."

"Different reasons?"

Vasili pulled on his seat belt a little, as though testing it. "Unicorns feel peace and tranquility when they are in the presence of a maiden. Dragons . . . tend to get a little more excited. For us, the scent of a virgin makes us eager to mate."

"Mate?" Tasha did not mean to squeak the word, but she did.

"Be easy, little one. While your scent is irresistible, I have great self-control. I have no desire for a female ever again. I lost my true mate."

"You suffered mate grief? How are you still alive?" Tasha gasped. Her mother had explained what she knew of dragons, which included how mate grief worked. But her mom clearly didn't know everything about their world.

"Yes. As to why I'm still alive . . . I do not know. But I suppose I must continue to live if this is to be my fate." There was a quiet desperation in his voice that had her reaching for his hand.

"My mother says sometimes a dragon has a second mate out there, that there are other possible mates. Maybe there's one out there somewhere . . ."

At this, his lips curved in a sad smile. "Your mother is correct. There can be more than one possible mate for a dragon. Perhaps that is why I have not died from the mate grief. You finding me . . . I think if it had been anyone else, I would not have woken up at all."

"Wait, what are you saying?" Her heart began to hammer violently against her ribs.

"It took me a little longer to recognize it," Vasili said. "Normally, I would have sensed it sooner, but after watching Marina die, I fear both my dragon and I are still adjusting to staying alive."

"Hang on," she said, still catching up on his words. "Are you saying I'm a potential mate for you?"

Dear God, she was a true mate for a three-thousand-year-old dragon who didn't *want* a mate. She wasn't sure whether to be excited or disappointed.

CHAPTER 4

Excerpt from Barrow's Journal – My Year with Dragons

DRAGONS ARE NOT BORN AS DRAGONS FROM DRAGONESSES. They are born to women in human form and age as children do, but their minds, ah, their minds develop much faster, taking in languages and other subjects at a fascinating rate. A child of four or five might have the knowledge and vocabulary of an eight-year-old. But the shifting of man or woman to dragon form comes later, around adolescence. Until then, the dragon is alive only inside the child's mind, but it has been described to me as a living thing, one that some shifters can picture clearly in their minds. For others, they feel emotions, see only things the dragon conveys to them in images. The strength of the connection between a human and a dragon who have merged is unique to each shifter.

. . .

VASILI HAD SHOCKED THE ADORABLE LITTLE HUMAN with his confession, and he felt rather guilty about it. But it was the truth. For the last hour, he had been sensing things inside himself and watching the dragon inside his mind very closely. It had been centuries since he'd had to consider the signs of a true mate, but the signs were there.

Her touch soothed him. Her scent excited him, and not simply its virginal quality. She smelled like the forests in Russia—rich soil and clean breezes with a hint of jasmine and pine. She smelled like home, and that made her irresistible.

"You need not worry, Tasha. I shall not claim you. I am not worthy of being anyone's mate. Not anymore." He knew others would see her as a gift, but he was a broken man, a broken dragon. Tasha deserved a mate who was a vibrant young male with a bright and happy future. Vasili was out of place here in this modern world. He was also not certain if he could ever love again, and if he did survive his dragon's mate grief, he would still need time to grieve as a man. He needed time to process losing Marina. It would be selfish to try to love Tasha when he was uncertain of so much.

"Oh . . ."

The hint of disappointment in her tone was unexpected. Had she wanted him to claim her?

She remained silent until the journey in the car ended. The dragon heart stone sat carefully wrapped on her lap, and she held it protectively, though her gaze was distant and her thoughts turned inward.

Vasili wanted to say something, to apologize for not being the mate she deserved. But he needed to get his bearings before he could truly consider what his future—if indeed he did have one—held.

The man controlling the horseless carriage—or *car*, as Tasha had called it—stopped it in front of a series of buildings nestled at the base of one of the mountains. Vasili let out a breath he hadn't realized he'd been holding. He didn't trust anything he couldn't look in the eye, and these transmogrified beasts had only strange circles that emitted light where there should have been eyes.

The human spoke to Tasha in a language that Vasili did not recognize.

"Okay, we're here. This is the Romantik Hotel Schönegg." She showed him how to unclip the belt across his lap and chest. Then he watched her pull on a funny silver latch that opened her door. He did the same and was able to escape. Everything around him was new and different and unsettling. He was not afraid. He had lost his mate; little else in this world could scare him.

He stood barefoot and shirtless, looking up at the *hotel*, as Tasha had named it. She'd said it was like an inn, but this was no inn. No inn he'd ever stayed at was this massive. It was palatial. How many rooms did a place like this contain?

Tasha stood next to him and played with a lock of her hair, coiling it around her finger over and over, seemingly unfazed by the impressive size of the inn. A flash of memory of Marina doing the same thing caused a lump to lodge in his throat. Was he going to see her everywhere?

"You ready to go inside?" Tasha asked.

Vasili managed a nod, and they walked up the stone stairs to the interior of the building. He was startled by the warm, woodsy feel of the place. Lights glowed everywhere using this electricity, a marvel he wanted to know more about. To see fires that did not burn with flames so bright that posed no danger to those around them was marvelous.

He followed Tasha to a high table by the wall, and Tasha spoke to the woman there in that same strange but somewhat familiar language. The woman threw a worried glance in his direction. It was clear his state of clothing, or lack thereof, was of concern to her. Tasha still wore the dark puffy robe that covered most of her body and the strange clunky shoes, whereas the woman she spoke to wore tighter, thinner clothing. Vasili assumed that the puffy garment was not what all women wore in this modern age, and was simply to provide warmth. He found that to be a relief. If females of this age were hiding their figures with such styles, he did not think he would much like it here.

The woman handed Tasha a bit of colored paper and a flat rectangular object that Tasha clutched as though it was important.

"God, I am glad I had my travel wallet in my ski suit," she told him.

"What is a wallet?"

She held up a small blue bit of leather folded to be the

size of his palm. "It has my ID and all my credit cards, plus my money."

Of all that, he only understood the term *money*.

"Come on, my room is this way," she said.

Tasha led him up a set of stairs and down a long corridor. They reached a door, and she slid the flat rectangular card into a funny sort of lock. A green light flashed, and she turned the handle to open the door.

"When my father died, he left me a lot of money. I sort of splurged for the penthouse suite on this vacation."

These were more words he didn't understand. She entered ahead of him and flicked something on the wall by the door that made the fireless light come on above their heads.

He examined the little object she had touched and pushed it up and down. "What are these?" The light vanished and then returned.

"Oh, that's a light switch. They turn on the electricity so that it flows to the lights up there." She pointed at a circle of light in the ceiling. She tapped her chin, eyeing him. "I think what I need to get you is a dictionary or an encyclopedia or something. I think I saw some books down in the lobby. They have the little reading lounge area by the fireplace. I'll go check it out in a minute."

She set the dragon heart stone carefully on the center of the bed, as though she was afraid it might roll away if she put it anywhere else. It touched him that she would take care of it like he would. She didn't have any notion of how important that stone was, yet she instinctively protected it.

"Wait here," she said.

Vasili stayed still as she left the room, but he closely observed his surroundings. Much of the room had warm walnut wood cabinets, and the ceiling was paneled in walnut as well. Just beyond the bedchamber there was a white bathing tub that looked like frozen ice, but when he touched it, it did not burn. Could it be porcelain? The Chinese Serpents coveted porcelain almost as much as jewels.

The door to the room opened, and Tasha returned, her arms full of heavy books. He rushed to steady her before they toppled from her arms, and he set them down on a nearby table.

"Thanks. They were heavier than I thought. I'm glad this hotel has a bookshelf. I bet no one ever reads these. I think they just put them on the shelves to look pretty." She caressed the spine of one of the tomes.

He picked up the top book and flipped through it. He recognized the language. It was Germanic.

"Can you read German? I know you don't understand English."

"English?" He repeated the word, which sounded familiar.

"That's my native language. Anyway, these are in German, but if you can read them, it might help you get up to speed on the last seven hundred years."

The book he held had golden letters along its spine: *Encyclopedia.*

"It's a collection of information about a lot of different subjects. You'll probably find it interesting."

He flipped through the pages. The parchment was white and felt strange, and there were illustrations that looked as though a master artist had painted them. Was it not made of animal hide? He lifted the book up to his nose, sniffing it. Not animal. There was a crisp, foreign smell to the parchment that he couldn't identify.

"It has photos in it. Pretty cool, huh?" Tasha leaned against him as she peered over his shoulder at the books.

Photos... Another word he didn't know.

"Do you want to take a shower, or do you want to sit and read while I hop in? We could order room service and figure out some clothes for you."

"It's going to rain inside?" He glanced up at the ceiling, wondering where water could pour in.

"What? Oh no, a shower is like a bath standing up. I'll show you." She waved for him to follow her into the room with the porcelain tub. Beside it was a glass chamber paved with smooth stones.

"Welcome to the modern age, and something we call *indoor plumbing*." She twisted the silver latch, and water poured from a silver contraption above her head. "You twist this to the right for cold water, left for hot."

Vasili stared at it. This truly was a marvel. The Romans had indoor plumbing, as Tasha called it, but their designs had been rudimentary compared to this and only washed away waste. They had nothing that brought water in from the sky like this to bathe under.

She giggled. "Just wait until you see the TV. There isn't a man alive who doesn't love TV." She grinned, and the expression lit up her lovely face. "So, do you want to try it while I see if I can chase down some clothes for you?"

"Er . . . Yes, thank you." He stared at the water coming down in a perfect rain-like pattern. Then he looked at Tasha, thinking again of the confession he had made in the car. His dragon was convinced that Tasha was a possible true mate.

Marina's death had been centuries ago, but to Vasili it might as well have been yesterday. Soon he would adjust to the span of time, but for now, the wounds were still fresh in his heart. Yet Tasha was here, and the truth was, she could be a possible mate to him. Vasili didn't want to think of her that way, but it was impossible not to. She was beautiful and her scent was irresistible, yet this pull toward her came from something deeper than mere scent and beauty.

There was a kindness in her eyes and a bravery in her spirit that reminded him so much of Marina. It was clear she wasn't used to being the way she was with him—he'd sensed a hesitancy to her in those early moments in the cave—but now she was growing braver, taking pride in helping him in this new world.

He was a blessed man to find two women of quality as mates. But as much as she called to him, he could not claim her as a mate. He didn't know if he still might perish from mate grief. No dragon he'd ever known had been in such a position as he was. He wondered how many of those he'd once known were still alive. After all, if the merfolk and unicorns were no more, perhaps there were few of *his* kind left as well. But if there were, perhaps they would know more about his condition.

"Are you all right, Vasili?" Tasha asked.

"I was thinking I need to discuss things with my kind. Other dragons. Before I went into that cave, I had a younger brother, Ivan, and three nephews. I do not know if they are still alive." Dragons were almost immortal in terms of age, but they could still be killed, and wars between his kind were common. Most dragons didn't live beyond ten thousand years due to losing a mate, or losing interest in life. A mere seven hundred years could have taken everything that still mattered from him. The weight of those centuries was only beginning to sink in. He had missed so much—not just in the world, but with his family.

"Before you were in the cave, did you interact with the human world, or did you stay hidden?" Tasha's eyes were wide and curious as she watched him.

"We were known to some humans, but not all. There were many who feared us, but the ones who trusted us, we kept close in our confidence."

She tilted her head, thinking. "Maybe your family will have social media profiles or something. I don't know— they may not, given the way that could lead to people noticing them not aging. We can still check."

"Yes," Vasili agreed, even though he hadn't the faintest idea what *social media profiles* were.

"Well, once we have you dressed in some decent clothes, we can try to find your brother."

"Thank you, Tasha." He brushed the backs of his knuckles over her cheek, unable to resist. "You have sacrificed much to help me."

"It's all right. I feel, well, guilty that I woke you up."

Her eyes softened. "I mean, if you wanted to stay in that cave and sleep after what happened, I messed things up."

He knew she meant to say *die* instead of *sleep*, but she was too kind to say it.

"I'll just do the shower, then," he said.

"Take a shower," she corrected.

He nodded to show that he understood. *Take* a shower. He would remember that.

"Stay in the room after you're done. Don't go anywhere on your own until I get back. The people here will not understand why you're wearing only brown leather pants. It's not really acceptable to go around underdressed, and no one here knows about dragons. So please don't do anything too *dragon-y*."

An unexpected bubble of amusement inside him rose to the surface, but still he didn't laugh. "Dragon-y?"

"Yes, you know . . . no breathing fire, no flying, no turning your hands into dragon claws. It would scare the hell out of everyone."

"I shall endeavor not to be too dragon-y," he promised.

"Good. I'll be back as fast as I can."

He waited until he heard the door close before he unfastened his trousers and removed them. Then he stepped inside the glass chamber and closed himself in. Once inside, he reached out a hand toward the water, felt the icy storm against his chest, and flinched. He was tired of being cold. He needed *heat*.

Vasili turned the silver handle the way Tasha had shown him and sighed in relief as the water warmed him. He turned the handle more until the water was as hot as what he might find in natural hot springs. It felt like heaven.

He groaned as the stiff ache in his limbs began to ease. He closed his eyes and let the water rain down over his head and shoulders. Without warning, he relived those moments where Marina had fallen from the sky, her throat ripped, unable to heal, her plea to take the stone and hide it from the Drakors . . .

It was all seared into his memory as though it had happened yesterday and not seven hundred years ago. To him, frozen in that cave, everything felt like it had happened mere hours ago. How could his dragon not mourn Marina the way the human part of him was? How could it yearn for Tasha when all Vasili could feel was pain for losing his woman?

The rage he had felt at losing her was gone, though. That surprised him. He'd been certain rage would be all he had left. But the truth was, there was *nothing* left in him. He was empty of everything. His dragon was quiet, curled up inside his head, his tail twitching like a cat's would when it was distressed. If only they could speak to each other clearly. All his dragon could do was send flashes of Marina's face, then Tasha's, over and over again.

Vasili stayed in the shower a long time. Only when the water turned cold did he turn off the spray and step out. He glanced about and saw a stack of fluffy white cloths. When he pulled the top one off the stack, it unfolded. He grimaced. It was no bigger than a loincloth. He was meant to wear this? He reached for the next one and found with relief that he could wrap it around his waist after he dried.

Tasha was not back yet, and he was not supposed to leave. He then retrieved one of the books that Tasha had brought him and sat down on the bed to read.

THANK GOD SOME BOUTIQUE SHOPS IN THE VILLAGE stayed open late. They were a godsend, because if Tasha hadn't been able to find clothes to fit a big, sexy Russian dragon shifter, she would've had a problem.

Tasha perused the racks of men's clothing, taking a chance to buy a full wardrobe for him. She had the money and didn't mind spending it on him. It was kind of fun. There was also just something about his eyes, the way he looked so tortured, that made her want to heal him.

God, if she wasn't careful she would have it bad for the man, like some heroine in a romance novel. Okay, she had to admit she was a sucker for the plots where women wanted to heal a gorgeous guy who'd been hurt in some way. Turned out she was one of those women in real life, the kind who wanted to fix a broken man, make him whole. But she wasn't sure if she could fix a dragon's broken heart.

It took her a moment to remember what she was doing. *Clothes.* The man needed clothes. A lot of them, to cover up that ridiculously sexy body.

Focus on buying him clothes, not what he looks like without them.

She grabbed two pairs of jeans, holding them up to judge the size. Then she collected half a dozen T-shirts with logos of the village and the Alps. Then she got some dress shirts, socks, and boxers. He seemed like a boxers kind of guy. After that, she grabbed a pair of nice dress shoes that looked close to his size and a pair of comfortable all-weather boots. If something didn't fit, she'd just return tomorrow morning and get a different size.

When she unloaded her massive armload of clothing onto the checkout desk, the cashier's eyes lit up. Someone got paid on commission.

"Can I help you find anything else?"

Tasha glanced about and saw a rack with winter coats. Some were classy and casual, while others were designed for hiking. She wasn't sure what they would be doing over the next few days, so she chose a knee-length black wool dress coat and a red-and-black all-weather winter coat, just to be sure. Then she returned to the counter and handed over her credit card.

"Do you know if they sell suitcases around here?" she asked the clerk.

"Of course, the shop two doors down sells suitcases. They close in fifteen minutes." The girl swiped her credit card and then printed out her receipt.

"Thanks." Tasha took back her credit card and collected three big bags before she headed down the little lane of stores outside. She soon saw a shop with suitcases sitting in the windows. This decision was much easier. She took the first big black rolling suitcase she could find and then called for a taxi to get her back to the hotel.

Once she got back, she stopped at the front desk to have some dinner sent up. Then she carried her loot to the room. As she stepped inside, she glanced about for Vasili.

The room was eerily quiet. There weren't even sounds of running water.

"Vasili?" She was starting to worry. What if he had left the room and had gotten lost in town? What if something terrible had happened to him? He was like a three-thousand-year-old newborn. She dropped the bags and darted into the suite, cutting sharply around the corner into the bedroom, where she smacked straight into a wall of hard muscle. She rebounded and started to fall, but strong hands caught her waist.

"I am here, little one," Vasili said.

She stared at his bare chest and swallowed hard. That Christmassy scent was even stronger now after he had showered. Was it his natural aroma? Her eyes skated up his chest to rest on his mouth and then his eyes. They were a soft blue; the dragon gold was only a shimmer in the background now.

"I was worried. It was so quiet. Did you shower already?"

"Yes. I have been reading." He nodded toward the bed, where he had piled up the books.

"Oh good." She relaxed, but a moment later she realized that he was still holding her by the waist, their pelvises touching. She blushed as she glanced down and saw he wore only a hotel towel around his narrow hips.

Oh God . . . so much for not thinking about him naked.

"I . . . uh, found you some clothes to wear. I also ordered dinner. The food should be up soon."

"I am very hungry," he replied. "Thank you, Tasha. I wish I could care for you as you have done for me. I'm not used to being so helpless." To hear such a gorgeous man say that to her, that he wanted to take care of her the way she had him . . . Her stomach flipped in foolish girlish excitement.

"It's no trouble. It's nice to have some company."

"Yes, companionship is good for the heart," he agreed. His fingers tightened slightly over her hips before she stepped away. She retrieved the shopping bag she had dropped on the floor, as well as the suitcase near the entryway of the suite.

"Let me show you the clothes I got you. If something doesn't fit, we can exchange it for the right size." Tasha set the bags on the bed and started removing items.

Vasili reached out and peeled away the thin tissue paper covering the clothes. He looked with interest at the jeans he unwrapped first. Taking a moment to organize everything on the bed, she started to explain the various pieces of clothing. She blushed as she pointed out how he would know which way to put the boxers on. He took the blue plaid pair from her and, with a frown, poked his finger through the front slit of the fabric, then slowly nodded as he understood the mechanics.

"Do you feel comfortable enough with this to get dressed?" she asked.

"Yes, I believe so."

"Okay, good. I'm going to shower, then. If you hear the bell ring, it's just our dinner. Open the door and let them bring it into the room. You don't need to give them money."

Vasili stared at the clothes, and Tasha hastily gathered a

pair of boxers, socks, jeans, and a T-shirt. "Start with these."

"Thank you." He reached for the edge of the towel that hung around his hips. Tasha spun away and rushed into the bathroom, her face hot. It was far too easy to imagine how perfect the rest of Vasili would look without clothes.

Tasha turned on the shower and closed the bathroom door so she could have a bit of privacy, then started to strip and did her best not to picture how she would feel against Vasili if she was naked as well.

VASILI MUDDLED HIS WAY THROUGH THE NEW CLOTHES Tasha had brought. She'd explained that the little white tags indicated the back of the clothing, so the T-shirt he held would go on a certain way. He put on the boxers, then the socks, then the jeans, which were snug but far softer and more comfortable than anything he had ever worn. He pulled on the T-shirt next. The fabric was light and soft and stretched around his upper chest, though not uncomfortably.

He approached the mirror and studied his appearance. He looked strange to his own eyes, but compared to the other men of this modern age, he supposed he looked suitable.

A soft musical chime echoed in the air. Was that the bell that Tasha had mentioned would ring? He went to the door and cautiously opened it. A young man pushing a cart covered with trays smiled at him. He spoke and Vasili listened, even though he didn't understand the words. Vasili nodded to indicate that the man should come inside. He rolled the cart in and laid out a tray on the bed with two plates covered in domes made of silver.

"Thank you," Vasili said in Russian, hoping the man would understand.

"Ah, you're Russian?" he asked Vasili in a rough Russian accent.

Vasili smiled in open relief. "Yes."

"Welcome to Switzerland. Please enjoy your dinner." The man's knowledge of the Russian language was rather decent for someone who obviously didn't speak it regularly. He offered Vasili a warm smile before slipping back into the corridor and closing the door behind him.

Vasili studied the silver domes on the tray. The aroma hit his nostrils and made his mouth water. He desperately wanted to eat, but it would be rude not to wait for Tasha. He decided to see how much longer she would be and opened the door to the bathing chamber.

"Tasha, when—?"

Vasili's mouth fell open as Tasha stepped out of the shower. She was completely naked, with one delicately arched foot pointed down toward the cloth mat resting outside of the glass chamber. She reminded him of the young human women who would dance in the springtime to please the fertility gods. Her limbs were sleek with curves, her hips were full, and her breasts . . . Gods above, she was exquisite. No, she was more than that. She was a goddess herself.

"Holy crap!" She scrambled for a drying cloth and

stumbled out of the shower chamber. He dove to catch her, and her body tangled with his as they both collapsed on the floor. He managed to twist around so she landed on him. Vasili grunted as his head smacked the white stone floor, dazing him.

"Vasili? Oh my God, are you okay?"

Tasha's sweet voice reached him clearly through the momentary pain. Lifting his hands, he grasped her hips, groaning as she wriggled on top of him. His body reacted, his cock hardening, and he rolled her so that she was beneath him and his hips fell easily between her spread thighs. By the gods, she felt wonderful, soft and curvy and . . . Her scent enveloped him, drugging him with its comfort and enticement.

He stared deep into her eyes, eyes so golden he would always think of topaz when she looked at him. He had been born to hunt jewels, and he found that the best one was right here. Was he blessed or cursed to have found such a person?

"Vasili . . ." Her lips trembled as though she wanted to say more but wasn't sure what to say, just as he didn't know.

"Tasha," he murmured, looking to her lips, his hunger for her almost overpowering. That brought him up sharply. He scrambled off Tasha and put his back to the wall, burying his face in his hands. What was he doing? She wasn't Marina; he couldn't feel this way, not so soon.

"I'm sorry, I didn't mean to . . ." She didn't finish, and he didn't look up.

He heard Tasha moving about the room, no doubt clothing herself before she left. He was *alone* again.

A few moments later, her bare feet padded back to him, and he raised his head. She wore jeans and a loose sort of top. Her wet hair was now braided, and she held out a hand to him.

"Come and eat dinner. You'll feel better." He heard the compassion in her voice, her desire to help him. She was more gentle in many ways than Marina had been. Marina had been a fierce lover, and while compassionate, she wasn't as soft and comforting as Tasha. His dragon closed its eyes in contentment, clearly enjoying Tasha's attention, but Vasili was still racked with guilt.

He shook his head. He didn't want to eat. He wanted to go back to his cave and die. But as he looked at Tasha, she was a new future for him, one he had never dreamed possible, but one that was at its core a betrayal, a soft voice in his head whispered, *Do you think I would ever leave you alone? That I would not find my way back to you?*

It was Marina's voice, the echo of a ghost long gone.

But you did leave me, and I am done . . .

He heard her scoff in that way she did when he said something ridiculous.

Would you live for me, would you love again, if I asked you to? Will you trust me?

Yes. He would try, because that's what she would want, just as he would have wanted that for her if by some twist of fate their destinies had been reversed.

Vasili placed his hand in Tasha's and stood. She led him back into the main chamber and sat down on the bed, and he sat opposite her, the tray of food between them. Tasha removed one of the silver domes, revealing a plate with lamb and a light-brown sauce covering it.

"Let's see . . . diced veal with mushroom and cream sauce."

Vasili's nose twitched again as the earthy scents of meat and mushrooms made him hungrier than he wished to admit.

He pointed at a baked sort of dish that was next to the diced veal. "And this?"

"That's rösti. The front desk clerk said it's a potato dish, cooked like a fritter."

"Fritter?"

"It's something fried. In my experience, almost everything fried is amazing."

He reached for the fork next to his plate and took a small bite. Tasha watched him, her eyes lighting up.

"Well? Thumbs-up? Or thumbs-down?" she asked as she made a gesture with her thumb, pointing it up and down.

"Which means good?" he asked after he swallowed his bite.

"The thumbs-up." She grinned at him.

"Then this is thumbs-up," he echoed. "I taste a bit of cheese in this one."

"Let me try." She took a forkful for herself. "Oh, Gruyère. I love that kind of cheese."

He tapped his fork against the tray that had two bowls. "And what is this?"

"It's supposed to be a soup with pork, vegetables, and white wine. They said it's a good winter dish. I tried to get some hearty dishes that have meat like you wanted, but also vegetables." She reached for a metal object next to their plates about the size of her hand. She tugged at the top, and it made a hissing, popping sound. He flinched and then stared as she held it out to him.

"What is this?" he asked as he took the object from her. It was cold to the touch, and the metal was surprisingly thin.

"Beer. You said you wanted a stout tankard. Well, that's a *can* of beer, and it will have to do." She popped open a second can and took a drink.

After watching her, he did the same, and the crisp taste of beer hit his tongue. He sighed in pleasure and took a longer drink.

"What do you think?"

"It's good. Thank you for the food, Tasha."

"You're welcome."

They continued to eat in silence, but it was pleasant. Outside, one of the lights illuminated a balcony. He could see that snow was falling.

Seven hundred years. The passage of so much time was strange. It seemed impossible since his body had not changed except to heal his wounds from the battle with the Drakors. Yet the evidence of time moving forward was all around him. He cleared his throat as he came to a decision.

"Tasha, would you teach me about the world and help me find my way home?"

She set her fork down, and with a look of surprise, she nodded. "Yes. I'll help you."

He didn't know what to do about her. He was still unsure whether at some point he would suffer the mate grief. Until then, he needed to try to live. It was what Marina would have wanted. As much as he wanted to crawl back inside the cave and die, he knew Marina wouldn't want that. She'd want him to live on, no matter how hard it might be at first.

No, if you loved someone and they wanted you to live on, no matter how hard it might be at first, that was what you should do. And perhaps, one day, he might learn that destiny had given him a second chance after all. It was worth the risk.

As the thought settled in his mind and heart, he glanced at the dragon heart stone on the bed. It was glowing softly beneath the cloth covering, its blue hue pulsing like a slow, steady heartbeat.

Each beat seemed to say, *Yes, Vasili, yes . . .*

CHAPTER 5

Excerpt from Barrow's Journal – My Year with Dragons

THE MATING OF DRAGONS IS A THING OF BEAUTY, I AM TOLD. To embrace your lover with passion and to open yourself in return means you will see quite literally the life of your loved one as though it were you living out their memories. It is a sacred experience, one that firmly bonds the dragons together even more, for to know someone deeply, truly, without real secrets, that is to love someone. I have often wondered if that is why dragons die when they lose their mate. They have come to know their mate so intimately that losing them is like losing themselves and thus they too cannot survive.

.   .   .

Tasha set the plates outside in the hall, as the hotel staff would come to collect them at some point in the evening.

"Okay, it's really late. Why don't we sleep, and we can start fresh tomorrow?"

She couldn't believe how much her Russian language courses and audio learning had paid off. She was feeling more confident speaking it, but she would love to teach him English. He should learn it if he was going to travel, given how prevalent the language was in the rest of the world.

"There's another bedroom in the suite," she said when Vasili stared at the king-size bed.

"I will sleep in the other bed. Please show me."

He waited for her to lead him to the other room, just next to the bathroom. She hadn't planned to use the other bedroom, so up until now she had left the door closed. The bed was a twin, and she frowned as she looked between it and Vasili. He was clearly too tall for this bed. His feet would dangle off the end.

"Actually, this one is too small for you. I'll sleep here. You take the big bed."

"No," he said. "This is your dwelling, and I am the guest. I will take this bed. I must insist."

He had an adorably stubborn chivalric look on his face. Was this how men were back in his day? She sort of liked the idea of a man who would subject himself to discomfort for her sake. Not that she wanted either of them uncomfortable, but it was nice to be put first.

"I don't want to picture you sleeping in this bed with

your feet hanging off the end," she said. "You'd look silly, and it really doesn't make sense. I'm clearly much shorter than you."

Did his lips twitch? She could have sworn they did. She had a growing desire to make him smile, even laugh if she could manage it. But from what she knew of the mate grief, he was in pain, deep pain, and she couldn't imagine it would be easy to find joy or humor in anything.

"I slept in a freezing cave for more than half a millennium. This overly soft bed will cause me no strife, little one."

"Why do you call me *little one?*" She remembered her father calling her that as a child, and he'd always said it with tenderness.

She still hadn't told Vasili that her father had been a dragon. Something about that felt too intimate, too personal. Besides, it might change how he saw her, that she was a child born to a dragon who couldn't even shift into one. What if that lessened her in his eyes? She couldn't bear the thought that he'd think less of her—not that he seemed like the kind of man who would, but she knew so little of men and relationships.

"*Little one* is a term of endearment among my kind. It means something is small, like a jewel, but it is precious, so it must be cherished and protected. I do not mean it as an insult. Even my first mate, who was not very much shorter than me, was still my beloved little one."

That made sense. Her father had always called her *little one*, and her mother was his *little flower*. Thinking of her father brought back bittersweet memories. She shoved them away—not because she didn't want to think about him, but because she had so much else to worry about. There was a dragon in her life now. It didn't get more complicated than that.

What were the odds that she would be at *that* particular mountain when there was an avalanche and that *she* would fall into the cave and find him, let alone wake him up? Tasha didn't believe in fate . . . but she also didn't believe in coincidences. She'd seen a man in the snowstorm leading her toward the cave, yet she'd never found him. Instead, she'd found Vasili in the dark, cold ice. Vasili had said she was a possible true mate to him. Had her presence in the cave caused him to wake up? Or did it have something to do with the glowing blue stone she had found? Clearly, something was happening between them, and there were things going on that she didn't entirely understand, and it raised a thousand questions.

"Vasili, what is that stone that I found with you? The one that glowed." They had left it securely wrapped on the bed in the other room.

He eased down on the edge of the twin bed. "That is a dragon heart stone, the Heart of Sorrows."

After a moment, she sat down on the bed as well. "Why did it glow when I touched it?"

"It glowed when you touched it?" His voice had turned suddenly sharp.

"Yes. When I came into the cave, I was having trouble breathing. When I saw the stone glowing on the floor, it was all wrapped up and I didn't know what it was. I picked it up, and I thought it burned me, but I couldn't let it go. Then I collapsed next to you. That's when you woke up."

Vasili got up from the bed and went to retrieve the stone. He brought it back and set it down on the twin bed between them. He carefully unwrapped it. The gemstone was dark blue now, its sapphire depths seemingly endless if one gazed at it long enough.

"As I said, this is a dragon heart stone. There are more in the world—or at least there used to be. They hold the souls of my people. We aren't from your world, but a parallel one, one where dragons exist. But it's not like here. It's like an afterlife in many ways, a place where our souls rest. On rare occasions, a portal opens and the stones are created. Dragon souls are pulled into the stones and then deposited into your world."

"But I thought dragons could be born, like drakelings," Tasha said.

"They can be. When two dragons have children, they can produce drakelings. Those dragon souls are new to this world and the other world. But the ones in the stones . . . they are the old souls, the ones who died in our original world, and their souls were transitioned to the stones for safekeeping."

"And you think there are souls of old dragons in here?" Tasha brushed her fingertips gently over the blue surface of the sapphire.

"Yes. Perhaps many of them. The larger the stone, the more souls can inhabit it. That is why we dragons hoard jewels. Gemstones are potential vessels to hold our people. In my youth, we had ceremonies for when mated dragons died. We would help put the two souls together into one stone. From time to time, humans were true mates to my people, and we could use the stones to gift them with a dragon soul so they could be with their mate for a proper length of time. But as our kind went to war, both against humans and each other, this knowledge was all but lost."

Something about that tugged at Tasha's heart. "Was your mate human before becoming a dragon?"

"Marina? No, she was born to dragons, like her parents before her. Her line was an ancient one. Those of her bloodline could see the future and control the elements. Her blood held more magic than mine."

"Magic is in the blood?" Tasha was fascinated by the idea.

"Magic is in all things, from drops of rain to the strands of your hair." He smiled softly then, the first time she'd seen him do it. It changed his face completely, and he became even more beautiful to her.

She scooted closer to him on the bed. "Magic is in me?"

Vasili held out a hand. "Of course. Let me see your hand."

She placed her palm in his, and that undeniable surge of heat and raw attraction from before flashed through her. She was glad she was sitting down. He didn't seem to be affected by her the way she was by him.

"Do you feel that?" she asked, nodding at their joined hands. It wasn't like her to ask something so potentially embarrassing, but it felt important.

"The pull to you?"

Tasha managed another nod.

"That is the mate bond calling us to join. It will grow stronger the longer we are together."

"Oh." Tasha ducked her head. "And that's bad, because you don't want a mate." She hadn't wanted one either, at least not at first. But being near Vasili, knowing that he could be a true mate to her, knowing what that meant, at least according to her mother, made it all very overwhelming and yet incredibly desirable.

A true mate was someone's perfect match. They would never desire another the way they would desire each other. They would share dreams and memories with only their mate. Her mother had said that a true mate would know her down to her very soul and would love and cherish her. What greater gift could there be than to be loved so deeply, forever, by someone who knew all of you, even your darkest parts? It was a gift no one in their right mind would reject, not even her, even though she had been warned to avoid dragons.

But Vasili was resisting her. He didn't want her. He had found his true mate and lost her. Tasha wasn't worth a lifetime of love and longing, not to him. For some reason that hurt her in a way nothing else had ever hurt her.

He stroked his fingertips over her palm, traced the delicate blue veins in her wrist.

"You think I do not want you?" he asked, echoing her thoughts. "That I am rejecting you?"

She bit her lip, unable to meet his eyes. She didn't want him to see her feeling weak and vulnerable, but they were long past him seeing her at her worst.

He reached up with his other hand and lifted her chin. "Look at me, little one."

Gold swirled in the ice blue of his eyes like warm firelight illuminating a pair of glaciers. Looking into his eyes felt . . . right. *Right* was scary, but not in the way that made her hesitate.

Vasili's voice deepened. "I am not rejecting you. The truth is, I do *want* you, Tasha. You are exquisitely lovely, and you have shown such compassion to a man cast out of time such as me. I dread to think what would've happened if I had revealed my dragon nature to anyone else. But this world," he said with a sigh, "it is not *my* world, and I fear I may never fit in. I may not even live long enough to make any of this matter."

He wanted her; he'd said it. He wanted *her*. But why did the look in his eyes warn her that he was going to try to talk her out of it? There was a part of Tasha that didn't understand how she could be so fearless around him, how she felt like she could trust him with anything, including herself. Even her changing her mind and wishing to be a part of the dragon world if it meant being his mate was something she seriously wanted to consider.

"But dragons mate forever," he continued. "It's not something you accept on a whim simply because lust has overtaken you."

But this wasn't just lust. Yes, she barely knew him, but somehow she *did* know him. It was like she'd come across a faded photograph of a familiar face. She knew him, deep down, where it mattered. Sure, she didn't know the small details, like how he preferred his coffee (assuming he even knew what that was), or what side of the bed he wanted to sleep on, but that didn't erase the sense that he was familiar to her. A safe harbor in a storm. Home. She'd never felt that way about anyone, not even her parents.

Vasili's fingers moved from her chin down to her throat, his caress light and tender. "There are so many questions you should ask yourself first before tying yourself to one like me. Do you want a life beyond your mortal one, one where you outlive your family and friends?" There was a sensuality to his touch that Tasha couldn't deny, like he was tempting her and warning her at the same time. "And what if you tie your soul to mine and then this world I do not belong in rejects me?"

She trembled, not from fear, but anger. How could he think he wouldn't fit in? He was here with her, and he'd come so far already. How could he not see that? She knew deep down inside that other dragons in his situation wouldn't have woken up. They would have stayed in that cave, sleeping forever until the skies fell and the world crumbled. But not him. He'd woken up . . . for her.

He'd come with her, trusted her, desired her, and she trusted and desired him. She didn't care that it all sounded crazy, that the lust and affection she felt wasn't logical. All that mattered was him and whatever may lie between them.

"What if I am too broken, Tasha?" he asked, and she instantly shook her head. He pulled his hand to her chest, holding it there between his palms. "None have survived the mate grief. I may never truly be whole again."

"Don't say that." His skin was warm, and she wanted to

feel it bare against hers. "You can adapt. The fact that you're still here proves it. There are so many amazing things about this age that will give you hope for the future. Will you give it a chance? Will you give . . . me a chance?"

Vasili brushed the backs of his knuckles over her throat as he gazed at her mouth.

"You are tempting me."

"Then *be* tempted," she insisted. What happened next seemed so natural that neither of them had any hope of stopping it. She leaned in, and their mouths brushed together. In that moment, Tasha discovered fire, like the first hominids who created a spark from stone.

She clutched at his shirt as he growled and deepened the kiss. He toppled her back on the bed, his body hovering above hers as their mouths moved hungrily. She'd never felt like this before in her life, as though the next kiss might be the thing to save her or slay her.

Her heartbeat throbbed in her ears as he settled between her thighs, pinning her down. He gripped her hands, trapping them on either side of her head. His fingers curled around her wrists, dominating her but not hurting her. His control in this moment made her feel safe, and she trusted whatever he would do—she just knew she wanted *more*. Tasha moaned as her lower body came to life, throbbing almost painfully with the need for him to finish what his mouth had started.

Vasili moved his lips down to her throat, whispering softly to her in Russian. "Such a beautiful body, little one. You make me hungry, wanting to sink myself into you and give you all that I am." His words stole her breath. This was more than sexual; his desires went to the sharing of bodies but also far beyond.

"*Please*, Vasili. Kiss me," she begged.

His mouth returned to hers, and his hands on her wrists tightened as she rocked her hips up against his over and over, entreating him to give her what she needed. *Release*. No, *release* wasn't the right word. When she came apart, it wouldn't release her from anything. Instead, it would *bind* her to him and his dragon.

Something changed inside her, like the walls within her head were crumbling. Flashes behind her closed eyes began to play like clips of a movie, yet she *felt* what she was seeing too.

Clouds whipped across her body, cold and freeing as the currents lifted her higher toward the glorious sun. A golden dragon flew ahead of her, and her heart swelled with love.

My mate.

It was Marina, Tasha realized. Somehow, she was seeing his mate through the eyes of Vasili's dragon. Was this a dream of some sort?

She followed the golden dragon as they both plummeted down through the clouds, toward a glittering green-blue sea. They splashed into the water, diving below the surface and chasing schools of fish that flashed like lightning as they banked and turned in the blue depths. She snapped her jaws at them before using her wings to swim up for air. The golden dragon nipped her flank playfully as it joined her, and they glided along the surface until they rolled in with the tide to shore.

Now it was her turn to chase the other dragon. She

caught the golden dragon and playfully pinned it down in the warm sand. Her mate feigned a struggle until she sank her teeth into just the right spot, and the play changed to something more primal.

They mated in dragon form, their bodies bathed in sunlight, water cooling their scales. When they were finished, she stretched out to sunbathe while her mate tucked its head against her shoulder. Bliss, so strong and eternal that it shook Tasha to her core and rumbled through her like an earthquake deep beneath the earth's surface.

Then the images faded, and Vasili stared down at her in shock and wonder.

They shouldn't have kissed, but it was something neither of them could take back. The mating bond between them was beginning. A thousand things she wanted to say to him were trapped on her tongue, but in the end, one single little word slipped out.

"Oops."

"Oops."

Tasha's adorably innocent little sound had a devastating impact on Vasili, in more ways than one. It made him want to kiss her again, which was the one thing he knew better than to do. It made his cock hard and his self-control fray at the edges. It didn't help that her sweet scent wrapped around him and seeped into his skin. He hadn't expected to feel this way again, not so soon. To him, it had only been a day since Marina had died. How could he bond to Tasha so quickly? It felt like he was betraying her.

And yet his dragon was purring in reptilian delight. He had come too close to claiming this little female. His dragon was ready to go straight to mating her without another thought, but Vasili wasn't. He couldn't survive another heartbreak.

Remember Marina? Would you like to lose Tasha too?

The dragon inside his head bared its teeth. For the first time in his life, he and his dragon were at war with each other. Over a human woman.

"Vasili?" Tasha's topaz eyes glimmered with tears. "I'm sorry. I shouldn't have pushed you into that."

"Do not blame yourself," he soothed. "Possible mates have a hard time being close to each other. It is a challenge we must face." Even as he said this, it took him far longer than he thought to release her wrists and roll off her body. They both lay on the small bed beside each other, staring up at the ceiling. Their shoulders touched, and Tasha's hand lay close to his arm, her fingertips touching his skin. Even such a small thing set fire to his blood, yet he could have stayed right where he was forever so long as he could feel her skin. He suddenly had a brilliant idea.

"Do the Normans still rule Albion?" Vasili asked.

"What's Albion?" Tasha echoed, her tone baffled.

"Britannia. Before I ended up here, the Normans invaded Britannia. We dragons called it Albion."

"Oh. England! Hang on." She got up from the bed and raced to the other room, then returned with one of the thick books she had shown him. She opened the tome and plopped down on the bed beside him. He helped her hold the book while she flipped through a series of colored maps. Vasili stole a glance at her, worried she was still upset about his hesitancy over mating. He was surprised she seemed so unresistant to it. In his past, most humans tried to avoid mating with dragons. Yet she seemed, at least on some level, far more willing to bind herself to him.

She pointed a finger to a map that covered one full page. "Right, so this is England. Your Britannia."

He leaned closer to her. To see the map, of course, not because he wanted to breathe in her scent.

"So what's so important about England?"

Vasili stared at the island on the map searching for familiar place names. *London* was the only word he recognized. It was the more modern name for Londinium which was a name he had been familiar with, and it seemed to be in the right place along the river.

"I had friends there once, other dragons, Londinium drakes in the south and fire drakes in the north. They were more unified than other dragons in other parts of the world. Most of us end up in wars over territory, but the dragons of Albion were partial to treaties and had the most long-lasting alliances among our kind. If there are any dragons left in the world, they will be in London. They might know of other dragons who survived the mate grief."

"Well, it would be easier to go to London than Russia," Tasha mused. "It's closer and a lot less intimidating."

Vasili didn't question her statement about Russia. No doubt every country in the world was far different than it had once been, and he did not wish to return home until he had answers about his condition. The last thing he wanted to do was to find Ivan and give him hope, only to then die from the mate grief. That would be cruel. It was better for him to seek out the English drakes first, ones who might have answers about surviving the death of a mate and finding a second one.

"So we go to England," Tasha said, then paled. "You'll need a passport, a driver's license—a whole new identity."

"I have an identity"

"No, I mean legal documents. In this day and age, to be able to travel to different countries you must have certain documents."

Vasili shrugged, unconcerned. "We shall fly. You may ride upon my back."

"What? No, we *definitely* can't do that. The world has changed. All of these countries, they have radar. Their military will see an object flying, and they'll attack you."

He chuckled. "They cannot see a dragon, not when I am so far above them in the air."

Tasha sighed and pulled something out of her jeans pocket. It was a slender black object. She pressed a button, and the thing came to life with light. She tapped on it and then held it up to him.

"This is an airplane. Humans built them to fly. There are ones they use with weapons that could kill you. You can't fly, not unless other dragons we meet say it's safe."

Vasili stared at the image moving in his hands. A bird-like object was shooting across the sky almost faster than he could fly. He had thought the Romans were advanced, but they had never dreamed of flying anything like this, like dragons.

"So we must travel on foot?" he asked, still staring at the moving image.

"No, we'll fly in one of these."

He raised a brow. "I do not think I want to fly in this 'airplane.' I do not trust it."

"Don't worry. You took the cable car down the mountain—that's way scarier, I promise you."

"You didn't seem terrified when we went down together," Vasili pointed out.

Tasha frowned a moment. "Huh . . . I guess I just got used to it after the first time. Don't worry about the plane, okay? You might even like it."

She took the flat black object from him. "I should call Mr. Bovill, my father's attorney, and see if he can help us with some travel documents. The guy is very connected— probably a little *too* connected," she muttered under her breath.

Ah, yes, the documents. Proof of his existence in this new era. A sudden fear crept up on him. What if his family in Russia was no more? What if the Drakors had won the war? They'd always outnumbered the Barinovs because they produced dragons for their army while the Barinovs mated for love. If this new world was as advanced as he feared, his enemies may have a way of finding him if he used the name of Barinov.

He would take a different name. *Vasili* had been a common enough name when he was alive, and Russians always kept names in the family, so there would likely be lots of men named Vasili with whom to blend in. However, he would go by his mother's dragon family name of Morozov. Her bloodline of Nordic ice dragons was long gone.

Tasha suddenly started talking to nobody in the room. "Hi, yes, this is Tasha Bellamy."

Vasili stilled as he heard a voice coming from the black object in her hand. "Miss Bellamy," a man exclaimed in delight. "How may I help you?"

Vasili crept toward Tasha and examined the object she held out on the flat of her hand. It was the same object she had used to show him the flying inventions.

"I met someone, a friend. He's a dragon." Her gaze met Vasili's.

"A dragon? He isn't—?"

"No, he's safe. But he was asleep in a cave in the Alps for more than seven hundred years. He needs to get to England to see if any dragons he knows are there, but he needs a passport and a driver's license. Probably a record of birth and stuff like that. I'd really like to help him find his family."

"Ah . . . I see," the voice said. "Yes, I can help with that. Do you plan to leave soon?"

"I was hoping to book flights tomorrow," Tasha said.

"That may be doable. Send me a picture of his face against a white background, as well as the name he wishes to use, and I will have documents delivered to your hotel tomorrow morning." The man paused. "You will be careful, won't you, Miss Bellamy? Your father entrusted you to my care."

"I will be. Thank you for helping us." She pressed

something on the surface of the black object and then put it away.

"What is that? And who was that speaking?"

"This?" She pulled it back out. "It's a cell phone, and it will soon be your best friend. You need to read all the books I brought, and once we can get you your own phone, you'll need to learn modern English."

Vasili nodded in agreement. "I learn languages very quickly, and other things too." He stared at the cell phone, fascinated. It looked like polished obsidian. He wanted to know how to speak to others on it, and he wanted to know how to see the moving paintings on it again.

When she saw the way he stared at the phone, she laughed. "Like I said, wait until you discover TV."

He didn't know what this *teevee* was, but he was no longer dreading this new world as he once had. If learning about it meant providing him a second chance at life, a life with a mate again, he knew that Marina would've wanted him to take that chance.

CHAPTER 6

Excerpt from Barrow's Journal – My Year with Dragons

Drakelings are able to fly early on during adolescence. Their wingspan grows as their dragon bodies do, but occasionally there are minor bumps and bruises while learning to fly. The body of a dragon is immensely heavy, so the wings must be large and strong in order to lift the body upon the wind. I thought at first that dragons were like birds, but in truth, they are far more like bats, with bone and sinew forming their wings. Mikhail recently told me that a group of dragons together is called a "wing of dragons." I rather like that, thinking of their wings and the way their scales glimmer as they fly in the sun. There is no more noble thing on earth than seeing a dragon fly upon the horizon.

. . .

Tasha rolled over in her bed. The lingering dream of black and gold dragons lounging on hot sand was still fresh in her mind as morning sunlight kissed her skin. Dragons . . . she had dreamt of dragons for the first time in her life. The memory of them left her feeling warm and yet melancholy, as though what she'd dreamed about had been so terribly long ago. A time that was over and gone, never to be experienced again. For a moment she tried desperately to cling to the dream, to hold on to it with all her might, but like the sand she'd dreamt of it poured through her fingertips.

"Good morning, little one." The words were in stilted English, and Tasha bolted up in bed. A tall, masculine body was reclined in a nearby chair.

Vasili. The dragon from the cave. It all came flooding back. Somehow in her sleep, her mind had buried yesterday's events.

He seemed somehow transformed from the ancient warrior he'd been last night. He now wore a pair of jeans and a gray cable-knit sweater. He looked every inch a modern man. Still gorgeous, but in a completely different way. He looked ready to dominate the world . . . including her. Every inch of him seemed alive and utterly present in the moment. How had she ever thought him a man out of time? Was this a power of dragons? The ability to adapt so easily to their environment? Whatever it was, she was drawn to him, a moth spiraling toward a candle flame, its light too beautiful to resist.

"Did you sleep well?" he asked, and this time it registered with her that the words weren't in Russian.

"You're speaking English," she said, but her mind continued to fixate on how *good* he looked. It was hard to imagine he'd ever been a frozen black dragon in the depths of an icy cave.

Yesterday had been a wild rush of events that had barely left her time to think. But now . . . now she could appreciate him in a way she hadn't before. His strong, sharp nose, his dark hair falling into his heavy-lidded eyes as he closed the encyclopedia he held in his lap. His strong fingers curled around its spine, cradling it like a treasure while the rest of him seemed focused completely on her.

Such quiet confidence radiated from him. He'd *settled*, that was the right word, settled into life, into being here with her, now, in whatever way that may be. He was willing to try.

"I stayed up most of the night and early into the morning, reading. Then I discovered the *teevee*." He stressed the letters uncertainly, as if not quite grasping the idea of an acronym. "I've been learning words by watching the Bee Bee Cee?" His rueful smile was completely devastating. She never wanted him to stop smiling.

"BBC. It stands for the British Broadcasting Corporation," she explained as she ran her fingers through her hair to tame the wild waves. Her hair always looked like a mess after she slept. "And *TV* is short for television." Not that that would mean anything to him at the moment.

His eyes tracked her movements. "You look very lovely this morning." He offered the compliment quietly, almost shyly. Why did that turn her on so much that she had to clench her thighs together and hold in a moan?

"Umm . . . thanks." Her cheeks burned and she looked away, afraid he'd seen how strong her desire was. She wasn't used to wanting someone, anyone, so much as she wanted him. It was disorienting to go from being so on her own to wanting to spend every moment near him.

"Did you get any sleep?" she asked, trying to think of what rational people would say to each other, rather than a lust-struck human woman obsessing over her potential dragon mate.

"An hour, I believe."

"Aren't you tired?"

He chuckled, the sound gruff and almost hoarse, as though he hadn't laughed in a long time. "I slept for seven hundred years. I think that was more than enough for me to skip one night."

"Right . . ." She cleared her throat. "Last night . . . I didn't have a chance to ask you about it, but when we, umm . . .?"

"Kissed?" Vasili set the encyclopedia on the reading table and placed his hands on the arms of his chair, like an ancient dragon king upon his throne.

"Yeah, when we kissed . . ." She let out an audible breath. "I saw things. I saw dragons." She closed her eyes. "Actually, I think I *was* a dragon."

Vasili stood, his blue eyes mercurial as he approached her. He sat down beside her on the bed, and she was all too aware of the intimacy of the moment with him so close to her while she wore only a silk nightgown. Why had she packed the thing? It wasn't as though she'd expected anyone to see her in bed.

"What exactly did you see?" He still spoke in English, his words less halting as he grew more comfortable speaking with her.

"I was a dragon . . . and I was flying behind a gold dragon. We dove down into the ocean, and then we crawled up on the sand and . . ." Tasha pictured the mating so clearly, but she couldn't say the words. How was she supposed to tell him she'd seen dragons having sex?

"Ah . . ." Vasili's eyes widened. "You saw one of my memories. You were in my head, seeing my past. The gold dragon was my mate."

"I was? Is that normal?"

"Yes," he said with a smile that made her heart flip in foolish excitement. "Very normal. It means you are receptive to the mating. Your mind and heart are open to mine."

"Oh . . . Did you see . . . I mean, are you supposed to see any of my memories?" What kind of memories would he find? Good ones? Embarrassing ones?

A shadow fell across his face. "I did not see anything." His gaze turned distant. "I may need time."

"But wouldn't it be the other way? Wouldn't you see *my* memories if I was the open one?"

"Yes and no. You are open to me, but I must be willing to go searching for you through our connection. Sometimes mates grow so strong that they can communicate clearly through their mental connection alone. The deeper they reach into each other's minds and hearts, the more they can see and speak to each other." He reached up and brushed the backs of his knuckles over her cheek, his eyes tender. "Give me time, little one. I have decided I want to try to be your mate."

Hope she'd never expected to feel surged through her, warming her to the tips of her toes. "You do?" How funny life was for her to go from fearing dragons to wanting to be accepted as a dragon's mate.

"I do. Marina would want me to take that chance. I think she would have liked you." He smiled, and Tasha knew that smile was meant for her and the future they might have.

It was strange, but hearing Vasili talk of his long-dead mate didn't upset her. This other woman had been his world, his everything to the point of death. And now Tasha had the chance to mean as much to him, and he could mean the same to her.

It was terrifying, but also irresistible. To be loved so deeply . . . Yes, she did want that, but she wasn't a fool. Love wouldn't come right away; it would come slowly, even though they were potential true mates. He had been through so much, and he'd been given a chance no other dragon had. They would both need time to adjust.

"So we should—?" she began.

A knock on the hotel room door interrupted them.

"Stay. I will answer it." He met whoever was at the door and returned with a manila envelope in his hands.

"That must be your paperwork from my attorney, Mr. Bovill." She held out her hands, and he placed the envelope on her palms. She opened the documents and sorted through the birth certificate, driver's license, and passport for Vasili. She opened the passport so he could see it.

"When we get on the airplane this evening, you will need to show everyone this." She walked him through each document in the folder and told him what to do and say in case they got separated.

"I need to book a flight to London. Then I need to shower and pack."

"I will watch more BBC until you are done. Then we must eat." He placed a hand on his stomach. "I am still quite hungry."

"I bet you are—seven hundred years is a lot of missed calories. Last night's dinner probably didn't even scratch the surface."

He stared at her quizzically. "Scratch what surface?"

"You might want to try watching some sitcoms instead of the news."

"Sitcoms?"

She smirked. "Never mind." She slipped out of bed but froze when she heard Vasili inhale sharply. She glanced over her shoulder at him. His eyes now burned a liquid gold, and he stared at her with unconcealed hunger. Suddenly aware of the silk nightie she'd put on, she rushed to the bathroom and closed the door. She leaned back against the wood and closed her eyes. He had looked at her like he wanted to devour her. Every woman wanted to be looked at like that by a man she was interested in, but Tasha was unprepared for how much that affected her. Having lived so secluded a life, she'd never been this close to a man.

Vasili's animal magnetism was a minor distraction most of the time, but right now his intense focus made her want to do something crazy. Like strip off her lingerie and stand in front of him completely naked, just to see what he would do.

This potential mate thing is insane.

She hadn't even known him twenty-four hours and she was considering stripping off her clothes in front of him. Tasha needed a cold shower—a really cold one. This new, more fearless Tasha was someone she didn't know. This new version of herself wanted to take even more risks, especially where Vasili was concerned. It was as if the old Tasha was beginning to fade away, but was that a good thing or a bad thing? She wasn't sure.

She removed her clothes and stepped into the water but couldn't bring herself to turn the tap to cold. Instead, she let the hot water burn over her naked body.

Her mind drifted back to the memory of the dragons on the beach, how she'd seen his previous mate. What he'd felt. Watching it had felt strange, like looking at herself in the mirror. She wasn't a dragon, but she couldn't deny the almost eerie sense of déjà vu as she'd seen the memory in Vasili's head. She also couldn't forget how it had felt to have him on top of her, kissing her senseless.

Vasili was temptation, beautiful masculine temptation. Everything about him was hard, sculpted, and warm to the touch. She wanted to lie naked on top of him with sunlight covering her back and sun herself, just like a dragon. Was that part of this process? The desire to be a dragon or to do dragon-y things? She couldn't ask her mother. While Naomi had been married to her father, they had never been true mates. Yet Dimitri had still loved her like one; they just didn't have that supernatural bond the way true mates did. Maybe she could ask the English dragons about what happens to humans who are true mates to dragons—assuming she and Vasili found any English dragons.

She finished her shower and dried her hair before dressing in jeans and a pale-blue sweater. When she emerged from the bathroom, Vasili had a set of books out and was paging through them, his brow furrowed.

"Is it true that the world went to war *twice?*" The look in his eyes was hollow, an ancient pain that actually hurt her too.

"The world changed after you went into the cave. It's more connected than ever, and there were people who did bad things, but there were more of us to step up to stop them." It was hard to explain to him the social and societal changes of the last seven hundred years.

"And my people? We did not fight in these wars?" That seemed to bother him more than anything else.

"I don't know. The majority of humans don't know you exist. To most people, you are just a myth."

His shoulders slumped a little. "My people must live in hiding. Are we all trapped in caves and—?"

"No, it's not like that. I know dragons are not in hiding. They keep humans unaware of their existence, but they live amongst us and act as humans." She still didn't mention her father being a dragon. For so long she had been trained not to speak about him to anyone except her mother. It was a hard habit to break. "Wasn't it like that in your time?"

"It was, mostly, but there were humans who knew about us. It seems there is still much I must learn." He sighed, the sound centuries old.

Tasha sat on the bed beside him and touched his shoulder. That now familiar spark of heat flared between them, and it took her a moment to focus.

"Let's just focus on getting to London. We'll take it one day at a time."

Vasili grasped her other hand and raised it to his mouth, kissing the back of her hand. The gesture wasn't seductive; it was *reverent*. For a long moment they simply stared at each other.

"I . . . I should schedule those flights now." She slipped free of his touch and was glad to have something to focus on that would keep her away from Vasili—and the bed—a little while longer.

VASILI WARILY EYED THE METAL BEAST—NO, THE *airplane*—through the tall glass windows of the airport. To see so much glass in long, clear sheets . . . it was a marvel that partially distracted him from the anxiety of the airplane in front of him. Trepidation crept through him as he watched the people ahead move their boarding passes over an odd desk with red lights.

So far, his entire experience of the airport had been a mix of wonders and unpleasantness. It was a crowded place, with humans everywhere. And the sounds were too much. His hearing was stronger than most humans, and the airplanes roared almost as loudly as dragons when they took to the air. He had read about airplanes last night while Tasha slept, learning how they worked. All the evidence suggested they were safe, but he still wasn't comfortable getting inside one.

Tasha leaned in, and his body hummed with irresistible desire for her. "Are you okay?" Her sweet scent made his nose twitch and his hands tingle with the urge to grab her and pull her into his arms. It was becoming harder to resist touching her now. His dragon was all for claiming her in the ancient way—pinning her down, biting her neck, and mating her. But Vasili was only beginning to entertain the idea that he might truly have a second chance at a mated life.

But as his openness to the idea increased, so did the temptation Tasha presented to him. Even now, he had a hand on her lower back, quietly asserting his possession of her to the human males around him. Part of him wanted everyone to know she belonged to him. The best part was the way she leaned into his possessive grip as though she wanted every female around to know *he* was also claimed. He liked knowing she was as possessive of him as he was of her.

"I am not comfortable climbing into the belly of a metal beast."

"Try not to think of it like that, then," Tasha suggested. "It's not eating you."

He grunted, and she giggled.

"And I thought *I* was scared of flying," she murmured.

"Wait, you do not trust these machines either?"

"I didn't," she admitted with a look of bafflement. "It took all my willpower to get on one of these to come to Europe. After that, I took trains."

He studied her. She seemed completely at ease. "You do not seem afraid now."

"Huh . . . maybe it's because I realize how silly you look making such a big deal of it." She nudged him playfully in the ribs, and his heart turned over in his chest. How often had Marina done that? Teased him and nudged him just so . . .

Vasili stared at the tunnel that led to the plane as they approached a female in a blue uniform. She took their boarding passes and ran them under the red light.

"I am beginning to understand how sheep feel when I eat them," he muttered.

Tasha made a soft, startled sound. "You eat sheep? Like cute little white sheep?"

He arched a brow at her amusing look of horror. "When I am a dragon, I am a wild beast, Tasha. We have to eat what the land provides."

She shook her head. "Just don't eat any sheep now, okay? People own them, and they often have metal tags or trackers. I don't want any humans trying to find their missing sheep and tracking you down instead."

As they reached the airplane's mouth, he insisted on going first. If there was any kind of threat ahead, whatever it may be, he wanted to be between Tasha and the danger. As he stepped inside of what Tasha had called the cabin, he saw lines of plush gray leather seats. Tasha nudged him from behind toward a pair of seats on the left in the front part of the cabin.

He sat down by the window, and she joined him. Peering out the small oval window, he observed men and women in brightly colored orange vests loading the traveling cases of the passengers onto a ramp that moved into the belly of the metal beast. When he allowed himself to relax, the marvels of this age left him breathless. Even as a being of otherworldly magic, the advances that had been made from the science of the humans were absolutely incredible. Science was a magic in its own right.

"Science is like magic . . . yet different," he said to Tasha. Her eyes lit up with interest.

"Different how?"

He puzzled over how best to describe it after all the information he'd absorbed in the last day. "Magic is something one feels, whereas science is something one thinks through, but both lead to discoveries and wonders beyond imagining. To puzzle out the mysteries of magic, one has to delve deeper and deeper into self-understanding of one's connection with everything. Science takes the opposite approach; they seem to try to understand their connection through everything by puzzling it out externally."

"Which is the right approach?" she asked.

He shrugged. "Somewhere in the middle, I should think. The world needs both science and magic to survive. I fear the day we lose either completely."

Tasha was silent a long moment and so was he as they watched the rest of the people finish boarding the plane. Then a woman in a blue uniform passed them in the aisle, telling them to prepare for takeoff.

"Let's buckle in." Tasha showed him how to secure the belt around his waist that kept him in his seat. He did so apprehensively. These moving inventions like cars and airplanes all seemed to require belts like these. He couldn't help but question their safety.

"Vasili, can you tell me about the other kinds of dragons? I know there are a few different ones, depending on where they are in the world." Tasha leaned in to twine her arm with his, and he let out a breath he hadn't realized he'd been holding. Other passengers walked past them deeper into the main cabin, but none seemed to be paying attention either of them. If there was one good thing about these modern humans, it was their own self-absorption; their cell phones seemed to keep them all distracted. He had a feeling he could have changed into a dragon and half of them would not even have looked up from their little black devices.

He turned his attention back to her. "You want to know about other dragons? Why?"

"I grew up knowing nothing about dragons. I only learned about them a short while ago. I've never seen any before you. I'm just curious."

"Well, we have different species, but we all share similarities. Colors can be spread out among all of the types of dragons, but other details may not be."

"Like what?" she asked.

He gazed into her lovely topaz eyes, amused at her interest. "Take the Chinese Serpents. They have no frills about their necks and no spikes or clubs on their tails. They are more like snakes with legs. They are skinny, sleek, and when they fly, they have webbed fins of a sort on their bodies. Then you have the Nordic ice dragons. Their scales are less rounded and more triangular in shape than mine, almost like shark teeth. They tend to be mostly blue or silver in color."

"Their scales are sharp?"

"Yes, and the scales on their heads and limbs are tougher. It helps them dig through ice and form tunnels."

"What about you? You're a Russian Imperial, right?"

"We are built to fight, to survive vicious fights and crashes or impacts." He touched the scar on his side where he'd been wounded by Dimitri Drakor, and Tasha didn't miss it. She placed her other hand on his arm, her eyes wide with worry.

"I didn't think you would survive that deep of a wound."

"I am tougher than you can imagine. My mate only died when . . ." It took him a minute to compose himself. "We have very few vulnerable spots, but our throats and our bellies are thinner and more susceptible to attack."

Tasha shivered, her hand sliding to grip her throat protectively at the mention of his mate's attack, and he felt like a bastard for bringing Marina up. He knew it had to hurt her.

"Her throat was torn out . . . I'm sorry. I shouldn't have said—"

"No, I'm the one who's sorry." Tasha cupped his cheek and turned his face so their eyes locked. "She was your mate, your love. You should never have to minimize her importance in your life. I just know how much it hurts to talk about her, especially how she died."

Vasili was quiet a long moment. "Dragons have a different sense of time, of the way it passes. We feel it far more strongly than other creatures, except perhaps for vampires, but they often become crippled by it the more they focus on its passage."

"Wait . . . vampires are real too?" Her eyes widened.

"Almost anything you've ever believed a myth was likely a real creature at some point. Dragons, vampires, werewolves, witches, unicorns, merfolk. But dragons, we are different. Dragons embrace time and its march forward. We see time as the collective memory of the universe and each second as a memory, good or ill. When I woke, it was disorienting at first to see how much time had passed and yet not to have felt the changes within myself. But I believe I am growing accustomed to those changes. It feels like more time has passed. The seven hundred years I missed while I was asleep are . . . How do I explain it? Expanding? Yes, expanding in my head to fill the missing sense of time. Marina's death will always be a painful memory, but the sharp agony of her loss is beginning to fade to a dull ache."

"Maybe . . . maybe that's why the mate grief affects dragons so acutely?" Tasha suggested. "You feel everything so deeply at first that you feel you can't get past it, but time was frozen for you. Now the grief is less acute because on some level your body feels the distance involved, so it's more survivable."

Vasili had never considered that, but it was possible. "If that is true, I may be the only known dragon to have survived losing a mate."

"Hopefully, the English dragons will know more about it," Tasha added.

"I hope so. The English drakes are good keepers of history. If anyone knows of this, they will."

"Are the English drakes different from the other types of dragons? You mentioned the Londinium drakes and fire drakes. Is there a difference?"

"The Fire drakes live in Scotland to the north, but the are no different than the English drakes that live in the south. It's simply a matter of geography. When I was much younger, I knew the English drakes as Londinium drakes. I had a few good friends there. They are like all dragons. They are fiercely loyal to their familial lines. Their clan relationships are strong. They rarely war with other nearby families and are less territorial, but they certainly aren't afraid of a fight. I suppose you could say they are modern in their thinking."

Their plane shook then. Something below clanged, and Vasili tensed.

"They've just sealed the luggage area. We'll be taking off soon." Tasha covered his left hand with hers. He turned his palm up to connect their hands better, so she could thread her fingers through his. It was becoming so much easier to be with her now. It was almost as though he had known her his entire life, not just a day.

The next fifteen minutes were a challenge as he sat still in his seat while the airplane moved and then sped up before suddenly lifting. His stomach dropped as the air pressure changed. All of this was normal for a dragon, but experiencing it as a human? It was eerie and unnatural. His body's natural instinct was to let his dragon slide to the surface and take over, changing him so he could fly. It took more willpower than he liked to admit to keep his focus on staying human.

Vasili stared out the window, watching the clouds suddenly cover the windows. Then the plane rose higher and beyond the cloud bank. He was flying, but in the most unnatural way he could imagine. What was he, really, if he could not change into his dragon form and fly the way he was meant to?

CHAPTER 7

Excerpt from Barrow's Journal – My Year with Dragons

The universe has a memory of its own, the stars, the moons, the planets . . . every minute of it belongs to dragons. Mikhail has told me this is part of an ancient dragonsong. I could not fully grasp the words he said, but this is my best interpretation of it. Dragons are living memory.

LONDON WAS NOT THE LONDINIUM OF HIS MEMORIES.

The city he'd once visited had been a tiny village, a human population of less than twenty thousand. The buildings had been wooden then, but now they were all stone and glass. Even the newly built Westminster palace he'd visited in the eleventh century was no longer the same. The great tower built by William the Conqueror was no longer a single tower but a vast network of stone towers and courtyards functioning as a tourist attraction. The once-sturdy Roman walls still existed but were merely crumbled ruins.

Even the single wooden bridge once built to stretch across the Thames was stone now. The once-quiet country town with its St. Paul's Cathedral and monasteries was buried deep beneath towering skyscrapers. The sounds of nature were drowned out beneath the ever-present hum of traffic. He didn't like the crowds or the chaos, and his dragon liked it even less. It was pacing in his mind, huffing smoke softly from its nostrils as it fought the urge to surge to the surface and change him into his dragon form.

"So much has changed," Vasili mused. He and Tasha exited the cab they had caught from the airport.

"What was it like before?"

"In the twelfth century, it was lively, but not so crowded. It was a city renowned for its abundant wealth. The commerce and the grandeur of its buildings was a testament to the power of England." He frowned as he studied the tall pictures of men and women displaying various objects that hung from the buildings. "There used to be a horse market at Smithfield where they raced horses. I loved watching those." He gripped the handle of his suit-case as memories from long ago came back. He could almost smell the scents of stables and hay that had once been here.

After a moment, he continued. "Londoners adored dancing. If you had any open spaces, people would find an excuse to dance."

"Did you like to dance?" Tasha asked.

"I was rather fond of dancing. The humans here also loved archery and wrestling. Men would fight each other with mock swords and shields, and when it was winter, people would skate on the frozen marshes."

"Skate? What did they use for ice skates?"

"Carved animal bones."

"Really?"

"What?" he asked, confused by her surprise. "Do they use something different now?"

"Yeah, we use metal blades. It's just . . . I never thought the concept of skating went back that far."

Vasili chuckled. "Men and women have been skating on ice for as long as they could stand on two feet. In the days of the Vikings, they used rough rawhide smoothed and slicked with oil to slide. The idea of skating on a fine, sharp edge came later." He was intrigued at the idea of metal blades. The humans of this age had an abundance of glass and metals and something rather curious called plastic, which was unbelievably versatile.

Perhaps someday soon he could try this modern form of skating. He pictured skating with Tasha, then pretending to fall and take her down with him, with her landing safely on top of him, of course. He rather liked that idea—or really, any idea that could put her body against his.

"Why don't we check into the hotel? Then I can show you the London of today. I was here not too long ago, and there are some fun places to visit that I didn't get to see yet that we should go to." Her face lit up as she talked of the city, and it was clear that she loved London. With each new street they passed, she rushed to point out things she'd been just brave enough to try out on her own, and then with more excitement she pointed out to him all the things she wanted to do with him now that he was here with her. Her cheeks flushed with excitement, and he too was excited about the possibilities of exploring this new world with her. She was so vibrant, so alive; her spirit was infectious. It electrified him, like a bolt of lightning to his heart. No wonder his dragon had woken up for her in that cold cave. She was life itself. And yet, he realized with some fascination and wonder, her discovering him had woken her up too in a way.

"Well, what do you think? We could do the whole tourist thing and see if we run across any of these English drakes."

"That's a good plan." No doubt the English drakes would be hiding their existence away from humans, yet living among them, which would make it a little more challenging to find them. But if he got close to one, he was certain he would sense them.

As they entered the grand hall of the hotel, he saw the word *Dorchester* in large letters on the side of the building.

"This is one of the most iconic and expensive hotels in London," Tasha admitted. "I probably shouldn't spend the money, but I've never really had a chance to enjoy something like this, and staying in a cheap little hostel just seemed wrong, you know?"

He hadn't the faintest idea what a hostel was, but it sounded, well, hostile.

The bellman tipped his cap at them respectfully and

pointed them toward the check-in desk. Vasili was impressed by the golden glow of the entryway. The floors were so polished that they reflected whatever moved above them. Lavish furnishings filled the space, and elaborate bouquets of flowers in large vases covered many of the side tables.

It was far more palatial than anything he was used to seeing in his day and age. If this was a place where normal humans of wealth stayed, he couldn't help but wonder where the kings and queens lived. Were their palaces even more overwhelming than this?

He remembered the stone castle he had left behind in Russia with his brother, Ivan. It had been a strong and mighty fortress that should have lasted thousands of years, if kept well. But he'd learned that only a handful of castles from that era still existed, and most were barely more than a few stone walls and ruins, the rest preserved as monuments to the past. This depressing thought only made him more determined to find the English dragons.

Tasha spoke to a person at the front desk, and after a few minutes she turned and handed him a key card. She'd explained the use of these in Switzerland.

"This one is yours. Don't lose it."

He slipped it into the folded leather wallet she'd purchased for him and followed her to the elevators. His mind was still catching up with this new age, the changes in the languages and the technology.

"We have the Belgravia Suite." Tasha grinned. "I stayed in it when I was here last time. It's gorgeous"—she then flushed bright red—"and I just remembered it has only one bed." She peeped up at him through her lashes, innocent, seductive, trying to both hide and announce her intentions. He almost kissed her then, but his dragon's overeagerness had a strangely calming effect on Vasili's human side.

Over the last day, he had been changing. The desolation that had gripped him upon waking up in that dark cave was beginning to fade. Life felt like it meant something again, and it had everything to do with Tasha. Her smile, her laugh, her stubbornness, the way she took charge whenever he hesitated, and the way she showed compassion. He was obsessed with the endless facets of her personality. She was a woman he could spend the rest of his life learning about. He had felt that way about Marina too, that desperate need to know *all* of her.

Yet with Tasha, it was different. He felt like he wasn't in a hurry. He wanted to enjoy her, savor each moment. If she was to be his mate, he had to prove to her that he was ready, and rushing it could destroy her trust in him. So he would take his time, he would woo her like the dragons of old, and perhaps, if he was worthy, he would be lucky enough to have a second chance at life's greatest joy, to love and be loved through a mated bonding.

"So that's okay, right?" Tasha asked as the elevator doors opened. "The one bed, I mean?"

They rolled their traveling cases into the corridor. "Yes. So long as it's a *big* bed, since I am large. You are right. I did not like my feet dropping off the side." He'd been more uncomfortable than he'd wanted to admit. Of course, much of that was because his dragon had spent most of the night wanting to go into Tasha's chamber and wrap around her body. The dragon's intentions were clear, but Vasili wasn't going to let the dragon control his actions.

"Oh, don't worry. This one's a king-size, like the one I slept in at the other hotel."

"Good. It will fit us both." He chuckled at her expression, which deepened in its wonderful red. He enjoyed knowing he could affect her that way.

"Yeah." She brushed her hair back behind her ear as she unlocked the room door. He reached out to push the door open for her with one hand so she could pull her suitcase inside without hitting anything.

They took a few moments to put their clothes away and then stood at the window looking down over a beautifully forested area lit by electric lamps.

"I think we should go out for dinner and then go dancing or something. We could both use a bit of fun to unwind."

"Unwind?"

She smiled up at him. "Relax."

Vasili couldn't resist. He slid a hand around her waist, letting his fingers slide up beneath her sweater to touch her bare skin just above the waist of her jeans. "Perhaps I do not wish to relax just yet."

Tasha made a soft sound and turned into him, pressing the length of her body against his. They came together so naturally, so perfectly, her curves fitting the hard planes of his body in a way that made him feel so at peace, yet hungry for every touch and kiss he could steal from her.

"This mating thing is insane," she murmured as she pressed a kiss to his jaw. "It's like I want you touching me *all the time.* Is it like that for you?" Her hesitant tone made his chest ache. She still feared he didn't feel the same about her. How could he convince her?

"It is," he promised. "I could hold you in my arms forever, little one. But I am trying to take things slowly."

She kissed his throat. "Why do we need to go slow?" His dragon rumbled in pleasure.

"Because I need you to be sure you desire me. And I want to earn your trust." It was a risk to explain what fears and concerns lay in his heart, but he had been open with Marina about all things, and Tasha deserved the same.

"When do you think you will see my memories?" she asked as her lips feathered over his. He groaned as he cupped her face and deepened the kiss. He knew what she wanted; to see his memories meant letting go and trusting her completely, both focusing and relaxing at the same time. It wasn't an easy thing to do, but he tried. Once mates trusted each other it was easy, but it was always difficult the first time.

Trust me. She spoke to him inside his head, but he knew she wasn't aware that he could hear her. She was already connected to him more strongly than he'd imagined. He felt his own control release inch by inch until he was spiraling into her head, blasting through memory after memory.

He was a child chasing fireflies while his mother watched from the back porch. Now he sat on a wooden dock, dipping his feet into the warm lake water as the sun beat down on his body. Now he leapt from one memory to the next, drinking in the experiences of her life like a man who'd crossed a desert and stumbled upon a cool spring.

There were a handful of glimpses of Tasha's face in the mirror, her gaze growing solemn as she grew up and matured into an adult woman. *Lonely*. She was a young woman separate from the world. His dragon crouched protectively, wanting to reassure her that she wasn't alone anymore. She had him and his dragon now.

One last memory flashed past his eyes before the end of the twisting and jarring pass he had taken through her mind—a dragon falling from the sky and crashing into a snowy mountain. Only *he* was the dragon falling, his throat ripped open by a Drakor dragon. His own dragon's wings fluttered in distress inside his head as Vasili tried to grasp the fragment of memory and draw it back into the light.

What had he just seen? This felt like his memory of Marina's last moments, yet it could not be, because in his memory he was chasing her as she fell. This shred of memory in Tasha's head couldn't be Tasha's. It could only belong to . . . *to Marina*.

Vasili tore his mouth away from Tasha. She shook violently as she gazed up at him, pain and confusion in her eyes.

"What did you see?" he demanded. She had seen something of his past, something that frightened her.

"I saw you fighting . . . with black dragons, and I saw . . . I saw her fall. Oh, *Vasili*."

She threw her arms around his neck, hugging him tight as she whispered apologies in his ear. He hugged her back, holding her close until her trembling ceased. She had seen the same events, but from his perspective. Why was one of his memories—or rather, one of *Marina's* memories— locked inside her head?

"Tasha, you held the dragon heart stone in the cave when you found me, yes?"

She pulled back to look up at him and nodded. "It glowed when I touched it, and at first I thought it burned my hand, but I couldn't let go of it."

Vasili gently released her and went to his suitcase, retrieving the stone. He unwrapped it from the cloth and watched it pulse softly in his hands. The blue glow rose and fell like a heartbeat.

"What does it mean?" Tasha asked.

"I do not know, but I believe one soul in particular may have been inside the stone when you touched it. A soul that is trying to bond to you." He looked up from the stone to her ashen face.

"You mean a *dragon* soul?"

"Not just any soul, but the dragon that was born to my first mate." He frowned as he struggled to continue. "I saw a memory that was not yours, but hers. It was brief, but it was her. Now it's in here." He tapped her temple with a fingertip.

"But how is that possible?" Tasha asked. "How could it bond to me?"

Vasili shook his head. He had no answers. Only other more ancient dragons might be able to tell him.

"We need to find the Belishaws."

"Who are the Belishaws?" Tasha asked. "One of the dragon families?"

Vasili prayed to all the old gods who no longer held sway in this new world that he would be able to find dragons hiding in the city. He knew better than anyone that dragons who didn't want to be found were nearly impossible to find, but he had to try. Who knew how long he would have stayed hidden if Marina's dragon's soul had not sensed a possible true mate and drawn her to his cave. He was almost certain that was what had happened, but the Belishaws would know for sure.

"The Belishaws are England's oldest dragon family, even older than the fire drakes of what you call Scotland."

"Okay, so how are we going to find them? You make it sound like it won't be easy."

He gazed at her grimly. "It won't be. But we can use the one thing any hot-blooded dragon can't resist: a beautiful virgin."

"Where are we going to—" Tasha cut herself off abruptly as she realized why he was gazing at her with a grim expression.

"Wait, you mean me?" Tasha's voice jumped up an octave.

He didn't like thinking of using her, but it was necessary. "Yes. You will be the virgin bait."

CHAPTER 8

Excerpt from Barrow's Journal – My Year with Dragons

As a gentleman, I do not often discuss matters of sex or love, even with my closest friends. But the issue of "virgin lust" for dragons is too interesting not to comment upon, at least in this private diary of mine. Dragons have a clear primal obsession with a dragoness or human virgin of breeding age. I am told I must imagine the most favorite food I've ever eaten and how it tastes and smells. I instantly think of my cook's sticky cinnamon buns that she bakes only at Christmas. Even as I write this, the memory of tasting such sugary sweetness upon my tongue makes my mouth water. The scent of a virgin is ten times stronger to a dragon compared to that. And the scent of a true mate, one hundred times stronger.

. . .

Being virgin dragon bait was not nearly as scary as she'd expected it to be. They grabbed meat pies on the street and walked down the pathway while he explained, eating and talking. They stuck to the touristy areas, enjoying the sightseeing themselves.

It felt natural, to explore the world with Vasili like this, as though she'd done it all before. Which, of course, she hadn't. But being with him was just that easy.

The hard part was remembering their mission, to search for dragons, though that job was more on Vasili than her. Every now and then, his gaze would dart around, his nostrils flaring.

"How can you sense them? The other dragons, I mean," she asked.

"The smell. It's . . . unique to our kind," he mused. "It's like no other scent in the world, but it can be masked by perfumes or other scents that humans seem to douse themselves in these days."

"Do I have a smell? As a human?" she asked, more than curious. "I mean, of course I have a smell, but what do I smell like to you?" She'd never had that great of a nose for smells. His was the only scent that she had really ever noticed. It made her dizzy and homesick to be near him.

"You smell like Russia, like the forests of my home in the fire hills." His tone was soft, sweet, and his eyes were gently swirling pools as he gazed at her.

"You smell like Christmas, I think," she confessed, her face growing hot. "Like evergreen and winter, and spice. Everything I love most."

"That is the way of possible mates. Our scent, our looks, our touch—it drives us closer until we cannot bear to be parted for long. It is what makes the mate grief so strong."

The more she was around him, the more she began to understand what it would feel like to lose him, to never see him again. The mere thought made her chest burn with pain.

We aren't even mated, and I can't bear the idea.

Tasha licked her fingers of the last bit of pie crumbs as she and Vasili stopped at the gates of Buckingham Palace.

"It's lovely," he said, half to himself. He nodded at the palace, with its gilded exterior. "So much gold and light."

"Did you have palaces like this back in your time?"

"Nothing like this. We built fortresses to withstand sieges. They could be beautiful, but beauty and loveliness often mean two different things."

"What do you mean?"

Vasili tucked his hands into his black wool knee-length coat. His gaze still roamed over the palace. "Beauty can be harsh, austere, remote. Loveliness is warm. It grows and makes everything around it welcoming." He turned to look at her, his blue eyes soft and warm. "*You* are lovely, Tasha. You are warm and compassionate. It makes you glow."

She glanced down at her feet, unable to respond. She didn't feel particularly lovely. She never really gave much thought to her appearance.

"Did I embarrass you?" Vasili cupped her cheek and lifted her face to his, studying her eyes.

"Maybe a little," she admitted. "I've just never . . . I mean romance wasn't really part of my life goals. I was always busy studying, and then working, keeping my head down and staying safe. Always safe—" She halted as she realized what she'd said, what she'd almost admitted. But now she realized she wanted to tell him.

"Safe? Were you in danger?" His voice deepened slightly.

"My father . . ." She drew in a deep breath. She had to trust him with herself. "He was a dragon, like you."

Vasili's eyes widened. "Your father was a shifter like me?"

"Yes."

He was quiet for a moment. "That explains how you've behaved around me. A normal mortal would have been far less comfortable knowing dragons exist. Why didn't you tell me this sooner?"

"I was raised to never speak of him to anyone but my mother. My father was always worried about my mother and me. He had enemies . . . enemies who killed him." She closed her eyes. "I loved him, but there was so much about him I didn't really know. I didn't even know he was a dragon until after he died. His death left a scar inside me."

She touched her chest. What she'd lost, a man she'd barely known, couldn't begin to compare to Vasili losing his mate, the woman he'd hoped to love for thousands of years. It made her feel very small, very *human* by comparison. "It sounds silly, I know. I mean, how can you love a person and feel their loss so keenly when you barely know them?"

Vasili put his hands on her waist and pulled her into his

arms. She resisted only a moment before she burrowed her face against his chest. She shed no tears, but the ache, the empty place in her heart, was still there, and it throbbed painfully. Vasili cradled her in his arms, one hand threading through her hair as he held her head while his other arm circled her back, locking her into him.

"You have every right to mourn what you lost. Just because you spent only a little time with him does not mean that time did not matter."

Tasha took a deep breath, allowing Vasili's scent to fill her lungs. "He came one Christmas, just one, but it was wonderful. We had snow that afternoon, and when he arrived for dinner, he and I built a fort and a snowman. Well, I built the snowman." She smiled. "Dad made the fort. It had these perfect little bricks in the tower. The snow was thick enough and I was small enough that he could sit me down on the turrets and the snow wouldn't crumble beneath me. I remember how much he laughed that night."

Tasha had been so young then, but she had always believed that her father had suffered. There had been more darkness in him than light, and what light he'd had, he'd reserved for her and her mother alone.

"You loved him very much, and all your moments with him are important. That isn't silly. Would I know your father?"

"I don't think so. I think he was born after you were in the ice." She thought back to how modern her father had been; he couldn't have been as old as Vasili.

"What about you?" she asked, still burrowed against

him. He was so wonderfully warm, and London was quite chilly.

"Me?"

"Yes, what is one of your happiest memories?"

Vasili hesitated and went rigid against her. "I . . ."

"You can talk about her. It doesn't upset me." It didn't. Marina was a part of Vasili. Tasha would never make him pretend she hadn't existed.

Vasili relaxed. "It was so long ago, yet still so clear in my mind. Marina and I were lying on the beach. It was warm, the water was cool, and there was nothing I wanted for in that moment. I was at peace with myself, with the world. It was perfect. How often does someone have a moment like that? Where they are truly happy?"

"Not often enough," she said. She was happy now, in this moment with him. With him touching her, talking to her, letting her see and know him. It was one of the closest relationships she'd ever had, aside from her mother. That realization overwhelmed her with a sudden sense of loneliness.

She looked up at him. "When we kissed, I think I saw a part of that memory."

"Yes, I believe you did." He stroked her cheek with the backs of his fingers. His hands were fascinating. He was an ancient warrior, and she had seen his hands as claws, tearing through ice like paper. Yet now they were elegant, his strong fingers long and soft to the touch. She couldn't help but fantasize about those hands roving over her bare skin, exploring places she was too shy to think about anyone else ever touching but herself.

"Would you say no if I asked you to kiss me again?" she asked. "Is it safe?"

His blue eyes swirled with gold as he lowered his face to her.

"No, not safe at all. But right now, I do not wish to be safe."

Somehow under the darkness of the night, it felt safer to ask him for a kiss. But the kiss itself was dangerous. It was the type of kiss that poets have sought to write about for hundreds of years. So many centuries of love, pain, joy, and agony filled that kiss. It was in the fierce grip of his hands on her as his control simply faded away.

Something deep within her stirred, a fluttering that grew with every passing second. A voice whispered to her, and images blossomed in her mind.

He was in the dark, a fire lit in the stone fireplace. Several fur blankets lay thick upon her where she stretched out on the feather tick mattress. Her heart beat wildly as her mate came toward her. Vasili's naked skin glowed in the firelight, and his eyes were gold with a dragon's desire. He stopped at the foot of the bed and pulled the furs away from her little by little until she was naked to his ravenous gaze. He said no pretty words of seduction, and she needed none. He climbed onto the mattress and crawled over her like a lion. He was all hard muscle and lethal grace as he grasped her knees and pushed them apart.

Vasili entered her body swiftly, and she cried out. He stilled above her, his hot breath warming her skin as he murmured soft apologies. She raised her hips, hesitant, unsure what to do next. She'd always been so confident, always knew what to do, except for now. He withdrew from her body a little and sank back in, still stretching her inside, but the pain faded with the slow penetration of her body by his. He seemed more guided by instinct than she and for once, she let him take control, show her what to do as they learned to make love together for the first time.

He gripped her gently by the throat and held her still as he rode her slowly, letting her get used to being filled. The pump of his hips increased as he sensed she was feeling pleasure now rather than pain.

Their first coupling was quiet, only filled with moans and sighs and the tap of flesh upon flesh as the snow fell outside their small stone home. It was everything she'd hoped for, this union in the dark, their bodies coming together, their dragons content with the warmth of the fire and the blaze of love between them.

The memory sank back into the depths of Tasha's mind, and no matter how hard she tried, she could not make it come back. She only knew that it was *her* memory, not his. But that was impossible. Vasili's lips broke away from hers, but he held her close, their foreheads touching as he regained his breath. Tasha grasped his wrists, holding him to her. Her body trembled, as though it had relived that memory of lovemaking. Her thighs were weak, her womb ached, and she was sore. It was as though her body was remembering the sensation of being sore. But how could she remember a memory that wasn't hers? Dragons saw memories from their mate's perspective. This memory had been hers because she had been . . . Marina.

"The more I touch you, the more I am unable to stop," he confessed as he nuzzled her face. "It's so familiar at times, this mate passion with you."

Tasha didn't want him to stop touching her, but she was afraid—afraid of what it might mean to see a dead woman's memories. She didn't think this was normal, even for dragons.

"We . . . we should go somewhere more public so we can see lots of people."

She glanced about. Only a handful of tourists were out this late. If they wanted to draw a dragon out into the open, they would need to go somewhere with more people.

"Where do you suggest?" he asked. "We need somewhere that people would gather."

"Maybe a sports arena? There might be a football match on or something tonight."

"No, such a place would heighten our competitive aggressive sides, and we would not be focused on females. We need a place that would stoke our passion."

"A nightclub?" She couldn't think of a better place.

"What is a nightclub?" Vasili asked.

She took his hand, and they walked away from the palace to hail a cab. "A place where people dance. Thousands of people will be there. There will be a lot of stoking of passions there. Hell, some people almost have sex right there on the floor."

"Thousands of people come together to dance like this?"

"Come on, we'll be nightclub virgins together. It's not a total orgy. I promise." She laughed as his adorable, ancient dragon's eyes widened in concern. She leaned in to whisper in his ear. "I promise I'll be gentle." Another flash of memory hit her then. Another night in Vasili's bed, one where she was on top, riding him to her pleasure, his hands bound to the bed so he could not touch her—he could only feel what she did to him.

Vasili pulled her to a stop on the sidewalk, an intense look on his face. "What did you say?"

"I'll be gentle," she said, trying not to let him see her own shock.

The storms were back in his eyes, and a haunted look shadowed his expression. "You say things . . . things that remind me of her." He seemed reluctant to admit this, and she understood why. A woman didn't want to be compared to a man's former lover. If she hadn't had the confusing flashes of someone else's memories, then maybe she would've been upset as well. Instead, she was confused.

"Maybe . . . maybe Marina's dragon chose me because I'm like her?"

"Maybe," he agreed.

She waved a cab down and gave the driver the address for a nightclub.

It never ceased to amaze her how quickly he was adapting to the modern world. But dragons learned things more quickly than humans. He'd also developed an addiction to Wikipedia and looked up everything on his new cell phone. He'd picked up the nuances of the language and had read through more books than she could count, books about science, history, and technology. Except for his slightly formal speech patterns, he could pass for a modern man. He clicked his seat belt into place and settled into the back of the cab with easy confidence, such a stark contrast to the half-naked muscle god who'd believed the horseless metal beasts with no eyes meant her harm.

Vasili placed a hand on her thigh, and she covered his hand with hers, tracing the veins that ran the length of the back of his hand. She couldn't help but picture him as he'd looked when he'd been wearing nothing but a towel when they were in Switzerland. He was all raw muscle, all hardness and hot skin. It was impossible not to want to touch him whenever she had the chance.

The cab dropped them off at the Printworks, which was a nightclub housed in one of the largest former printing factories in Western Europe. She held Vasili's hand as they entered the club.

It was dark, except for the colored lights swerving over the room in dramatic patterns that matched the music booming from the hundreds of speakers hanging in the old factory.

The original aesthetics of the factory were still there. In the shadows, half hidden by fog, Tasha saw the giant machines and printing presses that had worked tirelessly for decades. Techno music swelled around them, and the second story of the factory's interior had people flooding the balconies while the DJ operated the entire show with lasers and music. Vasili kept her hand in his, and she felt his grip tighten. She glanced at him. His jaw was set in a hard line as he watched the crowd around them, all lost in the music.

Just then, the room was filled with streams of color

forming a rainbow down the avenue of people, and Vasili's face was illuminated in blue light. A woman crooned a haunting melody in a minor key as the bass thumped a rhythm as steady as a heartbeat.

Vasili began to relax, his eyes sweeping the room before resting on her. Tasha stepped into his arms, and they both began to sway, finding a rhythm to dance to.

This is how it was, how it is, how it will be with him, she thought. The endless shift between light and dark, as they moved to the steps of an ancient dance older than memory. Every slide of his hands, every soft breath on her cheek, and every twitch of his muscles was a symphony she had once known somehow, as though from a dream within a dream. It terrified her as much as it soothed her, to feel so certain that she knew him as well as she did, even though they'd only known each other for two days.

Was it the magic of dragon mating or something else? Something even harder to explain? Like a dragon soul hoarding the memories of a dead woman and keeping them safe in the heart of a sapphire?

Tasha lost track of time as they danced. If there were dragons here, she did not sense them. She was too absorbed in the moment and this man, *her* man, to think past the next song.

RANDOLPH BELISHAW STARED AT THE HUMANS DANCING in the Printworks nightclub. He remembered, as all creatures do who sense time beyond a mere hundred years, a collection of moments in a vast and ever-shifting kaleidoscope. He could see this place as it was now, and he remembered the fields that had lain here before humans disturbed the wildflowers and stone with equal clarity. He remembered the early thatched-roof structures, and then later the stone edifices, and finally the factory that still stood.

It was another empty night, a night that had him wandering the club restlessly. Ever since he'd found his true mate four years ago, he had been yearning for more, but more was not something he could have.

The woman fated to be his was an American witch, and her life was subject to the control of the Salem Witch Council. They had ruled against one of their prized witch bloodlines mating with an English dragon.

His woman had been forced to go home to Boston and had not been able to return to England. This hollow ache he now felt was all that was left of his future. He was more than a thousand years old, young by dragon standards, yet the thought of living another moment without Jodie in his life made even one more day feel like too many.

He swept a tired gaze over the crowd below, hoping to find something, *anything* to distract him. What he didn't expect to see was a familiar face among the crowd. A face he'd thought he would never see again.

Vasili Barinov. The Russian dragon who had once been his father's dearest friend. Randolph peered down at Vasili, who dwarfed the human males near him.

It *was* him. There was no mistaking the face of a Barinov, nor was Vasili's face unknown to Randolph. He had been a young dragon when Vasili had visited London, but he remembered him clearly enough. He remembered Vasili had a dragoness mate named Marina. Vasili wasn't alone, which was to be expected. A beautiful woman was dancing with him.

However, it was the *wrong* woman.

Why wasn't Marina here? Marina and Vasili had vanished in Europe, and the Barinov brothers now running the family had confirmed his death centuries ago.

But if Vasili was alive, Marina had to be too. So why was he dancing with this woman so intimately?

And if Vasili was alive, why did no one know before now?

Something was wrong. Perhaps the light was playing tricks on Randolph's eyes and what he was seeing was an illusion, an old memory resurfacing, convincing him that he was seeing his long-dead family friend when it really was a different man.

Randolph retrieved his cell phone and zoomed in on the man below, snapping a photo, and then he sent it to his father. He didn't say who he thought it was. He wanted to see if his father would have the same reaction.

He waited, keeping his eyes on Vasili and his female dance partner. It was obvious that Vasili had eyes only for the woman in his arms—a human, no less. The world could have crumbled around them and Vasili would not have noticed. A dragon only acted like that with a true mate.

What did it mean? Randolph pushed aside his thoughts

of why he had come here tonight. His hunt for vampires and blood cults would have to wait. A moment later, his phone vibrated. He pulled it out of his pocket and saw his father's name on the screen.

"Father?" he answered, ignoring the noise around him.

"Where are you?" Everett demanded.

"The Printworks. I was hunting those fools from the blood cults."

"And *he's* there?" his father asked. "Do you still see him?"

Randolph locked his eyes on the dragon one floor below. "Yes. Is it him?"

"I can't be sure. Follow him. I will send a team to you. If it *is* him, we need answers, and he may not be in the mood to give them politely. He has been missing for too long for something not to be wrong. Is Marina there?"

"No," Randolph said. "Do you think he has gone rogue?"

"I hope not. We have enough to deal with right now. A rogue dragon is not something I want to face, especially a Barinov. We'll have to call Grigori. He needs to be here if we must put Vasili down. He is his uncle, after all."

Rogue dragons were dragons who'd gone mad and killed their mates. The mate bond either never formed or it became somehow corrupted, and the dragon or dragoness severed the link by attacking and killing their mate. Those dragons didn't die of mate grief, but lived on.

"You don't think he . . . killed Marina?" Randolph hated even saying the words.

"I pray he did not," his father replied. "But if he did, we shall deal with him."

Randolph winced. His father's voice would've sounded calm to anyone else, but his son knew better. Everett was old enough to have seen and done much in this world and jaded enough not to be affected too much by it, but Randolph could still hear the hint of pain in his father's voice. If Vasili had gone rogue and Marina was missing, things were about to become dangerous in London.

Please let it not be Vasili, Randolph prayed as he stepped back into the shadows to keep watch on the couple dancing below.

ANDRE MURPHY LICKED HIS LIPS OF THE BLOOD HE'D spilled as he fed a little too vigorously on the mortal woman he held pinned against the wall. The techno music bounced off the walls, and the human woman's blood now coursed through him, making his body sing. She had been high on some designer drug, and Andre couldn't resist. It was the only way a vampire could enjoy drugs or alcohol, by consuming it through the blood of a mortal.

He let out a contented sigh as his vision splintered into shards of rainbow light as the spotlights in the factory swept around the crowd. The woman he'd lured into the dark crumpled to the floor as he released her. Another empty shell, another mindless twit to serve an immortal like him. Humans were sheep, temporary sustenance while he quested for rarer blood.

Only one type of blood had any real value, one that could give vampires a taste of true power. Shifter blood. The mere thought of it kept his fangs extended and his throat burning with an unquenchable thirst. Even now, he could imagine the sweet smell of powerful shifter blood nearby. Perhaps he was dreaming about it after so much unsatisfying mortal blood?

No, he *did* smell a shifter, and he heard a heartbeat pounding in a different rhythm from the loud bass of the music. Andre moved through the crowd, chasing that irresistible scent—ancient, powerful, full of magic.

A dragon. He halted as he spotted the tall man dancing in the crowd several yards from him. It wasn't one of the damned Belishaw dragons. This was good. The Belishaws were protected. They drank wine laced with a cocktail of spells provided by the Lancashire Witch Council, which made their blood boil inside a vampire. The Belishaws had been chasing his blood coven for months now. But this dragon wasn't putting off the scent of poisoned blood. He smelled mouthwateringly clean.

Andre weaved closer, taking in the air, sifting through the sweat and overdone perfumes of the human bodies until he found another smell, one softer and sweeter. A virgin . . . but more than that. She was unique. She smelled like sunshine, a scent he sometimes remembered with dark agony. The male dragon held the woman possessively, his cold eyes raw with lust.

A smile stretched Andre's lips. So, the dragon had a human mate—a virgin, no less. *Interesting.* Andre would wait and watch for now. When the moment was right, he would take the human female, and her dragon would follow.

His lord would be pleased, most pleased. Two delicious beings to feast on. He licked his lips, and his fangs slowly retreated into his gums as he disappeared, unseen by his prey.

CHAPTER 9

Dragonsong—I have heard it several times as I've stayed with the Barinov brothers, and I can honestly say there is nothing more musical. The notes and the patterns transcend time and space in ways I cannot begin to fathom, as though they are speaking back to the universe itself.

THE MUSIC MOVED THROUGH VASILI AS HE DANCED. IT was so much more intense than the music of the past. Each beat seemed to *actually* beat into him, matching his heart, and the haunting melodies played over and over through his mind as he held Tasha close. Her hips moved in time with his. These new hypnotic dance moves were so close to mating that his dragon paced hungrily at the corners of his mind with desire.

Soon he would take Tasha to bed. He would join his body with hers and see more of her life within his head. He wanted to be connected to her in all ways. She was beautiful inside and out. She was his future, the woman who'd saved him.

He smiled as he pressed his lips to her forehead. She was his rescuer and fast becoming his heart, and he would be her devoted mate, her fierce protector for however long they had in this life.

Vasili spun Tasha out on one hand, then tugged her back into his embrace. They swayed and whirled as the lights flashed all around them. Dancing. By the gods, he loved this more than he could say. He let the rhythmic moves energize him, and Tasha laughed along with him. Her silken hair fell down around her shoulders in wild waves, and her face glowed with light and joy. She was so lovely it hurt to look at her.

Only when the music slowed and changed did they take a moment to catch their breath.

"Sense anything?" Tasha asked.

Vasili, while quite distracted by dancing with Tasha, hadn't immediately sensed any dragons nearby. Of course, it was a lot harder to sense them with all the other things going on with the music and the humans.

"Not yet. There is so much noise, so many strange smells. I haven't had time to adjust to it."

She shook her head. "Why don't we try again tomorrow?"

"Yes, let's try tomorrow." He grasped her hand and led her away from the music to linger in an alcove.

"Do you want to get some ice cream and cool off?" Tasha leaned against him, her breath tickling his throat as he held her by the waist.

"Why would they put ice in cream?"

"Because it tastes like heaven. God, you're adorable. I can't wait to see you try it." She kissed his chin, and her pleasure was infectious.

"Let's go." She pulled him through the crowd to the coat check and left the nightclub. They stopped on the street while she hailed a cab.

"So what is this ice cream?" he asked, wondering if maybe he had misheard her and it was an aggressive form of skating where they made the ice scream. He honestly didn't know.

"Just wait," Tasha promised him as they climbed into a cab. Her small hand found his, and their fingers threaded together. It gave him a flood of strength to feel her hand locked in his own.

Once they were near the hotel, she took him to a small shop that smelled like food but was very cold.

"This is ice cream," she whispered in his ear, and he shivered with desire. She made him think of sex with just about anything, even this.

There was a counter of curved glass in the small restaurant. Vasili followed Tasha up to it. She ordered something called a waffle cone of chocolate marshmallow.

The young man behind the counter looked to Vasili next, and Vasili shrugged. "I will have the same thing, please."

They received two cone objects with brown-and-white lumpy balls of what he now assumed was frozen sweetened milk of some sort, based on what he could smell. Tasha paid for the ice cream, and they sat down inside a cozy booth in the back of the restaurant. He watched Tasha in aroused fascination as she licked the ice cream on the top of her cone. It was hard not to imagine her tongue sliding over his body in a similar way. Vasili closed his eyes as his body hardened, and he fought for control.

"Try it." Tasha's foot rubbed his calf beneath the table. She was grinning mischievously at him. She knew exactly what she had done to him.

"I think perhaps I would rather lick you," Vasili said before he attempted to eat his ice cream. Chilled milk and flavors he didn't recognize exploded in an abundance of sweetness on his tongue. He wasn't usually one for sweet foods, but this was delicious. It was also decadent.

He took another lick, and his eyes locked with Tasha's. She was licking her treat at the same time, while her foot rubbed up and down his leg. He had the sudden urge to strip her naked and melt this frozen treat all over her body so he could lick it up while pleasuring her.

"So? Do you like it?" Tasha asked as she began to crunch on the edible cone.

"Yes, very much. It has given me many good ideas, little one." He flashed her a wicked smirk, which made her flush red, and she smiled shyly back at him. He adored how one minute she acted like a wanton siren and next she was a shy, virginal creature. Life with her would never be dull. When they finished, he held out a hand across the table to her. She took it, and he wrapped his fingers around hers protectively.

"I want to know everything about you, Tasha," he confessed. "Tell me of your life, of your hopes and dreams."

She lowered her gaze, still shy, before drawing in a deep breath. "I want to know that about you too."

"We have time, all the time in the world," he promised. There would never be enough time with her, but he would savor and cherish every second he had. "Tell me about your parents. I saw your mother in the memory, but it was too quick for me to hold on to."

Tasha licked her lips and then sighed. "My mom is wonderful, but she's afraid of a lot of things, mainly the rest of the world."

"That *is* a lot of things."

"We had a fight before I left to go on this trip. She didn't want me to go."

"Why is she so scared?"

"As I mentioned before, my father was a dragon, a powerful man who had enemies who eventually murdered him. He only came to see us once a year. You can't imagine what that was like, to grow up loving a father but seeing him only once a year. Because of the dangerous life he led, my mother raised me halfway around the world." She was silent for a long moment. Her face paled even more.

"When I was little, I started having these daydreams about my dad. I could see him wherever he was, living his life. I thought for a long time that it was something I did to cope with him not being there, but after he died, the daydreams stopped, and I wondered if maybe . . . maybe they were real. That's not possible, is it?" She sighed, the sound so heavy that Vasili was crushed beneath the weight.

He squeezed her hand, wanting her to know he was there for her, for whatever she needed.

"I'm not used to talking about my dad, not even with my mom. The way I grew up, I know it wasn't normal. To live so remote and be afraid of everything. It took me four years after my father died to come this far and do the things I'm doing now." She squeezed his hand. "It's weird, but finding you, it's made me feel less afraid."

"I'm glad," Vasili said. "The last thing I ever want is you to be afraid, especially of me."

Her face reddened again, and she smiled bashfully. "The things I feel for you, they are so intense, and I don't even know you."

"I understand." Vasili leaned forward in the booth, wishing he was closer. "Ask me anything, little one. I am open to you in all things."

"What about your family? You said you had a brother and nephews?"

"My brother and his mate have three sons: Grigori, the eldest, then Mikhail, and finally Rurik. They were good men, my nephews. I hope they are still alive."

"What about your parents?"

"My mother was a Nordic ice dragon, and my father also had Nordic blood. My father was killed in 832 by a thunderbird. His death took my mother a few hours later."

"What's a thunderbird?" Tasha still held his hand, her eyes soft and gentle as she asked her probing questions.

"It is another shifting being like dragons. It is a human

and also a bird, just as we are humans and also dragons. Thunderbirds are rare and dangerous. They can create storms at will, and the powerful blast of their wings while in flight can kill dragons at close range or render them unconscious. They are the natural enemy of dragons."

Tasha's eyes widened. Vasili absorbed the look of her, memorizing everything he could. She was his private glory, one that he could gaze at forever and never lose interest. He wanted to count the endless lashes on her eyes, which cast spells on him. He longed to brush his fingers over the smooth, silky skin of her throat and taste the natural sweetness that clung to her lips. He loved it when her eyes crinkled at the corners when she smiled, and the breathless sound of her laugh filled him with joy. It was amazing how like Marina she was in some ways, and yet vastly different in others.

Marina had been born in an age when dragons were fearless and outgoing. They had to be in order to survive. But Tasha had been trapped by her life, caged by the fear of a parent who wanted to protect her, even at the cost of her living a full life. Yet Tasha had been brave enough to go out into the world and experience new things. She had found him, a creature that should have paralyzed her with fear. But fear hadn't ruled her.

Vasili was humbled by Tasha, humbled by the knowledge that fate had given him a second chance and that even his dragon, and *Marina's* dragon, wanted him to bond with Tasha. Perhaps he and his dragon would have a second chance and a second life after all, which was more than either of them deserved.

"I'm sorry about your parents," Tasha said, her sweetness and compassion making him feel gloriously alive.

"I'm sorry about your father and that your mother is still afraid. Fear is a powerful thing to overcome. Not everyone manages it. I hope you do not judge her too harshly."

"I don't." Tasha's lips twisted into a sorrowful smile. "But I sometimes feel like I let her down, you know? I wanted her to come with me, to see the world, but losing my father only intensified her anxiety. I don't know if it's a genuine fear of my father's enemies or a mental illness. Either way, I feel like I failed her."

Vasili joined Tasha on her side of the booth and curled an arm around her shoulder, holding her against his side. She melted into him. It felt so natural, as though he had held this woman for centuries, not just a few days. She lifted her head, and he met her in a soft kiss, open-mouthed and gentle.

He dived into her kiss, which tasted of honey and fire, and opened himself up to her as he quested for memories, desperately longing to know more about her.

A door opened. An old man holding an umbrella stepped in toward her, speaking words that were muffled in memory as he felt only the pain, the loss of Tasha's father, and the way her mother had crumpled.

Then he was staring at a snowy mountain, the icy night cold and sharp. The breeze carried the scent of rain and dragons, but Tasha didn't know what those smells were, not in her memory. The snow gave way in a flash, and she fell into the moonlit cavern that would lead her to waking a dragon and the glowing stone upon the ground.

Memories whipped about his head, faster and faster, flowing backward and forward until he was dizzy, before it all slowed down and Tasha's fingertips touched the cave floor. Pain exploded in her chest. Vasili felt the agony of the stone's power bleeding into Tasha.

One last memory sliced into Vasili. His aching heart. His face, in dragon form, as he leaned down to nuzzle Marina while she lay dying. He felt her breath leave her and then . . . a whisper . . . a whisper so soft in her head that he had not heard it.

It was spoken in the old dragon tongue. "Love, I'll never do without. I am yours and yours alone. I am bound to you now and always. No matter the face, no matter the form, by word and deed, I will find you again."

The part of Marina that had been slipping away now changed course. It moved through the dragon heart stone that Vasili had placed beside her and far above her into the sky, where a black shadow still circled.

Vasili tightened his hold on Tasha as he struggled to understand what he had just seen. The stone hadn't just taken Marina's dragon's soul. She had somehow removed her human soul. Had it gone into the dragon heart stone or perhaps the mountain? He didn't understand how, but the implications were clear—Marina was here, not just her dragon. She was part of *Tasha*.

Tasha broke from the kiss and clung to him, trembling. "Vasili, I . . . I don't feel like myself." Her worried tone made him pull back so he could see her eyes. They were wide and full of tears. "I have these memories in my head . . . but they don't make sense. They aren't yours, and they aren't mine."

He cupped her face in his hands. "I know. They are Marina's . . ."

A DEAD WOMAN'S MEMORIES WERE IN HER HEAD. THAT was frightening enough, but what if it was more than that? What if she was a vessel for a dead woman's soul? She shuddered.

Tasha burrowed into Vasili's arms. He was the only thing that made sense. She wasn't going to let go of him.

"How is that possible?" she mumbled against his chest. The T-shirt beneath his black wool coat clung to his skin, and Tasha absorbed the heat from his body into hers.

"I don't know." He tightened his arms around her and feathered her temple with soft, reassuring kisses. "Why don't we go back to the hotel?"

She nodded. Her head had started to throb. She needed a Tylenol and a chance to rest. They left the ice cream parlor and walked through the small park that led to the back of the hotel. The night had been clear when they entered, but now a misting rain was falling. It matched her mood. The rain grew heavier, and soon lightning split the sky.

Vasili put an arm around her shoulders before he halted abruptly. She jerked to a stop next to him.

"Vasili, what—?"

He put a finger to his lips. "Stay close to me, little one. We are being followed."

Tasha's heart lodged in her throat as she glanced behind them. A man in the darkness became illuminated whenever the lightning flashed overhead.

"There's someone behind us," she warned Vasili.

"There's also someone in front of us," he said just as quietly.

Tasha dug into her purse. "Should I call the police?"

"They wouldn't be able to help. We found them. Or rather, they found us."

"You mean . . . ?"

"The English drakes." Vasili's body tensed, and Tasha felt his muscles become as hard as steel.

"You can come out of the shadows," Vasili called out.

More figures emerged from the shadows, six in all, who formed a loose circle around Vasili and Tasha. One of them stepped closer.

"It's been a long time since we've seen you in London." His hair was slicked back with rain, and his brown eyes looked black in the distant light from the streetlamps. He wore jeans and a blue shirt, and steam came off his body whenever the rain touched him. He looked strong enough, but none of the men surrounding them could match Vasili's masculine build.

"Randolph, good to see you alive after all these years. Is your father still . . . ?" Vasili let the question hang in the air.

"Alive and waiting to speak with you. He has concerns, Vasili. We all do." Randolph nodded at one of the other men, who stepped forward and tossed something at Vasili's feet that thudded and clanked on the pavement. A pair of iron manacles.

Vasili shot the ancient handcuffs a brief, disdainful glance. "Really?" He kept one arm lightly around Tasha's shoulders, keeping her close.

"I'm afraid we must insist. If after you and Father talk he feels it's not necessary, you will be released from them."

There was a long moment of silence before Vasili replied. "You truly believe I am a threat?"

Tasha heard the surprise in Vasili's tone, but he didn't relax even a single cell in his body.

"I do not know, old friend. It's been seven hundred years. Everyone said you were dead. We have concerns, but if you trust us, we can sort it all out."

Vasili turned his head to whisper in Tasha's ear. "You must trust me now, little one. Do not fight them."

"Okay." Tasha felt that strange fluttering in the back of her head, stronger than ever before. Ordinarily, she would do whatever these English dragons said, but some new, deeper part of herself she did not recognize balked at the thought of surrendering to these men or letting Vasili be chained and weakened. That other part of her told her to fight. But that was ridiculous. She couldn't fight dragons. And besides, Vasili had asked her to trust him. So she would.

Vasili slowly lifted up the manacles and shackled them around his wrists.

"It's iron, the only thing that can keep me from changing," he explained.

Tasha leaned against him, wishing she could do something, *anything*, but she was surrounded by dragons. The last thing she wanted to do was jeopardize Vasili's safety.

Vasili called out to Randolph. "You must not harm my female. This is Tasha Bellamy." Vasili nodded at her. "She is under my protection and my family's protection."

Randolph came closer, his gaze narrowing on Tasha, who found the courage to face him in the pouring rain. "She will not be harmed, though she does raise other questions. Where is Marina?" Randolph's gaze stayed fixed on Tasha's face.

"She is gone," Vasili said quietly.

"Gone?" Randolph echoed, one dark brow arching as he looked once again at Vasili. "How?"

"It is a long story, one I can share in the comfort of the indoors, out of this rain." He looked to Tasha by way of explanation.

Randolph's face softened slightly. "I often forget humans are delicate. We have two vehicles at the other end of the park. You will ride in one. Your female will ride in the other."

Vasili growled, the sound deep with a dragon's anger. "I will not be parted from her."

"I must speak to her alone," said Randolph. "She will be safe with me."

"Oh? An unmated male renowned for seduction? You forget, I know you, Randolph."

The British dragon chuckled, a small smile enhancing his attractive face.

"Once that was true, but four years ago I met my mate."

Vasili inhaled deeply. "You do not smell of a female. Why?"

Randolph rubbed the back of his neck and looked away. "I haven't been able to claim her. The situation is complicated."

Vasili looked to Tasha, speaking to her softly. "I believe you will be safe with him."

Tasha wrapped her arms around Vasili. "I trust that you trust him. Be safe. I don't want anything to happen to you." She kissed him, the desperate hunger for him stronger in this moment than she had expected. She saw none of his memories—the kiss was too brief—but their foreheads touched as the sky cracked with thunder and lightning.

"I'll be okay," she promised Vasili. He nodded.

A moment later, they were gently pulled apart. Randolph led Tasha ahead of Vasili, who followed behind, hands manacled in front of him like a prisoner.

There were two black SUVs parked at the edge of the park, and Randolph opened the back door of the first one for Tasha. She climbed in and watched through the windows as Vasili was escorted to the vehicle behind her. Randolph sat next to her, and the moment the cars pulled away, he spoke.

"Look at me, Tasha. Please." His voice sounded smooth—too smooth. She turned to face him, unable to deny the natural command that lingered in his tone. His brown eyes swirled with gold as he cupped her chin.

"Tell me how you met Vasili." Again she felt a compulsion to obey him, to tell him whatever he wanted. It was almost overpowering. But that fluttering in her head hadn't gone away. It grew stronger now, like a hive of bees buzzing against her soul rather than the delicate rhythm of a butterfly's wings it had first been.

"Tell me all that you know about Vasili." Randolph repeated his question, and his look of concentration deepened.

Anger flooded her, smacking the walls of her mind like a violent wave. "*Stop that!*" She didn't mean to shout, but she did, and the three dragon shifters in the car all stared at her. The driver hastily turned back to focus on the road.

"Losing your touch, Randolph?" the blond-haired man in the passenger seat asked.

"Sod off, Magnus," Randolph shot back at the man. He gazed deeply into Tasha's eyes. "You are resisting me. How?" He seemed to be asking himself this question rather than her.

"Look, you don't have to do whatever that thing was. It made me uncomfortable."

At this, his brows rose. "That's certainly never happened before. It's supposed to feel soothing, reassuring."

"Well, it wasn't. It made my head buzz." Tasha rubbed at her temples. The buzzing had faded.

"Your head was buzzing?" Randolph echoed. He leaned in and breathed in deep. She shrank back. The only man she wanted that close to her was Vasili.

"What is it?" Magnus asked.

"*Her scent. It's off.*"

Magnus turned around in his seat and leaned toward her. "What do you mean, *off?*" He took a deep breath.

"Okay, this sniff fest is making me uncomfortable." Tasha gripped the seat belt strapped across her chest tightly.

"You are human?" Randolph asked.

"Yes," Tasha answered.

"*Fully* human?" Magnus clarified.

"Yes." She was growing frustrated with the questions.

"And your parents?"

"Yes."

Randolph reached out and gripped her wrist. "You're lying," he said, the accusation quiet but full of mistrust.

"It's true," she protested.

Randolph said nothing, and Magnus shook his head. "Tell us, or you won't like what we do to you to get the truth."

Again that flash of anger, white-hot, a rage that was ready for battle rippled through her, catching her blood on fire. Fine, let them have the truth.

"You want the truth?" she snapped. "My father was a dragon!"

Randolph winced and immediately released her wrist.

"Your father is a dragon?" Magnus demanded.

"*Was*. He's dead. But I'm just human. I can't change into a dragon. I can't even change a tire." One of these, though, she was going to learn, dammit.

The car was quiet for a long moment. Only the heavy clink of rain against the windows and the occasional click of the car blinkers broke the silence.

"My apologies," Randolph said. "Was he an American ridgeback?"

"What? No. He wasn't American. My mother was."

Magnus leaned around his seat, staring at her. "Then who was your father?"

"My mother said he was a Russian Imperial." Tasha didn't want to say anything more.

Randolph was eyeing her with a new frown. "You look familiar. What was your father's name?"

"You wouldn't know him." Tasha had no way of knowing that, of course. She was firmly in the world of dragons, and she hadn't forgotten her mother's warnings to avoid the Barinovs because her life depended on it. But these were English drakes, not Russian Imperials. Vasili trusted them, so she should as well.

"My father was Dimitri Drakor."

The man driving the car hit the brakes. The SUV came to an abrupt stop.

"What the bloody hell are you doing, Dane?" Magnus growled, now pressed against the windshield.

"Sorry, I didn't expect that," Dane muttered as he started driving again. A phone buzzed, and Magnus answered it.

"We're fine. I'll explain later," Magnus said to whoever had called, presumably someone in the SUV following them. He hung up.

Tasha's heart was beating so hard that it made her head ache and her stomach roil. She was beginning to think she'd made a big mistake.

"You're Dimitri Drakor's daughter?" Randolph's look was one of utter bafflement.

"Yes. Did you know him?" Tasha's heart fluttered at the

thought of meeting someone who'd actually known her father, then sank with the feeling that this wasn't a good thing.

"Yes, I knew him." Randolph's brown eyes were almost black again. "He was one of my family's most hated enemies."

CHAPTER 10

Excerpt from Barrow's Journal – My Year with Dragons

Men speak of dragons as dread, fierce creatures who should be slayed, as the devourers of maidens and the destroyers of worlds. That is not the truth of what dragons are. Dragons are fierce. Fierce in battle, fierce in love, fierce in hate. They believe and feel to extremes that humans cannot fathom. It is this extreme level of emotions that we fear, and we fear it so much we put it into myth to understand it.

She was trapped in a car with her father's enemies.

Great . . . just great.

Tasha swallowed hard as she fought against the fresh wave of fear. It threatened to drag her under like a dangerous riptide.

"Please stop the car—let me and Vasili go. We'll leave London and never come back."

Tasha tried to unbuckle her seat belt, but Randolph's hands covered hers, preventing her from freeing herself.

"You are not in danger. Your father is dead, and you are human. No one even knows you exist." His eyes searched her features. "A Drakor daughter. I've never seen one before. He must have hidden you because you aren't a shifter, yet you aren't susceptible to our ability to mesmerize. That shouldn't be possible. Even humans born to a single dragon parent cannot resist us. Most interesting . . ."

"It's dangerous, that's what it is," Magnus muttered from the front seat.

Tasha tried to calm herself, but the fear of knowing she was surrounded by people who had hated her father made that difficult.

"Where are we going?" she asked after an uncomfortable silence settled inside the vehicle. It didn't help that Randolph was examining her the way a scientist would a tiny organism beneath a microscope, like he wanted to experiment on her to see what else she could do.

"We're headed to our family's main residence in Belgravia Square."

They continued in that heavy silence for another ten minutes before Randolph spoke again. "So the fact that you are immune to our influence means you aren't with Vasili out of some unnatural compulsion."

"What?" She shook her head. "No, of course not. He didn't force me to do anything."

If anything, she'd forced herself on him. It had been

impossible to leave a gorgeous, muscled god of a man all on his own simply because he'd woken up seven hundred years into the future. Vasili cast off a strange sort of gravity that seemed to pull her into him, but she had no desire to be free of it.

Randolph's eyes narrowed as though he was thinking deeply. "Then what happened to bring you together? The Vasili I knew was mated to a fierce battle dragoness. They'd loved each other since they were drakelings, and he had no eyes for any other woman. Yet I find you and him dancing intimately on the dance floor after he's been missing for centuries."

"Seven, to be exact," Tasha sighed. "Marina died while helping him locate something called the Heart of Sorrows, a dragon heart stone. They were followed by a group of dragons and attacked. She died defending him and the stone, and Vasili crawled into the cave, expecting to die . . ." She stumbled over the words as Vasili's memories that she'd seen during their moments of passion filled her with pain.

"He sealed himself inside the cave to die. I guess he sort of hibernated while he protected the stone, until I fell into the cave and found him." She ignored the weight of Magnus's stare from the front seat. "He said I'm a possible true mate to him, which might be why he hasn't died of the mate grief yet. We were trying to find you guys."

"You were trying to find us?" Randolph and Magnus shared a look. "Why?"

"Vasili thinks your father might know whether it's possible to survive the mate grief and mate again."

"If anyone would know, it would be him," Randolph agreed.

The SUV stopped in front of a four-story stone building. The ground floor was made of white blocks of stone, surrounded by a black wrought-iron gate. A flash of lightning illuminated a black front door with gold numbers over the archway. Tasha glanced behind her to see that the second SUV had come to a stop behind them.

Magnus opened the car door and offered her a hand. Once he helped her down, he kept a firm hold on her forearm as he led her to the front door. It swung open, and another man, as handsome as the rest, blinked in surprise. He looked between Magnus and Tasha.

"What's this, Magnus? I thought you'd already gone out tonight."

"She's not here for me," Magnus grunted and scowled. "She needs to see Everett."

"Ah." The other man continued to stare at her in curiosity, but he stepped back to allow them both inside.

The interior of the townhouse was bright, with white painted walls and black trim. The floor was a mosaic of white-and-black polished floor tiles in a checkerboard pattern. Gold light fixtures hung from the ceilings, and mirrors were mounted in clever places to extend the narrow hall endlessly. Bright English landscape paintings covered the walls, their gilded frames shimmering under the soft light. At the end of the hall, it opened up to a series of rooms on the ground floor and a staircase that led up to the upper floors.

Magnus escorted Tasha into a large sitting room with

robin's-egg blue walls and a pair of dark moss-green velvet sofas that faced each other perpendicular to the white marble fireplace. Magnus led her to one of the sofas, and she was pushed down into it, sinking deeply into the gold-and-white accent pillows. The dragon shifter gave her a look that warned her not to move. Still, she shifted forward a little, her concern over Vasili far stronger than her fear of Magnus.

"Stay."

"But, Vasili—"

"Is coming," Magnus growled.

A moment later, Vasili came into the room, escorts on either side of him. All of the tension inside her bled away the moment she saw him.

"Tasha," Vasili said in relief, as though he'd been feeling the same way. Randolph passed by the open doorway and walked up the stairs and out of sight, possibly to find his father.

Magnus and the other dragons stayed in the living room, but they gave Tasha and Vasili a little space alone. Vasili joined her on the sofa, and she curled her arm in his, tucking herself against him. It wasn't because she was afraid or wanted his protection, however. She had the sense that her touch and closeness gave Vasili comfort while the iron manacles continued to keep him unable to change. Unable to defend himself. More and more, she felt protective of him, the same way he did of her. She even felt the urge to lash out at any dragon shifter who threatened them.

Vasili turned his face toward hers. "Did anyone harm you?"

"No, I'm fine. You?" She cupped his face, and he leaned down, their foreheads touching. That simple connection gave her such a sense of peace. When they were like this, the rest of the world seemed to melt into the background. She didn't believe in love at first sight, or anything like that. This wasn't love. It was something ancient, something deeper than words could express. She knew in her soul that she and Vasili belonged together. She was becoming dangerously attached to him, but that was something she'd have to face another time. They had far more frightening things to deal with at the moment, like the possible wrath of the English dragons.

Magnus and the other men straightened to attention as Randolph returned, a man following behind him. Both Tasha and Vasili watched him carefully. It had to be Randolph's father. He was tall, heavily muscled, like Vasili. It seemed that the older the dragon, the more they were built like a Viking or a warrior of old. Though he looked to be in his early thirties, there was a hint of silver in his dark hair at the temples. And his eyes, while beautiful, seemed to be filled with thousands of years of memories.

It was a strange thing to think of the life span of dragons. To know that these creatures had experienced and forgotten more history than she would ever know in her lifetime.

The depths of this man's brown eyes shimmered with gold as he looked at her and Vasili.

"Vasili Barinov, you've been gone a long time."

Barinov.

For a second, Tasha's mind didn't seem to process that; she was too focused on the ancient dragon walking toward them.

"Indeed, far too long, Elisedd," Vasili admitted as he stood to face Randolph's father.

"*Elisedd*," the man chuckled. "I have not gone by that name in almost a thousand years. We've modernized with the times. I go by Everett now."

Tasha blinked slowly as the name *Barinov* echoed in her mind, growing louder and louder as it sank in.

"Barinov?" she whispered. Her throat tightened, and her pulse spiked. "You're . . . you're a Barinov?" She stared at Vasili in horror. She didn't see the man she was falling in love with. She saw only the man whose family had murdered her father.

"Yes." Vasili's eyes narrowed as he studied her. "Tasha, are you well? You're very pale—" He reached for her, but she scrambled back on the sofa until the arm of the couch dug into her back and several decorative pillows toppled to the floor.

"No . . ." Tasha shook her head, wishing she could erase everything she'd just learned. This was her worst fear—she'd just never realized it until now. To fall in love with a member of the family that had taken her father from her, the reason he'd never been able to spend more than a day with her once a year, the reason she'd lived in hiding. The Barinovs had *stolen* her childhood and her father.

Vasili stared at her, worry darkening his blue eyes. The

thunder outside suddenly exploded, rattling the walls and making the lights flicker.

"What have you brought into my house?" Everett demanded in a low growl. "Who is she? The skies are opening above this house, and she is causing it."

Randolph cleared his throat. "She's a Drakor, Father. Dimitri's only surviving child."

Just like that, the air seemed to be sucked out of the room. Tasha leapt up, and all the men in the room tensed, hands half raised to try to show her they didn't mean her harm.

Escape, a voice whispered in her head. *Fight later, escape now. Fly . . .*

Tasha acted on an instinct that was not entirely human as she rushed toward the tall windows.

DRAKOR? THE WORD HAD FROZEN HIM IN PLACE. HE stared at Tasha as she ran toward the windows, clearly intending to smash through them. Magnus got to her first, grabbing her by the waist as he jerked her back mere inches from the glass. He grasped her throat in his other hand, holding her captive against his body. The sight of his female being held like that sent Vasili's dragon into a rage. Only the iron manacles on his wrists kept it trapped inside his head.

"*Let her go!*" Vasili roared. He may have had no power to change shape, but he could still fight as himself.

"You heard him, Vasili. She's a Drakor." Magnus's eyes

had turned gold; he was ready to shift if need be. "Don't tell me you didn't know."

Vasili locked gazes with Tasha. "She told me her name was Bellamy."

"And *you* didn't tell me your last name at all," Tasha countered in a raspy voice.

Everett stepped between Tasha and Vasili. "Magnus, please release Miss Bellamy. I believe we all need to have a calm conversation."

"But she'll run."

"No, she won't." Everett turned to Tasha. "Will you, my dear? I guarantee your safety under this roof. While we are at war against your family, we are not at war with you. We are not villains. It is clear you came here with no threat in your mind toward us and little knowledge of your heritage. You have a safe harbor here so long as you behave peacefully. Do you agree not to harm yourself or anyone in my home?"

Vasili saw the fear in Tasha's eyes. He didn't know how a Drakor had become his possible true mate, but she had, and they both needed answers.

"I . . . swear," Tasha breathed.

Everett nodded to Magnus, who released her. She rubbed at her neck, gasping, and staggered away.

Vasili raised his fists. "Set me free, Everett."

"Do it," Everett commanded.

Randolph undid the iron manacles and tossed them to one of the men.

"Now, the two of us will have a drink, I think." Everett

approached Tasha and held out his arm. "Please come with me, Miss Bellamy."

Vasili watched with confusion and jealousy as Tasha, without a glance in his direction, put her arm through Everett's as he escorted her from the room.

The other dragons filed after him, leaving Randolph and Magnus behind to keep an eye on Vasili.

He was numb. After two days of feeling alive again, he was back in that cave, his body giving out, his soul withering away.

Tasha was a Drakor. Not just any Drakor, but the daughter of the only dragon he truly hated—the dragon who'd murdered Marina.

"How did you end up with a Drakor as a mate?" Randolph asked.

"I don't know," Vasili admitted. "She said her name was Bellamy." He replayed every conversation he ever had with Tasha. "She told me her father was dead. Is this true?"

"It is. He's been dead for four years. Your nephews killed him."

"My nephews? Not Ivan? Where was my brother?"

Randolph cleared his throat.

"Ivan is gone," Magnus said, his usually brusque tone softening slightly.

"Gone?" Vasili sank into the couch, digging his hands in. Ivan, his beloved brother, was dead. "How did it happen?"

Randolph placed a hand on his shoulder. "Twenty years ago, he chased down a mated pair of thunderbirds and attacked them. He and his mate died, but she survived long enough to take the young hatchling to a human home to be raised as a mortal."

"What?"

"She refused to kill a child, thunderbird or not, and it was good she did not. The child grew up and became Grigori's mate."

It took a moment for Randolph's words to sink in. "A *thunderbird* is mated to my nephew?"

Randolph nodded. "It came as a shock to us all, but Father says we are entering a new age. Supernatural creatures are changing—some for better, some for worse. Humans are finding ways to merge with dragons and become mates to us again."

This was a lot to take in. Natural enemies mating, humans merging with dragons—he'd thought that magic had been lost.

"What happened to Marina, Vasili?"

Vasili didn't want to talk about it, but he had to tell them. "Dimitri ambushed us in Switzerland. She died defending me and the dragon heart stone we found from his soldiers. I crawled into a cave to protect the stone and to wait for the mate grief to take me."

"And now you're mated to Drakor's daughter," Magnus added. "How is that possible? How are you still alive? The only dragons who have ever survived mate grief are dragons who've gone rogue."

"That is what I was hoping your father could tell me— how I survived when I shouldn't have. It's why Tasha and I came here. We hoped Everett had answers. He's older than any of us."

"How did you meet her?" Randolph inquired. It was then that Vasili realized he and Tasha had been separated, carefully, cleverly, casually . . . so they could be interrogated. He should have been furious, but Everett had guaranteed Tasha's safety, so Vasili would tell his tale and she would tell hers. Then they would be reunited.

Reunited with Dimitri Drakor's daughter.

As much as he hated Dimitri, he could not . . . could never hate Tasha. She was not her father. If anything, she was the opposite of him in every way. His dragon had not even flinched at learning she was a Drakor. His dragon still wanted to claim her and protect her, no matter what bloodline she came from.

"I was badly wounded, and my will to live was fading. But it seems the cold of the cave took me before the mate grief could, and I slept instead of died." He could still remember his scales icing over and the sharp pain of his wounds ebbing into a numb ache before he sank into a deathlike sleep, unknowingly waiting for Tasha to wake him, to give him hope again.

Vasili forced himself to continue. "I was in that cave for seven centuries and woke only when Tasha entered. She later told me that she saw the Heart of Sorrows glowing on the ground beside me and picked it up. It burned her hands, and yet she could not let it go. She fell down and lay against me, believing I was dead and she would soon be too. Between her touch and the stone . . . something woke me up. I changed into my human form after I got my bearings, and we climbed out of the cave. My dragon sensed her as a mate almost right away. It took me a little bit longer. I felt so much pain at losing Marina—I still do." There was a level of shame inside him as he still feared that his survival meant his mate bond had not been strong. It was not a dragon's way to survive mate grief. Maybe there was something wrong with him.

Magnus made a noise of disbelief. Randolph shot him a look.

"What?"

"You know what I'm thinking."

"You want to see the witches." Randolph looked skyward as if beseeching the gods to save him. "They aren't the answer to everything. Lord knows they hate dealing with dragons."

"Says the dragon mated to a witch he won't claim," Magnus fired back.

"*Can't* claim," Randolph growled. "There's a bloody difference."

Vasili stayed silent, amused by their bickering, but it didn't ease his concerns. "May I see Tasha now? Or are you not done with your interrogation?"

"Yes, we're done." Randolph waved for him to follow as he left the room.

The three of them crossed the hall into a dining room with a dozen brown leather chairs. Half of them were filled with English drakes, all discreetly surrounding his mate. Tasha held a cup of hot tea and spoke to Everett, who sat opposite her at the table.

"I'm not sure why I wanted to go night skiing or why I chose that mountain," she explained. She paused when Vasili entered the room, and her breath hitched. "I . . . I just needed to go in that direction. I can't explain the feeling. It's not the sort of thing I would normally do. It started when I saw pictures of the mountain range in my travel books. I just had to go there. It felt like something was hitting me, but from the inside."

Everett's fingers were folded into a steeple. "It was a rhythmic beating, this feeling you had?"

Tasha nodded and placed her palm against her chest and mimicked the beat against her heart. *Thump thump—thump thump.*

"Ah," Everett said softly. Vasili moved around the table, trying to get closer to his mate as he saw the understanding in Everett's eyes.

Tasha noticed Everett's reaction too. "What?"

"His heart. You were called by the heartbeat of your mate, Miss Bellamy. It was his heart that drew you to the mountain. To him."

Tasha bit her lip nervously. "But why did it hurt my chest? It almost killed me."

Everett touched the handle of his mug of coffee on the table. "When I was a younger dragon, at least five thousand years ago, we learned that dragons could be so connected to their mates that they could synchronize their heartbeats. Your body was trying to match Vasili's, but he was nearly frozen in dragon form. As a human, you cannot safely have your heart pump blood that slowly. But when he changed into his human form you were safe."

Everett's focus turned to Vasili. He had come to a stop behind Tasha. He wanted to put his hands on her, to reassure her that he was there and that the revelation of who her father was hadn't changed his feelings toward her. Yet he was afraid she would reject him now that she knew that his family had killed the father she had barely known yet still loved.

"How far has the mating gone, Vasili?" Everett asked.

Tasha flinched. She didn't yet look at him.

"Our bond grows stronger, but we have not claimed each other."

"There is still time to walk away, Miss Bellamy. You have a choice, but your window of opportunity is closing. Do you understand? A claiming cannot be undone except by death."

Vasili gripped the back of Tasha's chair. The wood cracked ominously beneath the sudden pressure of his hands.

"Everett, we need your help." Vasili tried not to think of Tasha walking away from him. "Things are more complicated than you realize. I see Marina's memories along with Tasha's. I saw a memory, Marina's last, of her casting an old dragon spell. I believe it bound her to me while she died touching the Heart of Sorrows."

"You saw Marina's memories while sharing passion with Tasha?" Everett stood, his eyes burning gold with emotions as he looked to Tasha. To her credit, she did not cower beneath the intense gaze of such an ancient dragon.

"Could Marina and her dragon *both* be trapped inside the Heart of Sorrows? Are they both trying to bond to Tasha?" Vasili asked.

"It's not impossible. But we cannot know for sure unless . . ." Everett hesitated.

Tasha stared back at the ancient English drake. "Unless what?"

"Unless we consult the witches."

Magnus nudged Randolph in the ribs. "See? It *always* comes back to the witches."

Everett ignored the interruption. "The witches have means of divining such things. If you want answers, Miss Bellamy, we can get them from the witches, but it may carry a price."

Vasili held his breath, terrified that Tasha would choose to leave, to abandon their quest for answers, to abandon *him*.

Just a day ago, he'd been uncertain he could have another mate, but now, facing the possibility of losing her, he knew he wanted her in his life, in his bed, in his heart. It had nothing to do with Marina or her dragon or even the desires of his own dragon. It had everything to do with his human heart, which now beat for her. But Vasili would not force her to choose him. Everett was right. This was her choice.

Tasha exhaled slowly, the sound strangely audible in the silent room.

"When can we see the witches?"

CHAPTER 11

Excerpt *from Barrow's Journal – My Year with Dragons*

There is nothing more powerful in the world than a dragon's love for its mate. It outlasts all else; it is stronger than any bond. It is love and devotion in its purest form. To be loved by a dragon is to be valued as life's greatest treasure.

TASHA WAS EXHAUSTED. AFTER EVERYTHING SHE HAD been through tonight, everything she had *learned* tonight, she was overwhelmed.

"The witches are in Cornwall. We'll leave tomorrow after you both have rested. I insist you stay in here tonight. There are dangers in London that you are not aware of yet and we haven't the time tonight to tell you about them. It is safer for you to remain here. My men can retrieve your luggage and the Heart of Sorrows, if you wish, and bring them to you," Everett offered.

Tasha nearly said no, but the thought of driving all the way back to the Dorchester sounded completely unappealing when she really felt ready to collapse.

"Thank you, Mr. Belishaw. I would appreciate that." She didn't speak for Vasili. She wasn't sure she could anymore. It had cut deep when she'd learned her father was the dragon who'd killed Marina. Now she was standing in the same room as Vasili, and all she could think about was this new and horrifying truth about her father.

The man she'd loved, the man she'd thought she knew all about because of those silly dreams was a lie. She hadn't known him at all. It was one more deception on a foundation of secrets her parents had kept from her.

Her father was a *murderer*.

She found herself unable to even look at Vasili, who'd moved to stand beside her. He must hate her. How could he not? She represented everything that had been stolen from him. And if Marina was somehow inside her, or even just her memories, it was one more thing she and her family had somehow stolen from Vasili.

"We will see it done. In the meantime, Randolph will take you to one of our guest rooms."

"Thank you." Tasha followed Randolph out of the dining room but paused at the door. "Mr. Belishaw, how did my father die?"

Everett looked between her and Vasili before speaking. "He conspired to attack the Barinov family on many occasions. He nearly killed Grigori's mate—Grigori is Vasili's eldest nephew. Then he killed the possible mate of Rurik, Vasili's youngest nephew. Finally, he attacked Rurik's chosen true mate.

"It was the woman mated to Rurik who killed your father. She is a scientist and had reverse-engineered a powerful drug an enemy of ours had developed, one that deprives a dragon shifter of their dragon for a time. She turned your father human moments before he tried to kill her. They fell from a skyscraper. Rurik was able to catch her, but your father perished in the fall."

Tasha stared at the tiled floor, fighting back tears. "Thank you for telling me the truth." Then she followed Randolph out the door.

She was already upstairs when she felt Vasili come up close behind her, and she froze.

"Thank you, Randolph," Vasili said, dismissing him. He put a hand on Tasha's lower back and guided her through the open door of a bedroom.

Tasha stumbled into the room, desperate to put distance between her and the man who surely hated her. "What are you doing, Vasili?"

Vasili's eyes were frosty and his face thunderous. "You and I must talk, Tasha."

"No, please, I don't want to. There's nothing I can say to you to make this go away."

She spun away from him and crossed the room to the windows, gazing bleakly out at the rainy night. Then she pressed her forehead against the glass, her chest aching.

Vasili growled as he came toward her. "Look at me,

Tasha." She saw him reflected in the glass as he approached. She didn't dare face him.

He spun her around, hands firm but gentle on her shoulders as he pinned her against the window. The second his hands touched her, that gravity of his pulled her toward him. It was going to be that much worse when what he said next tore her heart apart.

"Please," she begged, tears burning her eyes. "Please don't."

His hypnotic gaze caught and held hers. "What is it you fear?" he asked, his voice a gentle whisper that pierced her soul. His eyes searched her face. "Do you fear me? Fear that I will harm you?" His face was so close to hers that she could feel the heat of him. He reached up to touch her cheek, but she didn't flinch. The cold window behind her no longer felt like an escape.

Her eyes widened. That hadn't occurred to her. She'd been afraid of what he would say—what he would do to her heart, not her body. "No, of course not."

"Then what do you fear?" He moved one hand up, his fingers curling around the back of her neck in a soothing way. They both seemed on a ragged edge, desperate to say a thousand things.

"My father . . . ," she stammered. "He . . . he killed her." For some reason, she couldn't bring herself to say Marina's name. "How . . . How could you want to . . . How can you even look at me?"

"Ah, little one." Vasili's shoulders sank as he closed his eyes. "I feared that you could not look at me because my family killed your father."

For a long second, their bodies were locked as that awful tension between them ebbed away. Their breath mingled and their eyes never left each other's faces as the fears they'd both been holding began to fade.

"I would never judge you because of your father," he assured her. "I knew Dimitri. You are nothing alike." He rubbed the back of her neck with his fingertips in the ghost of a caress. "But you must hate me."

"No," she protested.

"When you learned I was a Barinov, you looked . . ." He shuddered. "It was a look of horror and betrayal."

She had felt both horror and betrayal when she'd learned of his family, but she had never feared him. He had gone into the ice seven hundred years before her father had been killed. She couldn't, *wouldn't* blame him for something that he hadn't been a part of.

"When my father died, I was told the Barinov dragons murdered him," Tasha said. "I didn't know how or why. My mother explained that's why we'd lived all of our lives in hiding, because of my father's enemies . . . and then I found you."

"Yes, you found me, in more ways than you know. What we have, Tasha, goes beyond wars or rivalries. We are mates." He leaned in close, touching his forehead to hers, and she closed her eyes for a moment, soaking in that feeling of belonging to someone.

"You truly want that? You want me? Mortal and all? The daughter of a monster?"

Vasili was quiet, though his eyes were turbulent. "If Dimitri loved you, then some sliver of his heart was pure, the part that loved you. I can live knowing that that part of him existed. It does not undo Marina's murder, but I can't hate that part of him. Do you understand?"

In a way, she did. She still loved her father, but now she knew there was a large part of him that she could never accept or love completely, the part that had held so much greed and hate that he'd attacked the Barinovs and gone after their mates. "I understand."

"Good." Vasili pressed his lips to her forehead. "Will you be my mate?"

He stepped back, his hands letting go of her as he asked the question. He wanted her to make the choice without the influence of his touch. Her head cleared of the fog of need she felt, but it didn't change her mind.

She stepped into his embrace, wrapping her arms around his back and pressing her cheek against his chest. "If you want me, I'm yours."

Something clicked into place inside her as everything opened between them. Tasha raised her head, and Vasili claimed her mouth. The kiss was soft and tender, as though he wished to learn the shape of her lips in his gentle exploration. It was full of heart, full of unspoken words and dreams of the future.

She cupped his face, her palms rasping against the scruff on his hard jawline. She'd never been intimate with a man before, yet some ancient part of her knew exactly what to do. She gripped the edge of his T-shirt and pulled it up his body. Vasili broke the kiss to let her push the shirt over his head before tossing it to the ground.

His chest was a hard, chiseled work of art, scars and all.

She leaned in, pressing slow, soft kisses to his skin. That scent, the one that brought back Christmas memories, filled her head, making her dizzy in the best way. She kissed a path to one of his nipples and flicked her tongue against it. He hissed out a breath, his hands tunneling into her hair as he cradled the back of her head while she explored him. There was an undeniable sense of wonder at the thought that this man was hers alone, and she felt safe knowing she would only ever belong to him.

Vasili's hands moved to her waist, teasing up the edge of her sweater until he met bare skin, and she shivered in anticipation. Lifting her arms, she let him remove the sweater.

He gazed at her a long moment, eyeing her white lace bra, gold swirling in the blue of his eyes.

"What an age we live in," he murmured. "To display your lovely breasts in such a fashion. I feel as though you are offering them to me, to suck and nip at until you are begging for me to be inside you."

Her nipples hardened at Vasili's words. Tasha's mind was filled with thoughts of him playing with her breasts, rubbing his cheek against them, flicking his tongue over them, lightly pinching them. She wanted to feel all of it.

He stroked his fingers down her throat, down her collarbone, and finally to the peak of one breast. He rubbed his thumb over one nipple as it pressed against the thin barrier of her bra. She whimpered as a sharp bolt of need shot through her body at his touch. He stepped closer, and her breath came unevenly as he slid the straps of her bra down her shoulders. Then he slowly spun her to face away from him. It took him but a moment to unclasp her bra and let it fall to the floor. Then he pressed against her from behind, his arousal digging into her lower back as he cupped her bare breasts in his palms. She arched into the touch, wanting so much more from him. She felt empty inside, and only he could ease that feeling.

"Please, Vasili, I need you."

His warm breath tickled the fine hairs on the back of her neck as he rolled her nipples with the pads of his thumbs.

"I know, little one, but I wish to enjoy you. A dragon always savors their first mating."

"So you're going to torture me, is that it?" Her voice was breathless with excitement.

"Torture you with pleasure, *yes*," he promised before he pinched her nipples. She gasped as he lowered his mouth to her neck, kissing her and then grazing his teeth over her skin. Each kiss seared a path over her sensitive flesh.

His hands left her breasts and unfastened her jeans. She shimmied her hips as he pulled the jeans down, and she slipped out of her boots. Once ready, she squealed as he lifted her into the air and carried her toward the bed. He gently set her down on the edge and knelt at her feet, removing her socks and massaging the arches of each foot.

He slid his palms up her body and reached her hips, where he grasped her panties and tugged. She lay back on the bed and lifted her hips as he slid the underwear off and let them fall away. His hands settled on her inner thighs, spreading her wide for his view before she could regain her wits enough to close her legs.

Heat scorched her as he stared a long moment at the spot between her legs.

"Vasili," she said uncertainly.

"Oh, you are exquisite, Tasha," he growled, the dragon rumbling coming deep from his chest. "I wish to devour you." He bent over her, kissing her belly as he moved down toward her mound.

"You don't have to—*holy shit*." She strangled the curse as his lips settled around her clit, sucking on it. He flicked his tongue into her sensitive folds before he laved the flat of his tongue along her slit. The feel of it was unlike anything else she had ever experienced. It was heaven and frustration at the same time.

"You taste so sweet." Vasili lifted his head, and their gazes locked. His lips glistened, and his eyes were now fully gold, his dark pupils large with arousal.

"I want to bind you to my bed and devour you for hours." He slid a hand up to her throat, curling his fingers around the column of her neck, but he didn't squeeze. The possessive hold sent her pulse into the stratosphere.

"Yes," she panted. "Yes, do that . . . Do everything . . . Oh God . . ."

He pushed two fingers into her sheath suddenly, but not roughly. "Little virgin," he rasped. "You have caught your dragon, and now I will have you." He pumped his fingers deep, hard. "So tight," he praised. "You are wet and ready to be taken by your mate."

Tasha entered a strange mindless state where her head was no longer in control of her body. She rocked her hips, inviting him, teasing him, *begging* him to do as he'd promised.

"More, Vasili, tell me more . . ." Her voice was a ragged gasp.

"You like it when I tell you what I want?" He smiled, a wickedness to the expression that told her he would fuck her to within an inch of her life if she asked him to.

"Yes. Tell me what you want to do to me." She had never known this side of herself existed, but now that her usually stoic dragon was revealing his darker desires, she had to have more.

Vasili continued to penetrate her with his fingers. His other hand held her throat as he stared down at her.

"I will ram my cock deep into you, little one, and listen to your cries of pleasure. You belong only to me. My body will fill you until you feel empty without me inside you. Then I will part those pretty lips and fuck your mouth until I release."

She groaned at the thought of sucking on him and how it would feel to be used like that. She wanted it, wanted to know that she drove him to madness. There was a power in knowing her body made him lose control.

"Then," he whispered more softly, "I might claim *other* places." He moved his hand on her neck down to her bottom, cupping it before he gave it a light smack while still pushing his fingers into her sheath.

She exploded like a firecracker, parts of her igniting at different instances as she came undone.

Vasili quickened the pace of his fingers inside her, drawing out her climax until she was quivering with exhaustion. Then he pulled his fingers out and tore at his jeans, shoving them roughly down his hips, along with his boxers. He cursed softly in Russian as he struggled for a moment to kick off his boots and socks.

Tasha giggled at the sight of him, but the giggle died when she saw his massive shaft jutting out from his groin. *Oh God* ... She had felt it through his jeans, but seeing it, it looked far too big.

"How? It won't—?"

He grasped her thighs and entered her in a swift thrust. Pain tore inside her, and she cried out. He froze, holding still, half-buried inside her. The lust dimmed from his eyes.

"Breathe, little one, breathe. We must get this over quickly," he said.

Her breath was uneven at first and hitched when he moved out of her a little, then sank back in. Pressure built inside her lower belly as he worked deeper into her. The pain eased, and finally the pressure faded a little.

"I'm okay now. You can go faster," she said. She gripped the bedding, holding herself in place as he stood at the side of the bed and took her hips in his hands.

"Faster, you say?"

"Yeah." She needed faster, needed harder. She was so close to that glorious next orgasm.

His hips slapped against her body as he fucked her hard and fast. He murmured softly in Russian, his own breathing as uneven as hers as he pumped into her with frantic desperation, a desperation that she felt all too well inside herself. The perpetual need to be closer, connected, to feel no end or beginning between them. She surrendered to his strength and dominance, letting him own her body, heart, and soul.

Her thighs quaked as her body desperately tried to join in the movement, but he kept her still, taking her at his own pace, using her as a pleasure slave for his desires; and that single thought sent her careening off the edge. Bliss blinded her. Her head thrashed on the bed, and she screamed out his name.

Vasili came a few seconds later, ramming into her hard enough that the bed frame lurched several inches across the floor. Vasili threw back his head. The roar that erupted from him shook the room. Electricity arched between their bodies, and a deep heat spread inside her.

He braced his hands on either side of her shoulders as he leaned over her on the bed. Sweat glistened on his body, making him shimmer in the dim gold light of the nearby lamps. His dark hair fell across his eyes. With a shaky hand, she reached up to brush it away before she stroked his cheekbones. He turned his face into her hand, catching her wrist as he placed a kiss to the center of her palm.

"Was I too rough?"

She shook her head. "It was incredible." The pain of losing her virginity had been totally worth it. He rocked his hips into her, and a little aftershock of her climax made her body quiver again.

"How was it for you?" she asked, praying that it had been good for him too.

He closed his eyes, moving deep into her body again. His lips curved up a little before he opened them again.

"It felt like the first time, like I had never claimed a female before."

He confessed this with a look of wonder on his face. His eyes were blue again, the color as soft and vibrant as a summer sky. He started to pull out of her, but she tried to stop him.

"I'm not leaving you, little one, but I must clean up before we can sleep."

"Okay." She winced as he pulled out of her body. Blood streaked his cock and her thighs. She shifted awkwardly on the bed. He stepped into the bathroom for a few minutes before returning with a warm, wet washcloth. He cleaned her legs and himself and then he returned to the bathroom.

A little embarrassed now that the lust had worn off, Tasha pulled back the covers of the bed and crawled beneath them. The second her head hit the pillow, she yawned and started to drift. She was dimly aware of Vasili joining her, his body coiling around hers, enveloping her in a protective position. As she slipped into sleep, she had one last thought—that she felt guarded, like she was the most precious jewel belonging to his dragon.

VASILI LAY AWAKE LONG AFTER TASHA FELL ASLEEP. HE was too excited. The word seemed somehow inadequate for what he felt at that moment. He held his mate in his arms. The first link in their bond had been forged, and there would only be more of them over time. His relief matched his joy tonight. He'd feared he would not be able to complete the bond, but he had. His dragon had been eager the entire time.

Tasha's thoughts had flitted into his mind while they mated, like distant echoes as she opened herself to him. Perhaps the secret of her father's identity and the fear of the Barinov family had been the last barrier that she'd finally let go of, and it was the bravest thing he had ever seen.

She had put her trust in the man who had the most right to hate her because of her heritage, and she had dared to care about someone whose family had killed her father.

She was a woman who loved deeply and without hesitation once she trusted someone. He had felt that affection in her kiss, in the touch of her hands, and in the soft gleam of her eyes. Vasili planned to spend the rest of their lives earning her trust and nurturing her affection and love. Because he *loved* her. He'd come to that realization when he'd seen her under the brutal hold of Magnus, a dragon he'd known for a thousand years, one he generally trusted. He knew he would go to war against dragons he trusted, if they threatened her.

He nuzzled her hair and breathed deeply, letting her scent fill his lungs, and it carried his heart back to a time when he had been home in Russia, when Marina . . .

He stiffened. Marina's scent. He had forgotten it. It had become such a small thing in his mind compared to a thousand other memories of his first mate. But no, he hadn't forgotten her scent. It had been right here all along. She'd smelled *exactly* like Tasha.

Was that what had drawn his dragon and calmed the

beast? Something as simple as having the same scent? The mating was so much more than that, yet this new realization filled him with fresh concern. As far as he knew, he was the only dragon to ever successfully claim a second mate. They had ventured off the map of the known and journeyed into the blank parchment beyond.

What was that charming expression the humans used? *Here there be dragons.*

He closed his eyes, trying to focus on sleep, but as he finally let his own exhaustion settle over him, he dreamed of Marina trapped in a dark, icy cave . . . and a trio of English witches whispering spells over a glowing sapphire stone.

ANDRE BECAME ONE WITH THE MOONLIGHT AND shadows as he lingered on the rain-soaked balcony of the expensive townhouse in Belgravia square that belonged to the English drakes. Through the parted window curtains, he saw the Russian dragon holding his now-mated female close in bed. She was a virgin no longer, but that didn't matter to Andre. No, what mattered was that she was mated to a dragon whose blood was untainted by a witch's protection spell. But for how long?

After a moment, he flitted from window to window of the home, eavesdropping on the dragons inside, learning what he could of their plans. As he passed outside an office window, he craned his head toward the glass, keeping his body out of sight.

One of the younger Belishaw dragons spoke. "Are you sure the witches can help? You know how tentative our alliance with them is."

"They are our best hope, Randolph. They have spells that can see into the girl's mind. We need to understand how a second mate is possible, or how a dragon could survive mate grief. I have never heard of such a thing, but they may help us find answers."

Andre held his body still. There was a heavy pause in the conversation.

"I'm sorry Jodie was sent back to Boston. Give it time, Randolph. The Salem Witch Council has marriage contracts, but they often fall apart if the warlock and witch do not suit."

"You have no idea what it's like," Randolph muttered. "To have a mate so close, yet being unable to keep her. It's like a part of me is slowly dying inside."

"I do know what that feeling is like," the other dragon said, his tone full of sorrow. "Before I took your mother as a temporary mate to continue my bloodline, I met a young woman in a local village. She was a potential true mate for me, but she died of a fever that claimed half of the village. I spent three years waiting for her to be old enough to mate, and fate took her from me. After her, I gave up on finding a true mate and reached out to your mother."

Andre stopped listening to the conversation. He had learned enough, and the drama of this pair held little interest for him. The dragons would leave for Cornwall tomorrow. His master needed to be told if they were to grab the human female and use her to lure her mate to them.

He slipped back into the shadows and drew on the last bit of the wolf shifter blood he had consumed in order to change shape, then flitted off into the darkness on bat wings.

CHAPTER 12

Dragons have relationships with other mythical creatures and often act as emissaries between warring factions of these other beings. Vampires and witches sometimes go to war against one another, and dragons are crucial to bringing peace. If a dragon speaks, they will listen.

THE CAVE WAS DARK AND DEEP. THE SOUND OF TASHA'S breathing echoed off the icy rock as the chill of the mountain settled into her bones. She was barefoot for some reason, and yet she wasn't cold. Her feet padded softly across the frosted cave floor toward the monolithic shape of the sleeping dragon. Icicles dripped off the scaled eyebrows and the tips of the frill lying flat against the dragon's back. The dragon looked more like stone than a breathing mythical beast, as though an ancient people had spent a century carving the shape into the rock.

Next to the dragon was a barrier of ice that separated Tasha from a second chamber in the cave, and behind that, warped by the ice, was a person. She moved closer to the barrier, and the ice seemed to clear until a dark-haired woman in a blue tunic became visible. As Tasha watched, the woman pressed her palms to the glassy surface, her eyes looking past Tasha, toward Vasili's sleeping dragon form.

"Marina?" The woman lifted her gaze to Tasha's face. "It's you, isn't it?" Her heart beat faster as the woman nodded, her features slightly blurred by the wall of ice between them.

"You woke him." The other woman's voice came through as clear as day. Her lips curved into a smile.

"I did." Tasha swallowed past the sudden lump in her throat. "Are you trapped in the dragon heart stone? Vasili thinks you are, along with your dragon."

Marina once again gazed at Vasili. "I am inside no stone."

"But then, how are you . . . ? I mean . . . he sees some of your memories whenever we . . . ." She trailed off, not wishing to confess what she and Vasili had done.

"Human souls are not like those of dragons. We cannot stay in stone. But we can tie ourselves to other humans." She smiled sadly. "I had enough strength left for one last spell."

"You tied yourself to Vasili?"

Marina shook her head, the ice between them melting a little more.

"Then who . . . ?" Tasha's eyes widened as a possibility struck her.

"There was one other who was close enough when I died."

One other. "No . . ."

"Yes. I bound my soul to his, hoping someday to be reborn and find a way back, to wake my Vasili again."

Tasha's head filled with a sudden throbbing pressure behind her eyes. She didn't want to think, didn't want to hear any more. It couldn't be true. She couldn't be . . .

The ice barrier turned once more to stone, and the woman melted away.

"No . . . ," Tasha said to herself as the cold and the pain in her head became too much. Finally, blackness swallowed her whole.

TASHA BOLTED UP, GASPING FOR BREATH. IT TOOK A second to orient herself. She wasn't at home. She wasn't in the Dorchester either. She was in a foreign bedroom, one that belonged to Everett Belishaw.

Vasili slept beside her. He was stretched out on his stomach, one hand bunched under his pillow, the other slung loosely over her hips beneath the comforter.

She curled up a little at the realization that she was completely naked under the sheets, as was Vasili. She flushed and covered her face as everything they had done last night came flooding back to her.

Holy shit.

She definitely wasn't a virgin anymore, and she was glad she had shared that experience with Vasili. He had been so gentle and caring before, but last night she had seen another side of him. A possessive, dominating, sexual side that had not scared her at all. It had been something she had needed, and he had given it to her without thought, like two perfectly match halves coming together to make one whole being.

Tasha glanced toward the clock on the nightstand. It was close to eight in the morning. She'd gotten only a handful of hours of sleep, but somehow she felt rested. She had the sense that she had been dreaming again, but she couldn't recall the dream. Something about Vasili and the cave, but it was too foggy.

She slipped out of bed and tiptoed into the white marble bathroom and turned on the shower. The moment warm steam filled the stall, she stepped inside and moaned as hot water cascaded over her chilled skin. She scrubbed at her face and tried to recall the dream she'd had, just beneath the surface of her conscious mind.

A shadow loomed across the foggy shower door. For a second, she imagined she was in an icy cave, staring at a wall of ice, a figure standing just behind. She wiped away the fog on the glass and saw Vasili's face.

"May I come in?" he asked, nodding at the shower.

"Um . . . sure." She opened the door and shyly retreated as he stepped inside. He was gloriously naked. He closed the shower door and smiled, the expression so gentle and sweet that it made her heart quiver.

"When I was young, we would breathe fire into pools

of water in open rock formations and bathe in the water during the winter." He touched the nozzle of the shower. "Such marvelous inventions. When I first woke, I was uncertain that I could adapt to all these changes, but now I am enjoying the technology of this age."

Tasha was listening—honestly, she was—but her hands had a mind of their own. She was touching his chest before she knew what she was doing. He curled his fingers around her wrists, holding her hands to his skin when she apologized and tried to pull away. He was just too beautiful, too tempting not to touch.

"I am yours, Tasha. You are free to touch me whenever you wish. I love it when you do." His blue eyes were so open and honest she couldn't doubt his words.

She leaned into him bashfully. "It's just so not me. I'm used to keeping my distance with people, but you make me feel desperate for that physical connection."

He stroked his knuckles over her cheek. "That will lessen a little with time, but it is stronger now because we are newly mated."

"So this is normal?" She trailed her fingertips along his collarbones, watching the water form droplets on his skin. She had the urge to lean in and lick them away.

"It's very normal. In fact, we must strengthen our bond." His amused chuckle turned into a groan as her hand slid down his chest to grip his erection. She stroked the hard length of him, fascinated at how he felt so soft and yet hard at the same time. Such an interesting contradiction.

"How's that for strengthening?"

Suddenly his hand was between her legs, his fingers stroking the petals of her sex. "A good start."

Tasha whimpered as he gripped her wet hair and pulled her head back so he could kiss her neck.

"I need to mark you," he said between kisses.

She moved backward until he had her pinned against the shower wall. "Mark me?"

"Yes." It was the only warning he gave her. He lifted her up, spread her legs, which she wrapped around his hips, and then impaled her on his cock. The sudden pressure of being completely filled by him was something she wasn't sure she'd ever get used to, but she was desperate for it.

She cried out, still tender from before, but also hungry for him. He braced her backside on his hands, holding her up between himself and the wall as he began to thrust into her. It was raw and hard, more primal than what they had done last night. Barely able to breathe, Tasha dug her fingernails into his shoulders, holding on for dear life.

He spoke no words, but grunted with each thrust, his breath hot against her neck as he ravished her. He then sank his teeth into the sensitive spot where her shoulder met her neck, and she screamed. Pleasure flowed through her violently, as though she were on fire with it. She was aware of nothing beyond him, beyond the feel of their bodies and the bliss of this rough union.

Long moments later, she held on to him, wrapped around him, her mouth caressing his with light kisses of wonderment. He kissed her back in such a way that made her toes curl.

"Vasili," she murmured.

He kissed her cheeks and the tip of her nose, making her smile so hard it hurt. "Yes?"

"I like this . . . I like *you*." She'd almost said she loved him. But that word held so much power, and she was still learning what it meant to be in love with someone. She didn't want to tell him too soon, but she would when she was ready.

"I like this . . . and you too." He nuzzled her neck and kissed the sore spot where he had bitten her.

She touched the bruise growing on her neck. "Ow."

He apologized with more kisses, tender ones that made her heart turn over in her chest. "Normally a dragoness, even in human form, has tougher skin. I didn't mean to hurt you." He kissed her forehead before setting her down gently. Her legs weren't quite ready to hold her up, and she collapsed on the marble bench seat on one side of the shower.

Vasili lathered soap in his palms and knelt in front of her, slowly moving his hands over her body, cleaning her and caressing her. By the time he was done, she had found enough strength in her legs to return the favor by washing him. It was a long time before they found any motivation to leave the shower.

"We have to go," she sighed in his arms and finally turned off the water.

"We could stay in London. Forget the witches," Vasili said, his tone suddenly more serious.

"Forget the witches?" She shook her head. "This is too important. We need answers, and they might be the only ones who can help us." She locked her arms around his neck and held tightly to him. "No matter what happens, we're in this together, right?"

"Yes," he promised.

"Everything will be okay. It has to be." Tasha tried to convince herself of that truth, but a gnawing worry was beginning to grow inside her.

What if the witches had no answers? What then?

VASILI MEANT WHAT HE HAD SAID. HE WOULD FORGET the witches and whatever they might discover if it meant keeping his mate safe and happy. He felt at peace now in a way he hadn't thought possible in a world without Marina. Tasha was a gift, and he would cherish every moment with her. But she wouldn't change her mind.

He allowed her to dress while he went downstairs to see what the Belishaw dragons offered by way of food and drink to break his morning fast. Randolph and Magnus were arguing as he walked into the dining room.

"Another body, and at the club you were in last night, Randolph. How the bloody hell did you miss the bloodsucker?"

"I was a little preoccupied with the *rogue dragon* I had on my hands," Randolph shot back. His coffee cup clattered loudly on the table. Both men wore jeans; Magnus had biker boots and a leather coat on, while Randolph wore a cable-knit sweater. The two presented such an odd picture as they argued—dragons older than nations wearing such modern clothing. Randolph looked like he belonged in those glossy paper magazines that Tasha liked to look at full of handsomely dressed men and women. Magnus looked like he was ready to go into the nearest pub and brawl. Vasili was so wrapped up in the moment, he didn't immediately realize what they were saying.

"What happened?" He stepped toward the table, worried that he might have to intervene, given the angry looks they were shooting each other.

"Bloody blood cults," Magnus growled. "Every twenty-five years or so, we get a nest of vampires who don't follow the rules. They kill humans without a care, and they hunt witches and shifters for the power in our blood. The London Blood Society can usually quash them, but this cult is more widespread, full of younger vamps, mad ones, ones who believe the world belongs to them and all other creatures are here to serve and feed their sick desires. They're like bloody millennial vamps."

"What are millennials?" Vasili asked. It sounded like a very old breed, not young.

"That's not important. Besides, millennials aren't all bad," Randolph said. "But we are dealing with a very moti-vated vampire cult. They worship the act of bloodletting. They enjoy the suffering of their victims. They killed a woman at the dance club last night. I was there watching for them, but I got distracted."

Vasili sighed heavily as he understood the argument he had walked in on. "By me."

"Yes."

"What's to be done?" Vasili asked.

"We have notified the London Blood Society, and we

will tell the witches this afternoon. The wolves and other shifters spread over London are more divided. It will take time to reach them all."

"We should get Vasili and his mate bespelled when we see the witches."

"Bespelled?" Vasili didn't like the sound of that.

"Just your blood," Magnus said. "It makes our blood poisonous to vampires. It keeps us relatively safe."

"By which he means it simply reduces the number of reasons vampires and their ilk would want us dead," added Randolph.

"Do you think Tasha is in danger?"

"I believe you might be in more danger, but if she's with you, they could kill her. They don't turn down succulent virgins, I can promise you that," Randolph said darkly.

"She's not a virgin anymore," Magnus chuckled.

Vasili let out a low dragon growl, his voice box changing to reach a deeper, more warning octave.

"It's not as though it was a secret. Randolph wasn't here, but your claiming last night damn near brought down the bloody roof on our heads," Magnus said, but he sounded slightly apologetic. Vasili relaxed a little.

"Do not tease Tasha about the mating. She is new to our world and shy. I will not have anyone make her feel uncomfortable."

Magnus shrugged. "Fine, no teasing. But you know, Vasili, we do have humor in this modern age."

Vasili raised a brow at him. "And women are more inclined to have men openly discuss their deflowering in this modern age?"

A rare blush darkened Magnus's face. "Point taken."

"Will you be ready to leave soon?" Randolph asked. "The drive to Cornwall is more than four hours."

"We will. She should be ready soon."

"Good. I'll call the council and inform them we're coming." Randolph pulled a phone out of his pocket as he left the dining room.

Vasili shot Magnus a look. "Where is Everett?"

"In his office—down the hall, last left."

He found Everett seated at his desk, facing a laptop, frowning in irritation. He glanced up at Vasili as he stepped inside, and the frown vanished.

"I take it congratulations are in order?"

"Yes. We had a successful mating last night." He wasn't embarrassed to talk about it, not the way he knew Tasha would be. To him, this was all natural.

"Interesting. Another piece for our puzzle. I wasn't sure if you would be able to. We are in terra incognita, after all, old friend."

"We are indeed." Vasili slid into a chair facing Everett. "I never dreamed this was possible."

"The witches may be able to figure out how this occurred."

"It must have something to do with Marina and how she died so close to a dragon heart stone, the Heart of Sorrows. But I cannot see how all of it fits together, or why Tasha and I see Marina's memories."

Everett was silent a long moment. "Whatever allowed it to happen, I'm not sorry. I'm glad you're back. I was worried I would be left alone with these younger dragons.

The world has changed. We dragons are changing. Gone are the days when we could fly without fear and live upon the land. Now we are in a world of cameras. Our every move is monitored by CCTV, the government, and even the phones of humans. Many supernatural creatures and other beings of myth have begun to die out. The rest, to survive, choose to crossbreed and make unique alliances. The world has less magic in it." Everett paused, his gaze distant. "I feel like we are approaching a great precipice. A kind of madness is sweeping the world. I fear magic and beings born of magic may not survive to the next century."

"Do not despair," Vasili said, sensing his friend's distress. "We dragons will survive."

Everett smiled. "You always were optimistic. By the way, I spoke with Randolph after you and Miss Bellamy retired last evening. He thought we should call your nephews this morning."

"Yes, that would be good. I was hoping you would know how to contact them."

"Luckily, I do. We helped Mikhail deal with a problem here in England four years ago. It brought our clans back in contact, and we have renewed our alliance with the Barinovs."

"I'm glad to hear it."

Everett picked up his phone and grinned. "Want to shock your nephews now?"

"Absolutely." Vasili settled back in his chair, chuckling as Everett began to dial.

❄

JACKSON BARINOV LISTENED TO HIS MOTHER HUM AS SHE cooked pasta in a large metal pot. The cooks at their palatial home took the weekends off—but they still got paid, at his mom's insistence. Jackson adored his mother for her kind heart. She was one of his two most favorite people in the entire world. The other being his dad, of course.

"Alfredo sauce or red sauce, Jackson?" she asked, holding up two jars of pasta sauce.

He pointed at the one he wanted. "Red!"

"Red it is."

Jackson swung his feet around on the high barstool while he watched. Then pain suddenly knifed across his mind, and he squeezed his eyes shut. It was happening again.

The cold came, revealing a sleeping black dragon. The glowing blue stone was there, but now he saw more. There was light flashing around his eyes, music deafening his ears . . . then rain. So much rain he thought he might wash away with it.

Aunt Tasha fled into the storm, but wraithlike hands snatched her, holding her down. The rain stopped, leaving only candlelight and the scent of old, dried blood. Voices echoed in the dark room, and awful things shifted in the sinister shadows.

Uncle Vasili was on his knees, a red light cast over his body as iron chains held him prisoner. The wraiths drew closer, their skeletal hands reaching for Vasili, sharp claws slicing open his chest. He didn't fight—he only hissed in agonized pain.

Jackson didn't understand what he was seeing. Why wasn't his uncle fighting back?

"Drink . . ." a voice rasped, and the obsidian shadows facing Vasili now lunged for him, death glowing in their red eyes.

Jackson gasped as the vision faded. He wiped the tears coating his cheeks.

"Mommy!" He didn't want to cry; he was a big boy, even though he was only four. But he couldn't stop it. This was scary—too scary.

"Yes, baby?" His mother turned to him, and her cheeks drained of color. "Jackson, what's happened?" She dropped the ladle into the pot of pasta and rushed around the bar to scoop him up into her arms. He buried his face in her neck.

"The bad ones . . . they are going to get Uncle Vasili and Aunt Tasha."

"The what?" His mother's hand stroked his hair, and the pain in his head eased a little.

"The bad ones. The shadows. They're gonna eat him."

"Eat Uncle Vasili? Oh, honey, that's not going to happen. Uncle Vasili is gone, remember?"

"He's not gone," Jackson protested. He had tried several times over the last few days to explain to his parents what he was saying. He was young, but he knew the difference between dreams and what he was seeing. They still didn't believe him when he said that Uncle Vasili had been found. His mother had been bothered by her own sense of something new, some dragon in the world, but she'd decided that it couldn't be Vasili—it was some other dragon being born. But Jackson knew it was him.

"Call Daddy!"

"Grigori!" Madelyn's shout carried through the house.

His father raced into the room, his eyes glowing gold.

"Something is wrong with Jackson," Madelyn whispered, still holding him against her chest.

"Another dream?" Grigori came toward them, and Jackson sighed in relief. He felt safe when both of his parents were near him.

"Tell him what you told me." His mother patted his back soothingly. Jackson explained as best he could what he'd seen.

"I tried to explain to him that Vasili is gone," his mother said.

Grigori's eyes fixed on Jackson's face. "Who is Tasha?"

"The bad dragon man's daughter, but she's not bad. She's good. Really good."

"The bad dragon man . . . ," Grigori murmured. "You don't think he means . . . ?"

His mother gasped. "Drakor."

"But Dimitri didn't have a daughter. We would have known."

"Would you? The man was good at keeping secrets, especially from you," Madelyn reminded him quietly.

"Still, I would have known."

Grigori's cell phone rang. He pulled his phone out of his pocket, glancing at the caller ID. "It's the Belishaws."

"Answer it," Madelyn urged.

His father looked at him with concern. "Jackson?"

"I'm okay," Jackson said. "Really."

Grigori let the phone ring once more before he answered.

"This is Grigori." He listened to the caller speak for a moment. "What?"

Jackson studied his father's stunned expression. Grigori

leaned back against the granite countertop next to the stove for support.

"I can't believe it," Grigori said into the phone. "Yes. We will come as quickly as we can. It may take us a few days. Thank you, Everett. Is he there? Could I talk to him?"

There was a long pause, then: "Uncle?" Grigori broke out in a grin. "How . . . ? I mean, I have so many questions. Is Marina there? Can I speak with her?"

The silence that followed stole Grigori's smile, and Jackson moved closer to his mother. He didn't tell them what he'd seen of the golden dragon's fall in the snowy mountains a few days before. They would know soon enough when they went to find his great-uncle.

"Oh . . . I see. Yes, Uncle. Be careful. We will be there soon."

Grigori hung up the phone and stared at Jackson.

"What is it? What did he say?" Madelyn asked.

But his father didn't hear her, still focused on Jackson. "What else did you see, Jackson?"

CHAPTER 13

Excerpt *from Barrow's Journal – My Year with Dragons*

Magic exists in all living things, even humans. But dragon magic, it is something altogether different. It is partly emotion, partly desire, and partly a willingness to sacrifice. When a dragon casts a spell, they cast it with such longing and are willing to pay much to achieve what they desire. The stronger the dragon's heart, the stronger the spells a dragon can cast. Even the tiniest dragon may have the strongest heart.

THE LANCASHIRE WITCH COUNCIL HAD ITS SEAT IN A manor house close to Tintagel in Cornwall. The drive took more than four hours, passing through Devon into Cornwall, and Tasha's nerves only became more strained with every mile.

The haunting land of Dartmoor had left her restless,

with its high moorlands and scores of ancient granite standing stones set in mysterious circles. The sight of the stones made her skin break out in goose bumps. She found some peace in the tranquil streams that tumbled through the woodlands and boulder-strewn ravines to form tiny hidden waterfalls.

Vasili sat beside her in the SUV, his arm around her shoulders, as they reached Cornwall and entered a sheltered valley with thatched cottages dotting the rainy green slopes. Then that quaint village gave way to the dramatic landscape of the Cornwall coast.

Something inside her stomach cramped slightly. An odd pressure filled her head.

"Vasili, what—?"

"It's the magic, little one." He stroked her cheek and kissed her temple as though he sensed her discomfort. "The witches have so much raw power here that you will feel it for miles."

"Do other humans feel it like this?"

"Not the way you do. Only those with a connection to magic or magical beings will feel it so acutely. To most humans, it may feel like someone is watching them, like a prickle on the back of their neck."

"How do you know so much about witches?" Tasha asked him. As far as she knew, she'd never met a witch. She was more nervous than excited at the thought of going into a house full of witches.

"When I was last in England, witches were quite powerful and influential. The Crown was displeased, but the royals had less loyalty from the people than the witches did. The witches here practiced white magic and were far more helpful to the citizens of England than a king when crops failed." Vasili pulled her a little closer against his side.

"Here's Tintagel," Randolph announced from the passenger seat. "We have to go a bit farther south and then enter at their southern gate."

Tasha leaned toward the left passenger window to peer at the landscape. The northern coast of Cornwall rose up in steep cliffs, and a ruined castle crowned the land as they passed by on a small country road.

"That's Tintagel Castle," Randolph said. "Birthplace of King Arthur."

"I've heard that legend." Tasha had always been fascinated by Arthurian legends.

Randolph chuckled. "Er . . . no, King Arthur was actually born there. The history books are not exactly accurate. He wasn't a myth."

She stared at Randolph and then at Vasili. Her mate shrugged.

"He was quite real. The wizard Emrys bespelled the world so that the name would only be remembered as a myth. It protects King Arthur where he rests in Avalon. He was wounded in his battle against his son Mordred, but Emrys could not bear to let the world lose him, so he was cast under a spell of sleep."

"You're kidding," Tasha stammered as she looked at Vasili. "He's kidding, right?" There was no way King Arthur was real.

"I would never lie to you, Tasha," Vasili said with intense honesty.

Her heart pounded in excitement. "But how . . . ? There's no record of him ruling. Wouldn't there have to be?"

"Emrys was powerful. He could adjust the flow of time itself when needed. A little thing like changing the memory of men was easy."

"But you . . . you both remember," Tasha pointed out.

Vasili smiled in gentle amusement. He spoke words that sounded like a song in a language she didn't understand.

"What does that mean?" she asked him.

"*When all the world has fallen away, only dragons will remember.* It's dragonsong, one as old as time. It means that much of what can be remembered will be remembered by dragons, even when everything in the world finally ends."

"Dragonsong is like poetry," Randolph explained. "Think of it a bit like folk songs."

"Do you actually sing?" Tasha gazed at Vasili, wishing she knew more about dragons than she did. There was so much about them that was still a mystery to her.

"Yes, we do, both in human and dragon form, but dragonsong is performed only when one is in dragon form."

"What does it sound like?"

Vasili traced her lips with a finger as he seemed to think over his answer.

"Have you ever heard whale song?"

Tasha nodded.

"It's something like that. Haunting, echoing. It's hard to explain."

Tasha wondered when she'd get the chance to hear dragons sing. She glanced back at the ruins of the castle on the cliff tops. King Arthur was real, and dragons could sing. What other wonders would she discover today?

A storm brewed over the sea, drawing ever closer, and it was starting to send thunderous swells against the shore. It was as though the very air could sense Tasha's trepidation as the car drove inland toward a distant valley and the manor house beyond.

A massive black iron gate blocked the two SUVs from entering. Randolph exited the vehicle and walked toward the gate's center padlock. A light breeze danced around him, tugging at his clothes and hair as he placed his palm on the lock. He flinched but didn't remove his hand for a long moment. Then the gate opened inward, and Randolph stepped back, allowing the gates to fully part before he turned and walked back toward the vehicle. As he came back inside, Tasha noticed his right hand was bleeding. He removed a handkerchief from his pocket and wrapped it around his injury.

"Are you okay?"

He smiled ruefully. "The witches use blood spells to protect the land and the witches who live there. This is their way to ensure that only those who are welcome are allowed entrance."

She looked at his injured hand. "Doesn't seem welcoming."

"Yes, well, the witches have good reason to mistrust

other creatures. They are often kidnapped and used for their spell work."

Magnus drove their SUV forward through the open gates, and Tasha got a better look at the manor house and the lush gardens that bloomed too early for England. Green ivy crawled in thick blankets up the stones of the house and framed the windows.

"How many witches are in the coven?" Tasha asked.

"Thirteen head witches. They have families, which make the covens larger, but at least thirteen must be active to lead the coven. They make decisions and form alliances with other supernatural beings, and the Lady or Lord Superior is elected by them."

"Who's that?"

"They rule as the senior witch or warlock," Randolph explained.

The SUV stopped in front of the manor house. The large oak door had a wrought iron knocker in the shape of a lion's head. The door opened, and a woman in dark-green trousers and a cream-colored sweater came out to meet them. Her face was smooth, yet silver threaded through the loose rippling waves of her shoulder-length hair.

Randolph and Everett exited their SUVs first. Everett bowed over the woman's offered hand, kissing her knuckles respectfully before he straightened.

"Lady Superior." He then nodded at the others who'd joined him on the steps.

"This is her? Miss Bellamy?" the woman asked Everett. Tasha approached the stone steps of the house, feeling like she was being observed under a microscope.

"Yes, this is Tasha and her mate, Vasili Barinov."

The woman's gaze slid to Vasili. Her eyes widened.

"It has been a long time since I've seen an aura like that," the woman said to herself, then cleared her throat. "Please come in. I've gathered a few of the others to assist in the spell casting, but it will take us a few hours to be ready. We have left the valley open. It is protected from human eyes if you wish to fly," she said to Everett, who smiled like a delighted child.

"You spoil me, Lady Superior."

The witch stepped back, and the dragons entered the grand old house. Tasha had felt the pressure in her head ease once they'd passed the gates, but now an altogether different sensation held her attention. She felt like she'd left home and suddenly remembered she'd left the oven on or a door unlocked. It was a niggling sense of worry, but she couldn't pin it down to any specific cause.

A lovely young woman with waves of rich golden hair tumbling around her shoulders rushed with excitement down the stairs.

"Grandma, what's going on? Who are these people—" She halted as she spotted the gathering at the bottom of the steps.

"Ah, there you are, Tamsin dear. Come and meet the Belishaws and their friends." Lady Superior turned to Tasha and the others. "This is my youngest granddaughter, Tamsin Batsford. She's spending the year here while she studies at the University of Cambridge."

"She's your granddaughter?" Randolph inquired. "She sounds American."

"Her father is. She's the seventh child of my seventh child. My seventh child, Tamsin's mother, accepted a marriage contract to Salem to marry a Batsford warlock. Tamsin and her siblings live in America but visit me every summer."

"The seventh child of the seventh child . . ." Everett gazed up at the beautiful young woman at the foot of the stairs as though lost in a dream. Tasha watched the ancient English drake's reaction. Everett's lips parted, his focus on Tamsin unwavering. It reminded Tasha of the way Vasili looked at her, as if she was the beginning and end of everything that ever mattered.

"Yes, you know the ways of magic, Mr. Belishaw. The seventh child of the seventh child is often more special, more powerful than other witches or warlocks. We expect great things from my grandchild. Once she turns twenty-one, she will be contracted in marriage to a Salem Witch Council member in America to make a powerful new bloodline of magic. Tamsin is already one of the most powerful witches of our day, even though she's only nineteen." Lady Superior beamed with pride at her granddaughter. Tamsin was clearly uncomfortable and nervously tried to tame her hair and looked down at the floor.

"Well, don't just stand there—come and meet the dragons," her grandmother insisted.

"Yes, Grandma," Tamsin replied and lifted her eyes. When her eyes fell on Everett she stilled, and Tasha sensed a strange vibration in the air, as though someone was running a wet fingertip over the rim of a wineglass. Tasha heard nothing, but she felt that strange note of energy winding through the room, coiling around everyone as the young witch stared at the ancient dragon. There was an intimacy to that look that Tasha knew all too well, the look of someone who'd seen their future revealed before them.

It was how she'd felt when she'd first seen Vasili. Her rational mind had been in control at the time, focused on all the wrong things, like panicking over finding a dragon in a cave, but her more instinctive side had seen him for what he was. Her destiny. Tamsin had that look now, as though she sensed that Everett Belishaw was her future, no matter what her grandmother had planned.

The air suddenly crackled, and the incandescent lights in the chandelier above winked out, leaving them in shadow. Vasili pulled Tasha against him instinctively, his body shielding her from any danger that might arise.

"Tamsin?" Lady Superior said softly, a question hanging in the air.

"Sorry, Grandmother, I was just startled. I've never seen dragons before . . ." The young witch's face was bright red as she snapped her fingers and the lights came back on.

Lady Superior's gaze drifted between her granddaughter and the dragon with open concern.

"Should I bring some tea into the library for everyone?" Tamsin suggested.

"Yes, and have the others meet us there. I shall soon have need of them," the witch told Tamsin before she turned to Tasha and the others. "Please come with me."

Tasha stared at the oil paintings of men and women in fine clothing as they wound through the beautiful old home. The eyes of the paintings seemed to follow them as they walked. And in a place like this, that wasn't necessarily an artist's illusion. In fact, she was quite certain she saw more than one portrait twitch or shift.

Tasha came up next to Lady Superior. "Who are they?"

"The witches and warlocks who were the leaders of our coven for the last five hundred years."

The library was a massive room lined with floor-to-ceiling shelves. In its center were several painted circles and a few comfortable couches and chairs that appeared to be expensive French antiques. Colorful glass bottles hung from the ceiling, suspended by no strings that Tasha could see. More bottles hung above the windowpanes, and a few floated in the opening of the fireplace.

"What are those?" Tasha asked Vasili.

"I believe those are witch bottles," he whispered. "They offer protection to anyone inside this house from black magic. Most witches are good, but there are outsiders who perform black magic, and they are usually at war with the council witches."

Magnus, Randolph, and the other dragons took up guard posts while Everett stared at the doorway of the library as if waiting for something.

"My dear, please come here," Lady Superior said to Tasha. Vasili followed close as Tasha approached the witch at a small table by the fireplace.

Tasha sat down, and the woman held out her hand. "Give me your palm, dear."

Tasha placed her hand in Lady Superior's. The witch bent over it and stroked her index finger over Tasha's palm, tracing lines and softly humming over broken lines and the curve of her mount of Venus near her thumb.

"I've never seen such a palm before. Normally, lines start on the inside and fork or break toward the outside of the palm. But yours . . . it's the opposite. Why would a life-line start broken and then converge?" the witch asked herself.

Tasha stared down at her hand. "What does that mean?"

Vasili, who sat beside her, shifted uncomfortably.

"Let me see yours, Mr. Barinov."

Vasili offered his hand without a word.

"And no broken lines at all in yours." The Lady Superior continued to stare at them both in puzzlement.

The library doors opened, and Tamsin returned, carrying a tea tray. Two others followed behind her, a redheaded witch and a dark-haired warlock. They joined Lady Superior while Tamsin poured tea into white-and-blue porcelain cups. Everett's gaze locked on Tamsin and didn't move, while the other Belishaw dragons turned to the newly arrived coven members.

"This is Arabella Langford and Jeremy Cavendish."

Arabella and Jeremy shook hands with Vasili, Randolph, and Tasha.

"We'll be working on a very specific spell this afternoon. We must procure a few special ingredients, and then we will summon you for the casting," Lady Superior explained. "Until then, please have some tea, and if any dragons wish to fly, you may do so anywhere in the safe space of the valley."

"Thank you, Lady Superior." Randolph nodded at his fellow English drakes, who all took tea from Tamsin. Everett was last. He halted at the table, taking the final cup from the young American witch. Tasha continued to watch their interaction out of the corner of her eye.

"Here you go, Mr. Belishaw." Tamsin blushed as Everett accepted the teacup.

"Please, call me Everett. And thank you, Miss Batsford."

She ducked her head but was smiling. "You can call me Tamsin."

Tasha's heart squeezed as she watched the lonely English dragon charm the young witch. Then she sipped her tea and noted the strange taste.

"Lady Superior, do you mind if I ask what kind of tea this is?"

"Earl Grey . . . with a dose of vervain, my dear. It will help purify you for the ritual. It also offers protection against dark magic."

"Oh." Tasha drank the tea until her cup was empty before she and Vasili decided to go out into the gardens. As they passed by Everett, Vasili slapped him on the shoulder.

"Come, Everett, it's been seven hundred years since I've flown, and I expect it's been a while for you too. Let's fly together."

"But—"

"Show the woman your dragon," Vasili whispered to Everett in Russian. "Impress her—it might help you entice her to your bed."

"Fine, but it's not as if I can. She's taken," Everett

growled back in Russian before speaking to Tamsin in English. "Would you like to come outside with us, Tamsin?"

Tasha bit her lip to keep from laughing at the exchange between Vasili and Everett who were acting more like teenage boys than ancient dragons when it came to girls.

"I am allowed to see you change? I would love that! I've never seen a dragon before."

Tasha smiled at the witch and waved for her to join them. Tamsin led them to the back gardens and showed them the valley that spread inland away from the sea. Several of the other dragons came to watch, including Randolph, who was also watching the way his father couldn't keep his eyes off Tamsin.

Vasili held Tasha close, smiling as she leaned into him. "You wish to see me fly, little one?"

"Yes, I really do," Tasha breathed. She needed to see Vasili as a dragon again, needed to see him alive and breathing so she could erase the image of his frozen body in the cave from her mind.

He gave her a long kiss and released her, stepping out onto the grass with Everett. Tamsin sidled up beside her.

"Will they . . . I mean, do you think they will take off their clothes?"

"I don't know," Tasha admitted. "I'm not sure how this works."

As if in answer, the two men began to change right before their eyes. Vasili's body twisted and elongated, his clothes transforming into obsidian-colored scales as he stretched out to more than thirty feet in length. Beside him, Everett turned into a ruby-red dragon. Vasili threw back his head and roared, shaking the nearby trees and sending a flock of starlings into the air. Everett fanned his frill out behind his head and nipped at Vasili's shoulder. It reminded Tasha of the way dogs or wolves played, the pretend fights and playful nips.

Vasili snapped back at Everett before both dragons took a running leap into the air and flapped their massive wings. The powerful rush of wind knocked Tamsin and Tasha onto their backsides.

"They're so beautiful," Tamsin gasped.

"They certainly are beautiful." Tasha watched the pair of dragons swirl in the sky in a sort of dance. They seemed to know exactly where the other dragon would move, like a pair of birds in flight.

"What happened to their clothes? I've heard other dragons leave them behind and have to strap them to their bodies," Tamsin said.

"Vasili said the older dragons who have harnessed their own magic can retain their clothes when they change. Most younger dragons don't know how."

"Wow . . . dragon magic. I would love to know more about that."

"So would I," Tasha agreed. It seemed dragon magic was different than witch and warlock magic. It required no ingredients or cauldrons, only the dragon.

Tasha studied their immense wings, the way the hide pulled tight over the bony structure of their wingspan and how their tails acted like ship rudders in the air. A soft, haunting sound reached her ears, not unlike those of a whale, and her heart stilled.

Dragonsong. Vasili was singing to her. The notes were more musical and more structured than she'd expected.

She had never heard dragonsong before, yet she knew the notes and the words they represented. She sang softly with Vasili, even though he was far above her in the sky.

"If the universe has a heart, its heart would be a dragon's. We who fly upon the wings of dawn remember the beginning and will sing at the end. We never die—we sleep until we wake once more, in a new dream, in a new world, to fly and love again."

"You know what he's singing?" Tamsin asked in awe.

Tasha blinked as she came out of the strange daze. "I guess I do. I can't explain how, though."

Tamsin gasped, her eyes widening. "Your eyes!"

"What?" Tasha reached up to touch her face but didn't know what the woman was talking about.

"They're gold. Tasha, your eyes are *gold.*"

"They can't be. I'm not . . ." Her words cut off abruptly as flashes of a dream came back to her. *An icy cave . . . a figure behind the wall of ice . . . trapped.* She clutched at the mental fragments, but they soon vanished, leaving behind a fierce ache in her skull.

"I . . ." She pressed her hands to her cheeks and closed her eyes. When she opened them again, Tamsin visibly relaxed.

"They're not gold anymore. Maybe I was just seeing things. I do that sometimes." The witch laughed nervously. "Being the seventh child of the seventh child can be a little frustrating at times."

The dragonsong died away, and the two dragons swept low over the valley. Vasili chased Everett, and then they arced up over the forest in the distance and wound their way back toward the house.

The dragons settled gently upon the meadow twenty yards away, and their bodies began to change back to human form. Everett grinned as he straightened and brushed the dust off his gray trousers, and Vasili combed his fingers through his dark hair before checking the state of his own clothes.

Tasha rushed out to meet them, Tamsin trailing behind her. She marveled at how they had changed without getting undressed. How did they do it?

Tasha melted into his arms as he opened them to her. "Vasili, your song was beautiful."

"Thank you," he said almost bashfully. He nuzzled her cheek, then kissed her slowly. She clung to his shoulders, forgetting where they were as his tongue dipped inside her mouth. Lord, the man knew just what to do to make her forget her own name.

"I will sing for you anytime, little one," he promised.

"Good, because I loved it. I love the meaning behind it too."

Vasili drew back to look down at her. "The meaning? You understood the words?"

"Yeah, when you sang, I just knew what it meant. I figured maybe that was a normal mate thing?"

Worry darkened his eyes. "No, Tasha, that is not normal. I've never heard of a human mate understanding dragonsong without being taught."

"Really? But—"

"The spell is ready," Tamsin said, and then her face

colored. "Sorry, I didn't mean to interrupt, but once the spell casters are ready they need to complete the spell within an hour, or it fades."

"Then we had better hurry." Tasha gripped Vasili's hand, and they followed Tamsin back to the house and into the library. The witches were waiting for them.

CHAPTER 14

Excerpt from Barrow's Journal – My Year with Dragons

When a dragon takes a mate, the passion, especially the physical, is almost impossible to deny. Once that bond is formed, a dragon and its mate cannot bear to be apart long, nor can they bear to resist touching each other when they are alone. This passion softens over time as the dragon and its mate learn to control their needs, but it never fades.

TASHA SAT IN A CHAIR CLOSE TO A CAULDRON THAT bubbled and emitted a purple light. Lady Superior and the two other coven members, Arabella and Jeremy, were pouring bottles of various ingredients into the cauldron. It made her think of a high school production of *Macbeth*, yet she didn't laugh. She could *feel* the magic in the room, like an eerie charge in the air that stroked her skin and made her shiver. Vasili stood behind her, and she could sense him frowning even though she couldn't see his face.

"We are almost ready," Arabella said. "The last thing we need is . . ." Arabella gave Lady Superior a look.

"Oh, yes, that one." Lady Superior cleared her throat and then said to Tamsin, "Be a dear and go play your new song on the piano for our guests."

Tamsin looked like she wanted to question this request, but with a sigh, she went to the small grand piano in the corner of the library. Tasha blinked. When had there been a piano there? She hadn't noticed it.

The piano bench creaked as Tamsin got comfortable and began to play. A simple string of notes, clear and pure, came out in a haunting melody that left a hum in the air. Then she pressed one of the dampener pedals, and her left hand began to play in perfect harmony with her right.

There were no words to the song, yet as Tasha listened, she began to see a life, hers with Vasili, as if the song played out their future. He was on his knees in the dark, bound by chains, bleeding. He roared as shadowy figures gathered around him and white fangs pierced his flesh. Then she saw herself, lying half dead, wounds upon her neck and arms, mere feet away from Vasili. She couldn't save him, because she couldn't save herself.

As the song faded and the notes slowly died, Tasha came back to herself. Tears streamed down her face. Lady Superior got up from her chair and came toward Tasha, holding a small glass vial. Without a word, she collected a tear that fell from Tasha's cheek. Then she went to Everett, who stood, like the others in the room, rooted in place by what he had seen in his head. He was pale, his eyes full of dark pain as he stared at Tamsin.

"She will never be yours, Mr. Belishaw. You will live alone until your last breath," Lady Superior murmured. A tear escaped Everett's eye, and she reached up to capture it with the vial before returning to the cauldron and pouring the tears inside.

"What was that?" Tasha dared to ask.

Lady Superior replied without turning around. "The tears required for our spell, one from the subject and one from a dragon."

"No, I meant the song."

"Oh, that is a possible future. Tamsin plays spells into her music. That particular song allows a listener to see one of their many possible futures, though none are guaranteed. Fate is still somewhat bound by free will. Your future can only be because of something you decide. Therefore, a particular fate is only possible given your choices and your decisions in any moment."

"Only a possible future," Everett whispered to himself, his gaze locked on Tamsin. She was staring back, her heart in her eyes.

"So what I saw . . . it's not going to happen?" Tasha pressed a hand over her heart as she tried to push away the pain of the vision she'd seen.

Vasili placed his hand on Tasha shoulders. "What did you see?"

She breathed a sigh of relief at hearing his voice. He was here. He wasn't dead.

"What I saw is not going to happen," she promised

both him and herself. She wouldn't let it. Lady Superior had said she had free will, that her decisions could stop a particular future from occurring.

Lady Superior stirred the contents of the cauldron, causing smoke to spill over and creep across the ground. Then Arabella dipped a blue bottle into the cauldron and pulled it out. A clear liquid was visible in the bottle. She passed it to Jeremy, who held it in his hand. Then he closed his eyes and murmured something in a strange archaic language.

The bottle suddenly glowed. Arabella unwrapped the Heart of Sorrows and held it out as Jeremy poured the glowing substance over the sapphire. Small sparks blossomed over the stone's surface, but rather than die away, they drifted up in the air like silver fireflies.

Lady Superior pointed her finger at Tasha and spoke to the glittering sparks of light. "Her."

The sparks shot straight toward Tasha. She flinched, instinctively shutting her eyes. Tiny cold prickles touched her face, and then she was falling through the darkness. Falling. Falling.

She landed on her feet in a snowy world. Everything was quiet around her, and then she heard some distant singing.

Dragonsong. Somehow she knew she was in the land of dragons, not the world that she had been born into, yet it felt like her own world was but a breath away, as though an invisible veil separated the dragons from the world she knew. The air tasted sweet, and the snow was warm as it fell around her. It was like a strange upside-down world, where not everything made sense. The distant evergreen trees covered in thick snow were almost a light blue rather than the rich forest green of her own world.

The songs of the dragons were still far off, but she could make out the words in the way she had when Vasili had sung earlier, as though she'd always known the language of dragons.

Love binds with dragon strength,
Love grows with a human heart,
Thine enemy will give thee new life,
So thy mate will waken and fly again.

TASHA STRUGGLED TO WALK THROUGH THE DEEP SNOW. Time seemed to pass differently here, the snow falling slower than it should.

"Tasha . . ." A voice spoke her name. When she turned around, she saw Marina behind her, wearing a heavy blue velvet cloak trimmed with white fur. She pushed the hood back and approached Tasha.

"Marina? Do you hear the dragons singing?"

"Of course I do—it is *my* song," she said. "The one they sing to remind me."

"Remind you of what?" Tasha knew she had a short time to ask all of her questions, but for some reason, she couldn't remember why time was short or even how she got there.

"It's to remind me . . . and remind you," Marina said.

"Remind us of what? Are you trapped here? Can we free you?"

Marina cupped Tasha's face. "It's to remind you of who you are."

"That I'm Dimitri Drakor's daughter?"

Marina shook her head. "To remind you that you are *me*."

You are me? Does she mean I am . . . Marina?

As if hearing her thoughts, Marina nodded. "We are one, Tasha. I am you, and you are me, if only forgotten. I used Dimitri to bring me back to the world, but I was only mortal. Our dragon lies waiting for you in the Heart of Sorrows. You must wake and join with her, or Vasili will die. The ancient dragons have foretold his death in hours if you do not."

"But how?" Tasha demanded. "I don't know how to join with a dragon."

The world of snow began to fade into a white fog all around her, and Marina could no longer be seen. "It takes an act of sacrifice."

"Sacrifice?"

"Sacrifice . . ." The word wrapped itself around her before it too faded away.

VASILI STARED AT TASHA'S UNMOVING BODY, HIS DRAGON pacing restlessly in the back of his mind. Tasha had collapsed the second the spell took effect, and all three witches involved in the spell had gone rigid, their eyes glowing with a pale blue otherworldly light.

"That's not at all disturbing," Magnus muttered sarcastically. Randolph elbowed him. Everyone else stayed quiet except Tamsin, who fidgeted nervously beside her grandmother.

"How long will the spell last once it's cast?" Vasili asked.

"Only a minute or two," Tamsin said.

"What does the spell do, exactly?" asked Everett.

"I'm not entirely sure," Tamsin admitted. "It's a memory spell, sort of. In a human, it goes to a core memory, one that the mind may be shielding. But with Tasha, well, she is not fully human. I don't know what she is."

Not fully human. What does that mean? Vasili wondered. Her father had been a dragon; maybe some of his dragon bloodline was in her even though she had no dragon bonded to her.

Suddenly the three witches spoke in unison, their voices deep and cacophonous, as if they were a thousand voices chanting all at once.

Love binds with dragon strength,
Love grows with the human heart,
Thine enemy will give thee new life,
So thy mate will wake and fly again.

THE THREE WITCHES SLUMPED OVER IN THEIR CHAIRS. Tamsin caught her grandmother before she collapsed.

Tasha suddenly bolted up from her chair, gasping. Vasili took his mate in his arms, and she began to cry as she shivered and burrowed against him.

"Tasha, are you all right?"

She wouldn't look at him, so he lifted her face with his fingers under her chin. Tears clung to her lashes, and she blinked rapidly. Her lovely topaz eyes were bright gold now. Dragon gold.

"It's me . . . ," she whispered in a shaky voice with a rich Russian accent. An *old* Russian accent. One he thought he'd never hear again.

She lifted a hand to his face, her fingers freezing as though she were holding ice.

"It's me, Vasili. It's *me*." It was a voice he recognized, but he didn't understand how it could be. This wasn't Tasha's voice.

"Marina?"

"Yes, my heart. I'm buried deep inside, but I am here. She is *me*. Since the beginning, we have been one."

"You are Tasha . . . and Marina?"

Tasha nodded. "I promised I would find my way back to you. I have kept my word." Tasha shuddered, and the gold swirled away from her eyes. She gazed up at him in confusion.

"Vasili? What happened?" Her voice was hers again, not Marina's.

Vasili stared at the woman in his arms. His mate had somehow been reborn? Tasha had been Marina this entire time? But Marina had always been so aggressive, and a force of nature, while Tasha was in many ways different. Marina was a stormy sea, Tasha a deep flowing river. Marina was born for battle, and Tasha was born to explore and discover. They were so vastly different he could not reconcile them.

"Mr. Barinov, this is highly unusual," Lady Superior announced. She smoothed her hair and eyed him and Tasha before she stood. Tamsin and the other coven members also rose to their feet.

"I don't understand," Vasili said. "Tasha is Marina reincarnated? How is this possible?"

"It can only be an ancient dragon spell, one so old that even we were not aware of it. Marina tied her soul to the nearest living dragon other than you."

Flashes of the fight came back to him, fresh and clear, painful as ever. The grief and rage at what had happened to Marina left him trembling.

"Who did she attach herself to?" Vasili clenched his fists, trying to contain his pain and anger.

"Dimitri Drakor. Through his mating with a human woman, Marina's spell gave her a chance to bring herself back as Drakor's child. She may look like your enemy, but she is Marina reborn."

"Good God," Everett said, amazed.

Vasili stared at the witches and then down at Tasha. He had no words, none. The anger and pain bled away, leaving him strangely hollow, confused. He'd never lost his mate. She'd found her way back to him. It explained so much, and that emptiness inside his chest began to fill with heat and joy so suddenly, so swiftly, that it caught him off guard. He released a soft breath.

"I think I need a minute to be alone," Tasha said. She pulled free of Vasili's arms and rushed from the room. For a long moment, Vasili stared after her.

"You must go after her," Lady Superior said. "She won't feel like herself. The spell will leave her unsettled for a time. She should not face that alone."

Vasili nodded to the older witch in thanks and chased after his mate. He caught Tasha in the upstairs hall and stepped in front of her, blocking her path. Tears streak down her cheeks, leaving glistening paths on her skin.

"Tasha." He cupped her face in his hands.

"Am I? Or am I Marina? I don't know *who* I am anymore. I don't . . ." Her words faded, and she began to cry again. Vasili's heart fractured. He would've given anything to take her pain and confusion away from her.

"Please don't cry, little one, please." He pressed soft kisses to her head and held her tightly in his arms. He absorbed every tremble and quake into himself, wishing he could cure her, heal her, give her whatever she needed. He would think about what this all meant later. The only thing that mattered was Tasha, and right now, he wanted her feeling better.

"Tell me what I can do," he said. "Command me, mate. Let me help."

She rubbed her face against his chest, her hands curling into fists.

"Take me away. Make me forget all this." She spoke in a muffled voice against his chest.

"Come with me." He had an idea. He led her back down the stairs toward the door Tamsin had shown them that led to the back gardens.

Tasha halted as he tried to lead her toward the field. "What are we doing?"

"You asked me to take you away." He turned back to her. "Let me show you how to fly."

Tasha stared at him with wide eyes as he held out his hand. "Fly?"

"Do you trust me?" Vasili asked.

She nodded slowly and placed her hand in his.

"Then let me steal you away."

They walked out into the field as the sun began to kiss the horizon and the sky turned blood orange. Vasili let his dragon ripple to the surface. As he changed, he kept his focus, and when he was done, he lowered his head toward the small human female.

My mate.

That was the only thing that mattered to his dragon. Tasha, Marina—names were transient things. *She* was his mate, a fact he had never doubted, even though his human soul had, but his dragon forgave him for that. Humans were, after all, far less perceptive than dragons.

Vasili crouched down low, bringing his head level with his little female. She reached out with hesitant hands, first touching the tip of his snout, then stroking down the bridge of his nose and coming up to caress his cheek. He leaned into the touch. Though his hide was thick, the touch of his mate was something he could always feel as though she were touching human skin.

"You're so beautiful," Tasha whispered. "The most beautiful thing I've ever seen."

He saw his reflection in her eyes, and she smiled, leaning against his left front leg. When her hands stroked over his frill, he let out a huff of pure contentment. She explored him a moment longer before he nudged her hip with his tail, urging her to climb up on his shoulders.

"Oh my God, you want me to . . . ?"

He nodded and waited to feel her clamber up his body and sit between his shoulders.

"What do I hold on to?" she asked.

In answer, he ruffled his frill, where his hide was stronger, and she clasped it. Then he moved slowly to the top of the hill and flapped his wings before he jumped into the air. They caught an updraft and surged skyward. Tasha squealed, and for a second he feared she had fallen, but her hands still held him tight. He kept his body level and slowed down as he spiraled around the valley. Together they watched the world as it was bathed in rich gold light, the way it appears only on rare evenings.

Let her feel free, his human thought inside his head. *Let her feel free to be whoever she wishes with me.*

He soared a while longer until he was certain Tasha was feeling better. Then he landed by the woods where he had spotted a stream that led to a tiny waterfall. He waited patiently for her to slide off him before he transformed back into his human form. Tasha ran to him, and he held open his arms, catching her.

"Thank you, Vasili. Thank you," she whispered before

her lips found his. They came together like lightning, the touch of their mouths more electric than ever before.

Tasha pulled at his sweater, and he lifted it off his body. Her hands were frantic to undress him at first, but he caught her face between his palms and kissed her, slowing everything down. He could feel her eager breaths against his cheek, and their hearts began to beat the same rhythm. They'd done it so often before, this sharing of heartbeats, but he knew it was something Tasha hadn't experienced yet in this life. He wanted to take his time and make sure she enjoyed every moment of their joining.

Vasili? Her voice was clear inside his head.

Yes?

Everything has changed, hasn't it?

The way I feel about you hasn't. You are my world. He swallowed tightly as he owned the truth of this fact. She was his everything. Always had been.

How can I be when I don't know who I really am?

He nuzzled her neck, kissing her softly. *You are who you've always been. A different lifetime doesn't change that.*

How could he explain it to her? Her soul was still hers. The name it now bore, the life it once lived—none of that mattered in the end. She was simply herself.

Love me? she questioned in his mind when she kissed him back hungrily.

Always. He had gone to his death loving her, and he would do it all over again if he had to.

In a slow dance of subtle movements, their clothes soon littered the grass, and he was carrying Tasha to the ground, lowering her beneath him. It was cold all around them, but his elevated body temperature would keep her warm. Tasha lay on the ground and held out her hand to guide him down on top of her. He took his time, was as gentle as he could be as he settled between her thighs. He had made love to her a thousand times before, and yet this felt like the first, felt like the one time that mattered most. He kissed the tip of her nose, her forehead, her closed lashes, whispering sweet words to her as he entered her body. She gripped him tight, her wet sheath welcoming him and her sigh of bliss a symphony to his ears.

His dragon wanted to sink his teeth into her shoulder, hold her down and take her, to remind her of their passion, of the years they'd spent together. But there would be time enough for that rough passion. Right now, the human part of him wanted to savor her sweetly.

Vasili rocked his body against hers, and Tasha's hands dug into his shoulders while her thighs gripped his waist. Above them, the evening sky bled into the hues of twilight, and the forest stirred to life around them. The world itself seemed to sigh and wake with Vasili and Tasha's lovemaking. The magic in the forest had been dormant for so long, but it couldn't ignore the presence of these two magical beings within its shelter as they created love between them. The purest magic was always drawn to love, and theirs was strong tonight in this hidden glade.

She shivered beneath him and cried out as she climaxed before biting his shoulder, and Vasili experienced the most intense climax of his life. It overwhelmed him, changing him to the very core of his soul. A lifetime—*two* lifetimes —of her flashed before his eyes. Marina . . . Tasha . . . Marina . . . Tasha . . All of her was there before him, and all of her was beautiful. Her lips danced along his skin in light kisses as he caught his breath. When he rolled to the side and pulled her against him, he gazed up at the blanket of stars through the opening of the trees overhead.

"Do you feel better?" He ran his hand over her silken hair as she laid her cheek against his chest.

"I feel a little more like myself. It's like even though she and I are one person, we can't both fully be present in my head. Either she is there or I am. Does that make sense?"

"Yes, I suppose it does."

"Do you wish it was her instead of me? Do you want her back?" Tasha asked, her voice more hesitant.

Vasili held her closer. "You are the same person."

"But I'm not. She is the one you lived with, the one you loved for so many years. The one you almost died for. You've known me for less than a week."

Vasili lifted her head so she met his gaze. "I understand your confusion, but I do not share it. I may be the only man who's ever been blessed to fall in love with his mate twice. Falling in love with you, Tasha, that was a gift beyond measure. All of my guilt, my doubt about betraying Marina's memory, it's gone. I know you act differently, your looks, voice, and mannerisms. But ask yourself, had you been raised by your father instead of your mother, would you be the same person? Had you been raised in Russia instead of America, would you be the same person? Had you been born a thousand years ago instead of a few short decades ago, would you be the same person? You and Marina are the same soul that has experienced two wildly different paths in life, and I love all versions of you, my mate. Every single one. You could be reborn over and over and I know I would love each new incarnation of you as much as the one that came before." It was the truest thing that could ever leave his lips.

She laid her head back down on his chest. "What happens now?" she asked.

Vasili chuckled. "I honestly don't know. My nephews are on their way to London. If you want to, we could go meet them. But I will understand if you don't wish to, because of your father."

"No, I want to meet them. My father is . . . well, that's a problem I'll have to face another day when I'm ready."

"Then let's get you dressed and return to the house. I don't want anyone to be worried about us."

Vasili helped her stand, and they collected their clothes. Once dressed, he stood there, laughing softly as he plucked bits of grass and twigs from her hair.

"I look like a mess, don't I?"

"An adorable mess of a woman who has been well fucked on the forest floor." He didn't miss the way her eyes heated at those words.

"I really love it when you talk dirty to me," she admitted with a blush.

He couldn't resist kissing her again. "Good. Because we dragons are primal. We mate fiercely and tend to be 'dirty,' as you called it. We see no reason to feel shame for who we are."

Their lovemaking in the forest had been such a different thing for him, but he had loved it as much as when he'd claimed her roughly. The way he had gently possessed her body and how her surrender had been that much sweeter—it had been different, but just as lovely.

"Tasha, I—" There was a loud *pop*, and pain lanced through his chest. He growled and staggered as he clutched his upper body while blood poured through the cracks between his fingers.

"Oh my God, Vasili!" Tasha tried to catch him, but she was suddenly pulled away by a shadowy figure.

Vasili fell to his knees, pain blurring his vision. When it cleared, he saw a man—no, a *vampire*—holding his mate by the throat. The pale-faced man with glowing red eyes sneered as he gripped Tasha like a child would a ragdoll that he might throw at any moment.

"I have your mate, dragon. You have been shot in the chest with an iron bullet. You won't die, but you cannot change. If you come along willingly, I won't kill her."

Vasili curled his hands into fists, but the dragon inside him was already weakening. There was no way he could fight now and not get Tasha killed.

The vampire smiled, his lips tainted with blood and his fangs gleaming in the moonlight. "Good."

Vasili's body seemed like it was being pulled apart cell by cell. He roared in defiance before everything around him winked out of existence.

CHAPTER 15

Excerpt from Barrow's Journal – My Year with Dragons

Most other supernatural creatures pay heed to dragons. It is not often that they dare to make enemies of dragons. Who would wish that fate upon themselves? For a dragon's wrath is often just, and justice can be mighty in its deliverance.

Tasha fell to the floor with a painful grunt, her palms scraping on rough stone. Vasili's body was dropped beside her moments before a cell door clanged shut. Their vampire captor stared at them, a cruel smile twisting his lips.

"When your dragon pushes the bullet out, tell him these bars are iron, and if he wishes to keep you alive, he will do what he is told." He then walked off into the darkness.

A single lit torch near the iron-barred doors was the only light left to them. Somewhere nearby, water dripped, the sound echoing in the silence. Tasha put Vasili's head in her lap and brushed his hair out of his face. With trembling hands, she lifted up the hem of his bloodstained sweater to see the wound. The hole was small, and she glimpsed a metallic sliver at the edge of the skin. He really was pushing the bullet out.

"Vasili?" Tasha whispered.

When he didn't stir, she took stock of their prison. By the chilly air and the damp stones around them, she guessed they were underground. She didn't have a clue where they were or how they had gotten there, however. The vampire had done something to her. One second they had been in the forest near the witch house, and the next she was coming to her senses as the vampire tossed her into this cell.

The man had to be a vampire. His fetid breath had smelled like death and decay, and she'd glimpsed fangs just below his lips when he spoke. But how had a vampire found them?

She counted the minutes in her head until she almost went mad. Tasha gasped in relief when Vasili finally groaned and touched his chest. The iron bullet was nearly expelled, his fingers prying it free the rest of the way. Vasili slowly sat up, bracing himself on the rock wall behind him.

"Tasha?"

"I'm here." She brushed her fingertips over his cheek as his eyes opened, seeking hers.

"What happened?"

"You were shot by a vampire."

Vasili raked his hands through his hair, pulling hard at the strands, and Tasha squeezed his arm, trying to calm him. "Where are we?"

"I don't know. He did something to me shortly after he shot you. I blacked out. I think we're underground now."

"I must have taken us past the witches' boundary and into an unprotected area. Even the London Blood Society must have permission to enter witch lands; at least, that's what Everett told me." Vasili put an arm around her shoulders, pulling her against his side. Tasha was glad she wasn't alone, though she feared for Vasili and whatever the vampire had planned for them.

"How long was I unconscious?"

"I can't be sure—I was unconscious too. We've been here maybe half an hour. The vampire said the bars are iron and that you would have to do what he says in order to keep me alive."

Vasili's blue eyes turned ice-cold as he stared at the iron bars. "I fear I already know what they want."

"They?"

"They. The one who grabbed us would not be working alone. Randolph and the other Belishaw dragons have been hunting vampires like these. They told me about vampires in a blood cult in London who were leaving bodies everywhere, without a care."

A chill raked along her spine. "Wh—what's a blood cult?" She really didn't want to know, but the question slipped out before she could stop herself.

"Vampires in a blood cult are not properly sired. They

are considered feral and have next to no control when it comes to feeding. They engage in a sort of bloodlust that's not only dangerous but homicidal."

"All vampires aren't like that?"

"No. Most vampires are not the monsters I have heard about in your horror entertainment. But the ones who have us?" He paused, the silence deafening. "They are true monsters."

"What are we going to do?"

"For now, we play their game. It's *my* blood they're after, not yours."

"But why?"

"Shifter blood gives them power. The Belishaws warned me, but I never dreamed we would be at risk so close to the witches."

Tasha rested her head against his shoulder as they leaned back against the wall, their legs stretched out side by side. "Why not?"

"The witches have a way to bespell their own blood, and they provided the same protection to the Belishaws. Their blood becomes poison to a vampire. Randolph told me we needed protection, but I thought I did not need to act immediately because we were still on witch land. I planned to ask for the spell before we returned to London. It's my fault we are here."

Tasha shook her head. "No, it's not. Let's just concentrate on keeping you alive."

That proved harder than expected. Half an hour later, the vampire returned, and he wasn't alone. Four others were with him, all big, hulking creatures with bright red eyes and pale skin, who moved in unnatural ways for their bodies. They were so clearly inhuman that Tasha recoiled as they opened the door. They were dressed normally, yet the black spots splattered on their clothes hinted at old blood. The thought made her sicker than she'd already been.

"It's a bird! It's a plane! It's a *dragon*!" the one who had captured them joked as he reached their cell. The other vampires behind him didn't laugh. The vampire held up a pair of iron cuffs and a chain. "Time to come out and play, dragon. We're quite hungry."

Vasili and Tasha both stood up. Vasili moved Tasha behind him with her back pressed to the wall.

"Fight us and she dies. Never forget that," the first vampire warned as he removed an old set of keys that clinked against the lock as he opened the door.

"What is this place?" Vasili demanded. Tasha hoped it would distract the vampire and delay whatever was planned for them.

"Oh, this? Do you like it? Apparently, Queen Elizabeth was quite the dragon hunter. She imprisoned several of your kind during her reign. My old master served as one of her advisors, and he knows all about you."

"Elizabeth?" Vasili repeated. "I was not awake when she reigned," he murmured to Tasha.

"Yes, well, you didn't miss much, dragon. She was a real bitch," the vampire said. "At least, that's what my master says."

Tasha peered around Vasili's shoulder, trying to keep the conversation going. "Who is your master?"

"John Dee. Surely you know of him."

Tasha gasped in surprise. "John Dee?"

"Who is he?" Vasili asked her.

"Queen Elizabeth's court astronomer and an alchemist," she explained quietly.

"Stop whispering. It's not as though we can't hear you," snapped the vampire. He jerked his head toward Vasili as he barked orders to the others. "Grab him so we can chain him."

The four vampires swarmed into the cell and seized Vasili. He jerked free once, but when one of them snatched Tasha by the neck, she couldn't help but yelp in pain, and Vasili stilled.

"An amazing thing, dragons and their mates," the head vampire mused as the iron chains and manacles bound Vasili. "Kill the one, and the other dies." He smiled. "I do hope we won't have to test that out."

Tasha's skin crawled where the vampire's hands touched her. His nails were clawlike as they dug into her flesh. He dragged her ahead of Vasili, leading them down a narrow dungeon tunnel and into an open atrium. There, a ring of hissing creatures waited for them just beyond the edge of the torchlight that filled the room.

A man in long black robes with a shaved head stood in the center of the room. He was unnaturally still, except for a slight flare of his nostrils as Tasha was thrown to the floor at his feet.

"His human mate," the vampire told the man in the robe.

"No longer a virgin," the man said in a hard voice. "Such

a disappointment." He stared down at her with frightening intensity.

"I'm sorry about that, master."

"It does make us have to be more careful with our guest. We wouldn't want to lose him if you kill his mate, Andre. So be careful when you play with her." The man's gaze fixed on Vasili, who stood defiant, even though bound by iron chains.

Tasha dragged herself out of the way as the man approached Vasili. She was certain he would have kicked her or stepped on her if she hadn't moved.

The man gripped Vasili by the throat, staring at him. "Such a beautiful specimen."

Vasili's blue eyes flashed with fury, but no dragon gold surfaced.

"Tell me your name, dragon."

"Vasili Barinov. I assume you are John Dee? I am told you are someone who once had the ear of a queen, but I confess I see no power in you."

"He thinks he's such a clever beast," Dee mused. A slim blade appeared in his hand, and in a flash, he slashed Vasili's neck. Tasha screamed.

The cut wasn't deep, and Vasili barely flinched. Only his heavy breathing gave away the fact that he felt pain. Dee stroked a finger along the small cut and then brought it to his nose, sniffing carefully.

"Not poisoned." He smiled cruelly. Then he licked his finger. The moment Vasili's blood touched his tongue, he let out a sigh of satisfaction. His dark eyes flashed bright red.

"I will feed first," John Dee told the others. And with that, he lunged, sinking his fangs into Vasili's neck.

Vasili roared, but the sound was human, not dragon, and full of human pain.

Tasha scrambled to her feet and threw herself at John Dee. "Stop!"

Before she could reach him, she was grabbed by Andre and tossed aside. She collided with the wall, and darkness swallowed her.

Vasili howled in rage as Tasha fell to the floor, limp. Several pale-faced vampires prowled toward her prone form.

"Andre, please take her back to her cell." John Dee waved a hand at Tasha. "We can feed my children later."

With another howl, Vasili jerked against the chains, but the four vampires holding them dragged him to his knees and adjusted the chains on the floor so that he was stuck kneeling in place, arms pulled out and away from his body, exposed. One of the vampires ripped his sweater from him, leaving his chest bare. The dragon tattoo on his skin shimmered and rippled, moving from his arm to his chest to his back. John Dee watched the moving tattoo with curiosity.

"Dragons and unicorns are such curious things. You both taste like pure power. I've never seen the like with any other creature." John Dee licked his lips.

"Of course, there are no more unicorns. They need hope and beauty and pure hearts to survive. The people of this age are not capable of saving unicorns, let alone believing in them. Even you, the nearly undefeatable dragons, have lost ground to humans. Your dark caves are crumbling, your gems stolen and exploited. It's a pity, really," John Dee sighed. "What shall I feed on when the last of you are dead?"

Vasili said nothing. His hands held the loose slack of the chains binding him as he tested his strength. As a dragon, he was one of the strongest of his age. He could have fought the Belishaw dragons easily before if he hadn't been worried about Tasha's safety. But now he had only mortal strength. His dragon could not rise to the surface while iron touched his skin.

He barely listened to Dee's rantings, instead focusing on Andre as he hissed at the other vampires, chasing them away from Tasha. Andre lifted Tasha's limp form up into his arms and walked out of the atrium. The rip of his mate vanishing into darkness with that creature nearly destroyed Vasili. He wanted to cleave heads from bodies and shred these unnatural creatures to pieces. The vampires in the room all turned their eyes to Vasili, either sensing his bloodthirsty thoughts or simply realizing that he was the only warm-blooded creature left in the room to satisfy their hunger.

Fuck. He wasn't going to like this . . .

"Be patient, my children. You shall feed soon," Dee called out to the creatures at the edge of the light. He turned to Andre when the vampire returned and four other creatures gathered behind him. They had to be Dee's next level of command. The rest of the creatures slithering in the shadows had to number well over a hundred, and the thought of so many ravenous creatures wanting his blood made his entire body rigid with the need to fight and escape.

"Andre, you and your men may feed next."

The wraithlike vampires swamped the center of the open floor where Vasili was chained down. Vasili roared at them, not that it stopped them, or even slowed them down. Rough hands held him while needlelike teeth cut his flesh as mouth after mouth tore into his skin.

It felt like a hundred years passed before Dee's shout stopped the vampires and they retreated. Vasili sat back on his heels, his head hanging down, chin touching his chest as he struggled to breathe. He'd lost too much blood, was too weak to move. He opened his eyes, trying to orient himself since it felt like everything around him was spinning. His skull throbbed as though someone was smashing it repeatedly with a stone club. Vasili's pulse thrummed erratically as his body tried to heal. Even bound by iron, he would heal faster than any human, but replacing the lost blood would still be slow.

"Your blood will make my children strong." Dee leaned down and peered into Vasili's face. "Your blood will let them shift into other creatures. Isn't it fascinating? Each kind of shifter blood confers different abilities, though dragon and unicorn blood are the most powerful. I've always wondered why. Perhaps it's your longevity, how you perceive time so differently than other creatures. You make it possible for us to manipulate moving between places in the blink of an eye." Then, in a swirl of black mist, Dee vanished. A split second later, he reappeared behind Vasili.

"That's how your minion got us here," Vasili guessed.

"Yes, Andre, my devoted child, scooped you up and transported you here instantly. Such a useful skill. It makes us nearly impossible to kill. You can't kill what you can't catch.

Vasili might not have been able to catch a vampire in his dragon's jaws, but he could easily roast him with flames . . . if only he ever got the chance to do it.

"How did you become a vampire?" Vasili asked Dee while he carefully tested the strength of the chains again.

"*How* doesn't matter. All that matters is that I am now free of my earthly torments. I see the world now for what it is, an endless river of blood and suffering"

"Which you cause," Vasili added with a growl.

"Hardly. We simply ride the currents that humans themselves create. Once I claimed immortality, I saw all that was truly possible and all the power that was within reach." He chuckled. "Such fools, my fellow alchemists. They thought gold and immortality were the key to understanding, but it's always been blood."

The vampires in the shadows rustled against each other, their bodies rasping like the dried, empty husks of cicadas. Vasili would have given anything to be able to unleash his dragon's fire upon them and burn them all to ash.

"My children grow hungry," Dee mused softly. "But once I let them feast, they cannot be stopped. You will be ripped to shreds in their frenzy, and I do so want to enjoy your blood just a little longer." Vasili braced himself for the attack this time, but nothing stopped the agonizing pain of John Dee's bite.

THE WOODS OUTSIDE THE LANCASHIRE WITCH HOUSE were searched for an hour before Tamsin's grandmother, the Lady Superior, found evidence of where Vasili and Tasha had last been. She knelt on the forest floor and touched the earth with her hand, then gave a nod.

"Here!" Tamsin called out to the surrounding forest. Within seconds, the Belishaws were charging into the glen, Jeremy and Arabella with them.

Her grandmother lifted up a handful of leaves and grass and cast them into the air.

"Reveal thyself," the witch murmured. A sparkling silver mist caught the leaves and grass, swirling into misty figures in front of them, playing out what had happened here like ghostly echoes.

Tamsin watched with some embarrassment as Vasili and Tasha finished making love and lay beneath the stars. After they stood and dressed, they were attacked. A vampire snatched Tasha away, and Vasili clutched his chest as a silvery liquid poured from his apparition. Then the three figures vanished.

"It's that damned blood cult," Everett growled. His hands curled into fists, and his warm brown eyes glowed a bright gold in the gloom.

"I fear you are right, Mr. Belishaw," sighed Tamsin's

grandmother. "They knew where the boundary was and took their chance when Vasili and Tasha strayed outside of it. We must return to the house at once. I need to check the wards on the estate and make sure the rest of us are safe. Then I can figure out how to locate them."

Everett nodded at his fellow dragons. "We must contact the Barinovs." He and the other dragons turned toward the council house.

Tamsin started to go after Everett, but her grandmother caught her wrist, gently holding her back.

"He's not for you, child. Do you understand? We must marry within our own kind, as must they. If you care for him, leave him be, or else he dies when you do and you've killed one of the world's most ancient surviving dragons. We cannot afford to lose any more such creatures in this world." The reminder was politely given, but Tamsin felt the weight of it like a boulder upon her back.

"I know, Grandma, but I can help them. Please let me."

"Your magic is still unstable. The awakening hasn't happened yet. Until then, I do not want you risking such spells. Let me handle it."

Tamsin persisted, pulling away from her grandmother and racing to catch up with Everett. Even if she couldn't be with him in the way her heart said she should, she wouldn't miss this opportunity to be near him. It was foolish, but it was all she had.

He glanced her way when she caught up to him. "Tamsin." He spoke her name in that husky voice that made the fine hair on the back of her neck stand on end and her heart pound as she became hyperfocused on everything in her environment.

"I was thinking—there has to be a spell, one that will help us find them, something my grandmother hasn't thought of."

"If you know of anything, we need to act fast," Everett said. "These vampires must be stopped before they kill my friend. I must call Vasili's family and then the London Blood Society. They will want to help if they can." He and the other dragons stopped in the meadow and looked up at the house far in the distance.

Everett held out a hand to her. "Care for a ride?"

"A ride?" Tamsin had barely agreed when the Belishaws started to change in front of her. Now a dragon, Everett stood waiting patiently for her. He lowered himself down into a crouch, and she climbed up onto his back. When he ruffled the beautiful frill right behind his head, she reached out and grabbed on to it. The second she did, he took flight, and she let out a shocked squeal as they took to the sky. She'd ridden a broom plenty of times, but this . . . this was different. She was riding another being, a dragon, a creature so linked with Everett that they shared bodies. It felt immensely intimate to see his dragon, let alone ride on top of him like she would a horse.

They landed less than thirty seconds later right beside the house, and she slid onto the grass, her head still spinning from the quick flight and sudden stop. He nudged her hip with his snout, huffing softly. She placed a hand on the dragon's scaled cheek and smiled. His reptilian gaze fixed on her, and she couldn't help but wonder what the dragon thought of her. Did he like her as much as his human side seemed to? The dragon puffed out air through his nostrils and nudged her again as though concerned.

"I'm okay. Just need a sec . . ."

His golden eyes gleamed in dragonish amusement.

"Yeah, laugh at the girl who's never ridden a dragon before."

Everett blinked his large catlike eyes at her before becoming human once more.

"That's not the only way to ride a dragon," he said. "Maybe someday you can try the other." The seductive way he said this made her thighs quiver.

"Maybe . . . ," she said, wishing more than anything she could. She was sure that it would be everything she'd dreamed it would be. But she would never even get the chance. But to do so would cause a war between witches and dragons. Dragons could not interfere in the affairs of witches, especially their marriage contracts.

He held out a hand to her. When she grasped it, an electric spark shot between them, and the magic beneath her skin buzzed wildly in response. Everett's eyes flashed gold. For a long moment, they didn't let go of each other.

"Father, Grigori has texted my cell. They've landed. Where should I send them?" Randolph interrupted the intimacy of the moment.

Everett continued to stare into Tamsin's eyes. "Tell them we will bring them here. If they go to our residence in London, Lady Superior can open a portal between the two houses. Call them now."

The dragons and Tamsin entered the house. It amazed

her to see these men side by side, father and son. They both looked to be in their early thirties at the oldest. Only a faint streak of silver at Everett's temples betrayed his ancient status.

"Let's go back to the library," Tamsin instructed. "I need to start looking for spells."

Randolph was on his cell speaking to someone—Grigori Barinov, if Tamsin had to guess.

"Yes . . . we have a problem. He was taken, and so was his mate, Tasha . . . A blood cult." Randolph paused to listen to Vasili's nephew. "What? Just a moment." Randolph glanced around and came over to her and Everett by the reading table. Randolph seemed unsure of what he was about to say.

"This is a little unusual, but Grigori said his son needs to tell you something."

Tamsin was shocked. "His *son*? A child?"

"Yes." Randolph listened to Grigori on the phone, then he put it on speaker. "Okay, she can hear you now."

A little boy's voice spoke up uncertainly. "Miss Tamsin?"

"Yes?" Tamsin replied. Everett drifted a step closer to her.

The little boy continued. "Did you know that butterflies remember things from when they were caterpillars? Even though they totally melt when they are in their cocoons, they still remember things after they change into butterflies. They don't remember *being* a caterpillar, but they remember stuff they learned *as* caterpillars."

Tamsin stared at the phone. What in the world was he talking about?

"My aunt Tasha . . . She's a butterfly, but she needs to remember what she learned as a caterpillar," the little boy added more insistently.

"That's all he told us." Grigori Barinov's voice cut in. "What does it mean?"

"I have no idea what—" Tamsin cut off her own words with a gasp. "She's a butterfly!" Tamsin cried out and raced through the library, hastily running her fingers over the spines of old spell books. Everett was on her heels, yet she didn't lose focus on the task at hand. If she could only find the book she was looking for . . .

"Where is it?" she muttered. "We don't have time . . ."

Everett put a hand on her shoulder. "Call it to you."

She had never called a book before. Tamsin closed her eyes and imagined the old book with its blue leather cover and the symbols of power carved into it in pure silver. That was the book she was certain could help them.

Come to me . . . come . . .

She felt the welling of power in her, like a still lake suddenly rippling. Far above her head, a shelf rattled and a book slid free, floating gracefully down to her. Motes of dust followed in its wake, swirling in the moonlight that streamed in through the windows. Tamsin grasped the book, and Everett let go of her shoulder. She carried the book to a reading table and then began to thumb through the old parchment pages.

"What are you looking for?" Randolph asked. He and Everett, along with the other dragons, now surrounded her.

She paused halfway through to point to a page that had a glittering painted illustration of a blue-and-black winged butterfly emerging from a gray silk cocoon. "This. A chrysalis spell," she said.

"A chrysalis spell?" Randolph asked, his brows drawn together. Tamsin couldn't help but notice how much like his father he was. They both frowned the same way, like mirror images. For some reason, that made her want to smile, but the urgency of the situation crushed any humor she might have felt.

"Yes. It's an old spell, very hard to perform."

"But what does it do?" Magnus asked.

She was about to answer, but Everett seemed to read her mind. "It's a spell to remind Tasha that she's a dragon."

"But she's . . . human," Magnus said.

"Yes, but it's as Grigori's son said," Everett explained with clear understanding. "She was once a dragon. We have to remind her of who *Marina* was. That she was one of the fiercest battle dragons the world has ever seen. If we can bring back that part of her, we won't have to find her—she will be able to free herself and Vasili."

"Exactly." Tamsin stroked her fingers over the image of the butterfly. It was a powerful spell, one she was certain would work, but it would take someone with immense power to cast it. Someone like her grandmother. And a spell like this would cost that person something. Magic like this *always* had a price, and she feared her grandmother couldn't pay it.

CHAPTER 16

Excerpt from Barrow's Journal – My Year with Dragons

In the oldest of days, the battles between dragons were fierce. Battle dragons, above other dragons, carry a need to fight. The other types of dragons carry this burden well, but others not so easily. The hunger to fight, to defend, to attack, is an almost overpowering instinct. To be mated to a battle dragon means living with a creature who will bring danger and destruction to your door. Most battle dragons do not take mates for this reason. They cannot bear to put that burden upon another soul they love.

It was hours before someone came for Tasha. She paced in her cell, head throbbing, her mind playing out every terrible scenario of what could be happening to Vasili. When Andre finally came down the narrow tunnel for her, she froze, her fingers curled around the iron bars.

"Where is Vasili?" she demanded.

Andre's lips curled into a sneer. "He is feeding my master."

Tasha's stomach turned at the thought of Dee sinking his fangs into her mate.

"Bring him back here *now*." Where Tasha's bravado came from she didn't know, but she was tired of being afraid. Tired of letting the world keep her from living. If she was going to die, she wasn't going to let this asshole have even a second of her fear.

Andre chuckled as he placed his hands on the bars, leaning toward her.

"No longer a little mouse, eh?"

His face was close enough that she could see the blend of blood red and brown in his eyes. Tasha moved one of her hands away from the bars to find the slender bit of shale rock she had picked up from the floor.

"Come closer and you will see my courage," she challenged.

The idiot actually listened to her. His pale hand reached through the bars to grab her throat, but she moved a beat faster, lashing out and slicing his arm deep with the sharpened edge of her rock.

Andre hissed and reared back, clutching his arm. Blood dripped onto the floor in thick droplets.

"Little bitch, you don't even know the torment that awaits you."

"I know you can't kill me, not without losing Vasili too. Guess that makes me valuable, huh?"

"You overstate your importance. You are only alive so long as he is alive."

She stroked her thumb over the edge of the shale rock, feeling the vampire's blood on her fingers. A surge of victory swept through her, and she smiled at him. "Why don't you come back in here and see what happens."

Something full of primal fury slithered beneath her skin at the thought of attacking him, of killing the creature that threatened her mate. Andre stared at her a long moment before he turned and rushed into the darkness.

Good, bring your friends, she thought. *I'll take you all down.*

She sat back in the semidarkness and closed her eyes.

All she wanted in that moment was for Vasili to be beside her, safe. She couldn't stop replaying every moment she'd spent with him. From finding him frozen in the ice to escaping the mountain with him. The way he'd made love to her, how he'd held her and touched her as if she were the most precious thing on earth. Being with him had been earthshattering. The way he'd looked at her when she'd stepped out of the shower that first time and he'd seen her naked—there had been so much she'd missed in his eyes in those first few days. She'd thought she'd seen only pain and later lust, but looking back, she now saw him with fresh eyes, saw his face each time he'd looked at her.

It was the way she'd wanted someone to look at her for her entire life, like she was the key to a universe she didn't even know existed. Like she could unlock a world of glorious things with just a smile or a laugh. Vasili had gazed at her like that so many times, and she'd always missed it. She'd been so focused on keeping herself safe, keeping her heart protected, dealing with her father's death and her mother's fears, that she'd missed out on living her life.

Vasili had been her chance to be all the things she'd ever wanted, and yet she'd been so blind to it. She'd lusted after him, and she'd realized that she loved him, but it went so much deeper than that. She'd only dipped her toe into the pool of emotions that he'd dived into headfirst, despite his insistence that he couldn't. He had trusted his feelings for her far quicker than she had for him. He'd given her his whole heart, even when he said he couldn't. She should have trusted his actions, not his words.

The thought that it might be too late, that she'd never get the chance to tell him what he meant to her, filled her with pain.

Try to rest. You need to be strong and ready for when Vasili returns.

She wouldn't think about what she would do if he didn't.

A short while later, her head was leaned back against the rock wall, and she was just starting to slip into sleep. Suddenly, she felt herself falling over and over into a vast abyss. When she landed, she couldn't see anything around her. A distant ball of light came toward her, like a large firefly. It zipped around her head and then stopped inches from her face.

"What are you?" She reached toward the light but halted as a voice came through the glowing orb of light.

"Tasha?"

"Tamsin? Is that you?"

"I found her!" Tamsin seemed to be speaking to

someone else. "She's here! Tasha, where are you?" The ball's glowing light pulsed with every word.

"I'm not sure. We're in an old tunnel. There's a dungeon. I think we may be beneath London. The vampire said it was a place Queen Elizabeth held her dragon prisoners."

"The old tunnels?" an unfamiliar Russian voice asked. "I know where that is."

"Tamsin," Tasha said. "Who is with you?"

"Vasili's nephews, Grigori, Rurik, and Mikhail. They just got here. Listen, we have a spell. It might help free you, but it's dangerous, and it's not going to be easy on you."

Tasha wished she could see Tamsin's face. Being trapped in the dark with the glowing orb as her only source of light made her feel very small and alone.

"Whatever you need to do, do it fast. The vampires are feeding on Vasili right now, and I don't think they have much control over themselves."

"How many are there?" another Russian voice asked, one of Vasili's other nephews.

"John Dee is their leader, and he has maybe four others right beneath him, but there's at least a hundred others down here, all feral and deformed." She didn't want to remember the ghoulish faces she had seen at the edges of the firelight in the vast domed room where Dee held court, but she had seen them. Their emaciated faces and hollow eyes would haunt her for the rest of her life.

"John Dee?" one of the Russians asked. "You don't mean . . . ?"

"The one who once served Queen Elizabeth," Tasha confirmed.

There was a muttered curse and several voices speaking quickly in Russian.

"Tasha, when we cast this spell, you're going to feel different. Do you understand? It's going to change you. Try not to be afraid."

"Okay . . ." Tasha didn't like the sound of that, but she would do anything for Vasili.

"I'll be with you. You just need to trust me. This is the only way we can get you out. Just hang on."

"I will." The light winked out, and Tasha was falling again. When she landed, she woke up back in the cell. She let out a shaky breath as she heard footfalls in the tunnels. Andre was coming back, and he wasn't alone.

TAMSIN SANK BACK IN HER CHAIR, EXHAUSTED. THE will-o'-the-wisp had done its job and found its way to Tasha's mind. It was an old witch trick to reach someone you could not physically locate—and possibly the easiest part of what they were about to do. She stared at the glowing wisp in the lantern on the table in front of her.

"Thank you, friend. You found her for me." Tamsin touched the glass, and the will-o'-the-wisp fluttered toward her fingertip. "But I need you a little while longer. As soon as she is safe, I will send you back to the forest."

The will-o'-the-wisp fluttered about before settling down to a steady glow.

"John Dee," a voice growled behind her. Tamsin turned to the three intimidating Russian dragons who had recently arrived. The one who'd spoken, Mikhail, was glaring at her, but she knew he wasn't angry with her.

"You know him, brother?" Grigori asked.

"I know him," said Mikhail. "He is the one who poisoned Elizabeth against me and all other dragons. She was convinced his alchemy would someday give her the immortality she wished for. I had no idea he had been turned into a vampire."

"Where are these dungeons?" Rurik asked. Rurik was a battle dragon, like Tasha had been in her former life. He already looked ready for a fight.

"She had many—*too* many—dungeons," Mikhail muttered in frustration. "She moved many of her prisoners around to keep them from being rescued if they were discovered."

Tamsin listened to them, but a plan was forming in her head. She rushed back to the bookshelves, sorting through the various books. "We need a solar spell."

Her grandmother, Arabella, and Jeremy came into the library, stacks of spell books in their arms.

"A solar spell?" Jeremy asked, having overheard her.

"Yes, something we can set off in the tunnels. It could weaken them if it's strong enough. Perhaps even kill them. We can't have any of them getting away." She returned to the reading table and set down several books.

Everett pulled a chair out for her. "Tell me what to look for," he said, taking a seat beside her.

She reached for the top spell book. "Something that has an illustration of light or a sun in it."

The others came to help as best they could. As they all paged through the dusty spell books, Tamsin prayed they could find something useful. After a few minutes, Everett slid a book toward her. "What about this one?"

"Witch light . . ." Tamsin read the name of the spell aloud. "Yes, this could work." She looked at the other three witches on the opposite side of the table. Her grandmother was too weak now to do more than aid the others after she'd opened the portal that had brought Vasili's family here.

"Jeremy, could you open a few portals so Arabella can perform this spell once she gets into the tunnels?" Tamsin carried the spell book over so the other witches could see what needed to be done. "If you do that, I can perform the chrysalis spell."

"But you have to be close to Tasha for the chrysalis spell. That means you would have to go into the dungeons with her." Jeremy shook his head. "Let me go in your place. I am a senior warlock."

"She won't be going in alone," Everett announced. "She shall be fully protected."

"Tamsin," her grandmother began. "Your powers aren't stable yet. The awakening—"

"I will be awakened, or at least close to it." Tamsin gave her grandmother a meaningful look. "You must trust me, please."

"Remember your promise, Tamsin," her grandmother reminded.

Tamsin wouldn't forget. She had signed a marriage contract with a warlock in Salem. Whatever she did now to awaken her powers, it would only be fleeting—it would not be forever. That made what she had to do all the more important.

"If the Belishaws don't mind helping, we still need to collect the ingredients for these three spells." Jeremy held up a handwritten list so the dragons could see.

"If the Barinovs would please come with me," Arabella said. "I will bespell your blood for your protection. The Belishaws have recently been bespelled and are already protected."

Tamsin had a brief moment alone as the other witches and the dragons began to prepare. She slid her hand into Everett's and led him from the room. He came behind her without question. She didn't stop until they reached a secluded alcove on the second floor. The gazes of her ancestors were all about her, their painted faces filled with disapproval of what she was about to do.

"Tamsin, what is it?" Everett asked as he stepped into the alcove with her.

"I need your help," she confessed.

"Name it, and I will find what you need."

"*You* are what I need." Her face heated with embarrassment, but she had to cut to the chase or they would spend an hour dancing around the issue. "You know that witches and warlocks must awaken their powers by a certain age or risk losing them altogether, right?"

Everett nodded. He braced a hand on the dark wood

paneling of the wall beside her head and studied her intently.

"And you know how we are awakened?" she asked, her voice turning into a whisper.

"With passion, I believe. I admit, I know very little."

"Sex, Everett. Awakening comes from sex. It's a process, and it doesn't always happen all at once."

"Sex." He spoke the word in that seductive British accent, and she knew that he would star in every one of her fantasies for the rest of her life.

"Yes."

"So you want me to . . . ?" The ancient dragon trailed off. At any other time, she would have delighted in his utter disbelief, but the situation left her without time for such things.

"Kiss me. That's all I need right now." She hoped that was all she would need; it would be too dangerous for them to go any further.

"A kiss," he repeated.

"Now, if you please." She grasped his gray wool sweater in her hands and pulled him toward her.

His startled lips met hers. Tingles of delicious warmth spread through her, and she felt it—that strange sense of something awakening inside of her. A witch or warlock's magic was present at birth, but its full power didn't manifest until they were an adult, and only if they learned to let go and trust their body, heart, and soul to another. Hence the sex, but it had to be with the right person.

Everett teased her with his lips, and she curled an arm around the back of his neck as she pressed closer to him.

This wasn't enough. She needed more. She broke their mouths apart.

"Kiss me like you want to get slapped," she said. "Like you want to enrage every warlock who might lay claim to me."

The growl that rose from Everett's chest was not human. He slammed her against the wall, his hands pinning her wrists to the wood on either side of her head. His mouth slanted harshly over hers, forcing her lips open as his tongue thrust against hers. But he didn't stop there. He wedged his knee between her legs, forcing them apart. The pressure of his body against her as he rubbed at just the right spot sent her spiraling. She wriggled against him, desperate for what that friction promised. He bit her lip and licked away the sting before possessing her mouth again in a raw kiss.

The arcane power of the natural world exploded inside her, filling every cell of her body. The lights above them sparked as little pieces of magic escaped her, dancing away in firefly sparks. This was enough. She could perform the spell now. She pushed at Everett's shoulders, but he growled and moved his mouth to her neck, nibbling and kissing as he rocked their bodies against the wall. There was an insane wildness to this kiss, as though he had waited thousands of years to kiss someone this way, and that thought sent Tamsin over the edge into exquisite pleasure. She opened her eyes and gasped for breath.

Everett pulled back, his eyes white-gold as he consumed her expression. The air around him was blinding bright as her magic surged to life. She could have performed any number of spells in that moment, reshaped the world itself. For a second, they breathed together, their bodies fused in a tight tangle of limbs.

"Was that enough?" he asked, a cocky smile on his lips.

"More than enough," she replied, but that single kiss had doomed her. She had glimpsed the truth as her magic woke around her. She was his mate. She had seen flashes of a life she couldn't have, a life he must have also seen when she had played the piano earlier and he had shed a tear. Everett threaded a hand into her hair at the nape of her neck as he pressed their foreheads together.

"You know I'll never let you go, not after this." He let the silence fill her head with the memory of the kiss.

"You will have to. We've both made promises, and right now Tasha and Vasili need us."

The gold faded from his eyes, and his expression darkened. "We aren't done with this conversation, but you're right. This is not the time." He took her hand, kissed it once, and they walked back to the library together.

Grigori held his wife in his arms, kissing her deeply. Madelyn dug her hands into his shoulders, holding on as if she feared he would never come back.

"You know I hate this macho bullshit," Madelyn whispered. "Do you think Piper or Charlotte are happy with this either?" She nodded at her sisters-in-law, who were scowling while their husbands tried to convince them that leaving them behind was necessary.

"Little flower, you know how much I trust you, but Piper is pregnant. You and Charlotte need to protect her and our son. The witches and their portal must be kept safe. If any vampires were to escape . . ."

"It would be bad," she agreed.

Grigori chucked her under the chin. "I know how brave you are. How strong you are. Let me have a chance to protect you for once," Grigori said.

Madelyn closed her eyes, clinging to his shirt. "If you get hurt, I'll kill you."

With a chuckle, he kissed the tip of her nose before turning to his brothers. They carried short, machete-like blades given to them by the Belishaws.

Their plan had been set. Lady Superior would cast another spell to find where Tasha and Vasili were being held. Jeremy would open a portal to that location and send Tamsin and Everett there. Then he would open other portals for the Belishaws and the Barinovs to stop any vampires who might try to escape down different paths in the tunnels. Arabella would use the witch light spell once all the vampires were herded into a single location.

While that was happening, Tamsin would cast the chrysalis spell on Tasha. It sounded like it could work, but no one wanted to discuss what would happen if that key part of the plan failed.

"We don't have much time to wait," Lady Superior announced. She held the lantern containing the will-o'-the-wisp between her hands.

"Does everyone know their job?" Rurik asked. Everyone nodded in agreement.

"Good." Lady Superior set the lantern down beside an old map of London's tunnels. Then she spoke softly to the glowing fairy creature inside.

Show us the way in the dark,
Find our friend before it's too late,
Lest the world share in her fate.

She opened the lantern, and the will-o'-the-wisp darted out into the room. Jeremy opened a tiny portal to London, allowing the glowing light to slip through before it snapped shut. Jeremy closed his eyes, conserving his strength to create a larger portal.

"I sense she's slowing down. She's close," Jeremy warned the room.

Grigori let go of his wife. Madelyn joined Piper and Charlotte as they stood around Lady Superior and Jeremy.

"Ready, brother?" Rurik asked as Grigori and the others faced the empty air a few yards in front of Jeremy.

Grigori tightened his grip on a short sword. "Ready." Beside them, Mikhail stared at the air in front of them, a grim expression on his face. Perhaps he was remembering the prison Elizabeth had kept him in for so long.

"She's found Tasha and Vasili," Jeremy announced, then chanted a spell as he held a white crystal up in the air. The air split with a lightning crack, and a portal opened up, leading into darkness.

CHAPTER 17

Dragons believe in one thing above all else: nobility of heart. Nobility is not a birthright—it is something anyone is capable of, if they but try. Often the greatest acts of nobility come from the greatest acts of sacrifice, which is why sacrifice is so important to dragons and so many of their most powerful spells require it.

Tasha stilled as Vasili was shoved back into the cell with her. He was covered in bites, most around his neck, wrists, and chest. Blood splattered his bare chest and legs. He staggered toward her, and she braced his body against hers to keep him standing. Andre smirked at them and then turned and walked back into the darkness.

"Tasha." He groaned her name and nuzzled her neck. "I

was so worried when he took you away from me." Vasili gently touched the cut above her right eyebrow. She winced.

She explored his bite wounds, her heart hammering with fear and dread as she counted the gash-like bites marring his beautiful skin. It must have hurt beyond imagining. "What did they do to you?"

"They did what their instincts demanded. They fed," Vasili said once they were alone. "They won't keep us long."

"How do you know?"

"The other vampires, the wild ones in the shadows, they are too hungry, too numerous. He will lose control of them before long. It's simple pack behavior. Even though he is their maker, he isn't a strong leader. He will not be able to command them to ignore their hunger much longer."

Vasili leaned back against the wall and Tasha joined him, her hand locked in his as they stared into the darkness of the tunnel ahead of them, which seemed to go on forever.

Neither of them spoke for a long while. When Vasili broke the silence, he first had to clear his throat.

"I'm sorry I failed you."

"Failed me? You haven't—"

"Tasha, we won't . . . we won't survive what comes next. The vampires will enter a feeding frenzy."

She shuddered as she imagined a mass of piranhas filling the water with blood. She feared what he was talking about would be a lot like that.

But she had this funny feeling that she couldn't lose

hope, not when she was with him. She'd had the strangest dream while she was unconscious. She knew she had dreamt of Tamsin . . . and there had been that strange and beautiful light. "We can't give up."

Vasili raised her hand to his lips, kissing it gently. "I will never give up, not for you." Tasha saw his dragon's ferocity in his eyes; not even iron could destroy that spirit.

"I won't give up either." She felt a rippling of power beneath her skin and clenched Vasili's hand tighter in her own. After everything they had been through, the things she couldn't even remember, in this life and the one before, she would not allow her time with Vasili to be wasted, not for John Dee and his vile creatures.

Suddenly the ground around them began to rumble as though thousands of feet were pounding against the stones. A faint hissing sound, like gas escaping from a pipe, echoed down the narrow tunnel.

"They are coming," Vasili growled, and he moved Tasha behind him.

The flickering torchlight showed their shadowy forms nearly twenty yards away. The vampires scrambled against each other, fighting to reach their prey, to the point where they bottlenecked the tunnel opening and trapped them-selves in a chaotic horde. Tasha pressed against Vasili's back, staring at the vampires. Vasili was right—they weren't going to get out of this.

"I love you," she whispered to Vasili. "I will never stop loving you." It was the truest thing she had ever said —and the most important. Whatever happened, even if death dared to separate them, she wasn't going to allow fear inside her. She would find her way back to him again.

Vasili clasped her hand to his chest above his heart. "I will love you in this life and wherever the next may take us." He wrapped his body around hers, shielding her for a second before the vampires broke free and collided with the bars of the cell. The iron creaked and groaned against the press of so many bodies, and Tasha buried her face against Vasili's chest as his arms tightened around her.

The world suddenly exploded around them, and they fell back against the rock wall, prepared for death. But it didn't come. Tasha opened her eyes and saw Tamsin and Everett stepping through what could only be described as a crack in reality. Tamsin held the Heart of Sorrows in her hands, and Everett faced the vampires. He swung a machete, slicing off several arms that reached through the bars toward them.

"Vasili, here!" Everett tossed Vasili a blade, and the two hacked at the vampires closest to the bars while Tamsin came to Tasha.

"Tamsin? How—?"

"Give me your hand," Tamsin commanded. Tasha did so in confusion and then cried out as Tamsin sliced her palm with a small knife.

"Sorry, I don't have time to explain. Hold the stone." She pushed the heavy sapphire into Tasha's hands.

"Tamsin, what are we doing?"

Her question went unanswered as Tamsin began to chant a songlike spell in a language Tasha didn't know . . .

only she *did* know it. It was a dragon spell, in dragon tongue.

Time's thread once broken,
Now must mend,
Her breath and life a vow spoken,
Let her past and future blend,
Or the fate of all this is forsaken.

Tamsin's eyes glowed with an otherworldly blue shine. Pain like Tasha had never felt surged through her like a bomb detonating inside her head. Everything around her vanished as she was surrounded by ice in a cold, dark cave. Marina's cave.

"It's time, Tasha," a voice whispered from the shadows.

Tasha's voice trembled. "Time for what?"

"Time for you to let me free . . ."

"But how?"

Marina's voice was stronger now. "It's easy. You simply let go."

Tasha had a terrible feeling there was something that she would lose if she did that. Something precious.

"What will it cost?"

Marina's figure stepped out of the shadows, her face full of pain as though she didn't want to say. "Cost?"

"Yes. Magic always has a price, doesn't it?" Tasha knew, deep down, the spell would cost her dearly.

"When you let go . . . it is forever. You will not come back. This version of you, the part of us that has been Tasha, will cease to be."

"And you . . . will be there?"

Marina nodded. "I'll be back. I know how to save him —our mate needs us. He needs my strength."

Ah, what a dear price it turned out to be. To lose Vasili when she'd had him for so short a time.

"But he'll have you after I'm gone?"

"Yes, he'll have me . . . and you, in a way," Marina promised.

It would be enough, to know she would be giving him back the true version of herself, the mate he had lost so long ago, the one he had loved first. There was no choice. Her love for him—*their* love for him—made this inevitable.

"Then I agree. Save him. Save all of them." Tasha drew in a breath. A moment later, she felt herself fade into shadow and ice.

VASILI SEVERED AN ARM THAT HAD SNAKED BETWEEN THE bars to slash at his chest. He snarled in Everett's direction. "Tell me you have a better plan than this?"

Everett's clothes were splattered with dark-red vampire blood. He nodded at Tamsin behind them. "Ask the witch."

Vasili shot Tamsin a glance. The stone Tasha held in her hands, the Heart of Sorrows, suddenly crumbled to dust, and Tasha threw her head back and let out a roar . . . a dragon roar.

What the hell?

Tasha slapped her palm on the wall, and flames exploded from her hand, spreading along the rock like quicksilver until the flames hit the first vampire they touched. The creature went up in an explosive blaze. The vampires around it scrambled back, but the nearest ones weren't fast enough. The fire spread quickly.

"You will all *burn!*" Tasha bellowed in Russian as she rushed at the iron bars, ready to fight. Everett and Vasili both backed away, recognizing a battle dragon's rage when they saw it. She curled her fingers around the bars, and the vampires backed away when the bars burned red-hot beneath her fingers. How was Tasha doing this?

"It worked," Tamsin said with a shaky laugh. "I can't believe it worked."

"What worked?" Vasili asked. Tamsin sagged against the wall behind him.

"Marina is awake. She remembers now." Tamsin slumped against the rocks, and Everett caught her a second before she would've collapsed.

"What's the matter, Tamsin?" Everett demanded.

"Need . . . another boost." Tamsin curled her fingers into Everett's shirt.

"Boost?" Everett echoed as he dropped his sword with a clatter to better hold Tamsin

"Kiss me," Tamsin breathed a moment before her lashes closed and she went limp. Everett lifted the witch's head up, cradling her in his arms before he leaned down and kissed her parted lips. The witch's eyes flew open as she clutched Everett, kissing him back deeply.

"Everett, now isn't the time," Vasili warned in a growl as the vampires seemed to regain their courage to come back in their direction.

Tamsin pushed at Everett's chest. "I'm okay now."

Everett pressed his forehead to hers for a moment and nodded slowly as he helped her stand, and then he retrieved his blade from the ground. Vasili turned back to Tasha, who was leaning against the iron bars, the flames slowly dying in her palms. The vampires huddled at the end of the tunnel continued to hiss.

Tamsin's words came back to Vasili about bringing Marina back, but he had to know for himself. He had to be sure.

"Tasha?" Vasili touched her shoulder. She whirled to face him, and he stepped back as he saw her eyes. They weren't Tasha's eyes. The topaz he'd come to adore was gone. In its place was a beautiful deep brown he'd never thought he'd see again. They were Marina's eyes.

"She's gone," Marina said.

"Gone?" Vasili peered at his mate. "But you are the same, are you not? How are you here and she's not?"

Marina smiled sadly. "I am not entirely sure. Things feel . . . blurry in my head still."

Vasili took her into his arms, holding her. "Do you remember being her at all? She remembered being you."

Marina shook her head. "We are one, but there is division. We cannot merge. I was buried before. Now she is buried."

Vasili's stomach dropped. Tasha was buried. He didn't like that. He wanted her back. But he wanted Marina too . . . and it seemed fate wouldn't let him have both.

"You were very smart, young witch, to cast such a

spell," Marina said to Tamsin. "You knew my magic is not dragon magic?"

Tamsin smiled. "I saw that when my grandmother and the other witches dived into your memories. That your bloodline had an extra power source that was not from your dragon soul."

"Are you strong enough to break the manacles?" Marina asked.

Tamsin blushed and shot a look at Everett. "I am now." She came to Vasili and grabbed the iron manacles around his wrists. His skin heated, and then the manacles fell to the floor. She turned her attention to the cell door and put her hands on the lock. "We came with friends. They will be in the other parts of the tunnel. We weren't sure if we could all fit inside this cell, and it is vital we kill every vampire here, so we split up. We can't afford to let even one vampire escape."

"It would expose supernatural creatures to humans, including witches and dragons," Everett finished for her.

"So be careful once we get clear of this cell. The other Belishaws and your nephews are fighting the vampires."

Vasili nodded. He would be very careful. "We are ready if you are," he told Tamsin.

Tamsin placed her hands over the lock and closed her eyes, chanting softly. There was a flash of blue light and the lock clanged. The door opened without resistance.

Marina stepped forward, the flames in her hand reignited, and Vasili joined her, machete at the ready. He was too weak to transform or use his dragon's power after losing so much blood, but he could still cut down anything in their path.

"Let's go." Everett nodded at the tunnels, and they charged the vampires clustered at the far end. Vasili let out a roar as his blood rage took over. These creatures would pay for all the death they had caused, as would John Dee.

MADELYN HELD HER BREATH AS JEREMY LET THE LAST OF the dragons and Arabella pass through a portal into another part of the tunnel network beneath London. They couldn't allow any of the vampires to escape tonight—they would be even more desperate for blood and beyond the influence of their maker. The human death toll would be significant.

"Did I mention how much I hate this plan?" Charlotte said to Madelyn and Piper as they stood behind Jeremy.

"None of us like this plan," Madelyn said. "But it's the only one we had time for."

The portals were now closed, and Jeremy was breathing hard from the exertion. It seemed like the spells had cost him greatly.

"Rest, Jeremy, or else we won't get them back," Lady Superior counseled. She too looked weary from her spell-casting.

Madelyn kept a close eye on Piper, who had a palm over her stomach. She was five months pregnant, and only a hint of a belly gave her condition away. But Madelyn remembered how she'd felt when she was pregnant with Jackson.

"Mom!" Jackson appeared in the doorway of the library.

Madelyn rushed to him, catching her son in her arms. "Jack! Go back upstairs, now! It's too dangerous for you to be down here. You need to hide, remember?"

Her son shook his head. "I can't. The bad men will open up the door and get me if I stay there."

"Who are the bad men?" Charlotte asked as she joined him. "What bad men, Jack?"

Jack's eyes were wide. "The ones with white skin. I gotta stay here. To warn you when the doors can open."

Madelyn now knew that her son had a gift, one that was thought long lost in the dragon world. She had to trust what he was saying.

"When is the door going to open, Jack?"

"Now!" He pointed toward Jeremy, who suddenly collapsed onto the floor, his body spasming. A blinding flash filled the room as Madelyn shoved her son behind her.

"Someone reversed Jeremy's spell!" Lady Superior shouted. "The portal is open!"

Madelyn, Charlotte, and Piper faced the sudden rush of vampires into the library.

"Jack, hide!" she shouted to her son a second before a pale, hissing creature launched itself at them. The thunderbird inside her screeched, and a pulse of energy escaped her hands, impacting with the vampire a second before it would have sunk its fangs into her neck. The creature vaporized before her eyes, white dust billowing all around her.

"Piper, look out!" Madelyn shouted as Piper, who'd beheaded one creature, was being stalked from behind by another. Nearly a dozen vampires had come through the portal, and Madelyn understood now why Grigori had left her behind. Had she gone with him, no one here would have been able to save their child.

She welcomed the surge of primal rage within her. She drew up the energy of the very air itself as her thunderbird went to war.

THEY WEREN'T GOING TO MAKE IT.

Marina cast a wall of fire to clear a path toward the other dragons. Vasili was right behind her, guarding her back as she forged a path through the danger.

"Grigori!" Vasili bellowed at one of the trio of men they found battling in a loose circle. Marina recognized them as the three sons of Vasili's brother.

"Welcome to the party, Uncle," Rurik shouted back before he kicked a vampire in the chest, sending it backward into another group of undead, knocking them all to the ground.

"Funnel them this way!" Magnus shouted from another part of the large underground atrium. He was driving a number of wild vampires toward the central room.

Marina saw John Dee holding a crystal in one hand and speaking words in front of an open portal that led back into a library. His lieutenants ringed him and protected him while he cast his spell. They had to stop that portal before the vampires could escape.

Marina made straight for the inner circle of vampires but jerked to a halt as one of the witches, tripped and fell. Feral vampires were upon her, biting her exposed arms, but they suddenly fell away, howling as their mouths frothed with blood. Marina slashed her way toward the fallen witch using her flaming hands as a blade. She lifted the woman up by the arm.

"They took too much," Arabella murmured before collapsing.

"We must get her to safety," Marina said.

"I'll take her." Magnus came to her side, and Marina transferred Arabella to him.

"Someone needs to perform the witch light spell," Arabella said. "Tamsin?"

"I'm sure she will be able to," Magnus told the witch soothingly before he shot Marina a grim look. She understood what he was telling her. Tamsin was depleted of much of her power. No one else had the strength to cast such a spell . . . except maybe her. Her magic was neither dragon nor human, but elemental, blood magic older than dragonsong, and not bound by words or potions. Perhaps if she used her dragon magic with it, she could manage to create this witch light.

With grim purpose, she fought through the masses toward Tamsin and Everett. There were easily another fifty vampires still outnumbering them in the giant underground room. Dee was still guarded by Andre and his chosen underlings, and none of them could reach him.

"Arabella is too wounded for the witch light spell." Marina had only a moment to tell Tamsin this before a creature leapt on her exposed back. She cried out as sharp fangs sank into her shoulder, and she threw herself forward in a somersault, crushing the vampire beneath her. She rolled up onto the balls of her feet and spun, catching a sword that Everett threw toward her so that she could sever the vampire's head from its body as it started to rise from the ground.

Marina was breathing hard as she faced Tamsin. "Tell me the spell for the witch light—we don't have time."

"It's not so much a spell as an explosion of power. It would drain any witch. I'm not sure what it would do to you."

"There's only one way to find out. Give me the incantation."

Tamsin breathed the words, and Marina spun back toward the battle. Her mate was facing off the guards around John Dee. Vasili was glorious, his bare chest covered in blood and sweat as he fought valiantly. He was the most beautiful man she'd ever seen. This was the mate she remembered, the mate she'd carried love for across hundreds of human lifetimes. She sprinted toward him.

Vasili cut one of Dee's lieutenants down and lunged through the opening he had created toward John Dee, but he made the mistake of thinking Dee fought only with spells. He didn't see the blade Dee held ready, didn't see the danger—

The knife sank into Vasili stomach.

Her dragon screamed, the sound rattling her body until it felt like her ears would bleed. Even as she reached Vasili, the whiplike crack of John Dee's laughter pierced her soul.

"By blood, I am reborn!" John Dee jerked the knife from Vasili, his eyes turning into twin red flames.

Marina caught Vasili as he fell to his knees, his hands pressing against his stomach. All around them the battle raged, but nothing mattered anymore. Her mate was dying in her arms.

Was this the agony Vasili had felt when she had lain on the cold mountain in the Alps, drawing her last breath? She had faded away so quickly that she hadn't had time to think about what he suffered that day. Now she *knew*. This was the cost of loving a battle dragon. This was why he had loved her other half, Tasha, the gentle, curious woman who had only wanted to explore the wonders of the world in peace.

I took that part of myself away from him—he wouldn't be here if he hadn't felt compelled to find out the truth behind my memories. I killed him.

It would not be long before her own life would be snuffed out by the raw pain slicing invisible wounds in her chest. She would not let Vasili's death be in vain.

This is our last time to fight, old friend, she whispered to her dragon. *Be brave with me, one last time, and we shall avenge our love.*

She lifted her head and stared at John Dee. He held the dagger raised, his ruby eyes fixed on the pulse in her neck as he prepared to take her down. Drops of Vasili's blood still dripped from the blade onto the ground. Marina snarled, her resolve to destroy Dee and his creatures absolute.

I call upon the inner sight,
To free me from this eternal night,
By the life blood of this witch's light.

The breath was ripped from her lungs, and raw power exploded from every cell of her body. There was nowhere to hide from this light. It blossomed out, expanding through the atrium, filling every hole, every corner, every crevice, so bright that none could see.

Marina slumped forward, Vasili cradled in her arms. She landed on the ground beside him. The screams of vampires burning up beneath the witch's light gave way to the soft sound of dragonsong as Marina surrendered to her fate.

CHAPTER 18

xcerpt from Barrow's Journal – My Year with Dragons

I have always felt lost in the world, my place uncertain. I feel differently than most men. I see love in a way that others often do not, and it has left me on the edges of society. But here, with the Barinov brothers, I feel more myself, more centered than ever. Dragons see love not as a physical sensation or even an emotional one—love to dragons is a pure experience that transcends body and mind and resides entirely in one's soul. To love someone, you must surrender yourself to the truth that when all else of you is gone, your love remains in the world, given freely by others who have loved you. To love means you are never truly lost.

TASHA WOKE IN A BED OF POWDERY SNOW, UNAWARE OF how she'd gotten there or how long she'd been there. The sound of dragons sang in her ears. Through the lightly falling snow she saw their shapes, like giant shadow creatures behind a veil of lace. There weren't words to describe what she felt in watching the majestic dragons as they moved in the distance. Was this the other world that Vasili often talked about?

The music of the dragons filled the air around her and seeped into her bones until she felt every note. Beside her, Vasili lay on the ground, snowflakes landing on his skin. He was unmarred by bite wounds, his skin perfectly smooth except for his ancient scars from old battles still evident in worn white lines in a few places.

What were she and Vasili doing here? The last thing she remembered was surrendering herself to Marina to save Vasili. Pain lanced her heart at the memory, of the sensation of fading away into nothing, hoping that he would be happy with the other half of her who now took her place. How was he here now? Surely he hadn't died, not after all she'd done to save him.

Tasha placed her hand on Vasili's shoulder, and he stirred, his blue eyes opening and focusing on her face.

"Tasha?" Vasili speaking her name was the most wonderful thing she had ever heard.

"Are you okay? What happened?" she asked as he sat up.

"We were fighting John Dee and his thralls. And you . . ." He shuddered and wrapped his arms around her, holding her as though he feared she would vanish. "You were gone. Marina was there, but you were gone." He buried his face in her hair, then frantically kissed her temples and cheeks before his lips found her mouth. His kisses were full of ardent longing and laced with a sweet agony she didn't understand.

"Vasili, what happened?" She pulled away to look up at him. "You shouldn't be here. I let Marina take my body so she could save you . . ." Had everything she'd done been for nothing?

He cupped her face and closed his eyes. "I was stabbed by Dee, and you . . . Marina . . . cast the witch light spell. But she was already dying, because I was dying."

His words were a punch to her stomach. She'd failed. She'd given up her life, and he'd still died. Part of her felt guilty at the thought that she was trapped here with him in this quiet, beautiful place that felt like the beginning and the end of a world somehow, like the edge of everything she couldn't even begin to understand.

"So we're dead?" She studied the snowy world full of dragons and dragonsong.

"Yes, but the pain is over now. We're together now, here in this next life," Vasili said, his tone quiet and thoughtful. "We are where we are meant to be." He held her close, wrapping his arms tightly around her.

Tasha shook her head. It couldn't be over. She'd fought too hard, as had Marina, to just die and let it all go. "Vasili, we have to go back." How could she explain what she was feeling to him? This sense of something left undone?

"She's right. You must go back," a voice said from behind them. They turned to see Marina standing there. She pushed back the hood of a midnight-blue cloak and offered Tasha a sad smile. Tasha understood the woman's sorrow. They'd both tried to save Vasili, and neither of them had succeeded.

"Marina?" Vasili stood up and looked back and forth between them, his hands curled into anxious fists at his sides.

"The dragons have spoken, Vasili. You must return," Marina said. "Two sacrifices were made this night, and only one was needed."

"Needed?" asked Tasha. "Needed for what?"

"To reunite me with my dragon through the Heart of Sorrows." Marina looked deep into Tasha's eyes. "We have a choice."

"A choice?" Tasha echoed.

"Yes. One of us can return with him, but only one." Marina's gaze was full of a thousand unfathomable thoughts, and also love. Love for her, the other half that had been so different from her.

Tasha's throat tightened. "But we are the same—we are one. That's what you said."

Marina's eyes softened with sorrow. "I was wrong. We haven't been one for many centuries. When I cast that spell, it left only a part of me to move forward. I didn't understand that until tonight. We can never be fully bound back as one, the way other souls might. My time in the world of humans is over. It is now time for me to dwell with dragons."

Tasha didn't want Marina to just accept her fate. How could she simply agree to leave her mate? As if sensing her thoughts, Marina came toward Tasha and embraced her fiercely.

"My mate is a questing dragon. He hears the call of our people's stones, and he runs toward adventure, not war. All those years I was at his side, I craved the fights his quests would bring. He didn't. He needs a mate who wants to explore a less violent world with him, a mate whose heart is full of hope. The spell I cast left you, my other half, with him. You are the one who must return with him to the world of the living."

"No, Marina, I *won't* leave you." Tasha stepped toward the other woman, toward the other half of herself, wanting to hold on to her so she would not vanish.

"Vasili will love you as he loved me. He would love us no matter who we were. But I was another life. I had my time with him. *You* are the part of me that never had a chance to exist in my much darker and more dangerous world. Now it's your turn." Her words were full of heartbreak, but her face was firm with determination.

It nearly brought Tasha to her knees.

Vasili stared at Marina, his face an emotionless mask, but his eyes betrayed his breaking heart.

"You haven't asked what I want . . ." He spoke with a broken voice that shook Tasha to her core. "I loved you . . . loved our life together. You can't ask me to throw that away."

"I'm not." Marina came toward him and touched his chest just above his heart. "I will be here with you always. You can never lose those you truly love—we're always just far enough away that you'll miss us, but too close for goodbyes."

"We should have had more time . . ." Vasili's words broke like waves upon a craggy shore.

"You will have time to be with another part of myself and let her have a new life, a new chance at happiness with you. I think, deep down, I've always known this part of me was buried and could not surface, not unless it was set free." Marina's smile became bittersweet as she turned back to Tasha. "I have lived. Now it's time for you to live."

The songs filling the air grew louder, the notes ringing like church bells all around them. Marina moved away, slowly vanishing into the snow, her voice joining the dragons. This time Tasha could understand the words.

> *I hold it true, whate'er befall;*
> *I feel it when I sorrow most;*
> *'Tis better to have loved and lost*
> *Than never to have loved at all.*

The words belonged to the human poet Alfred, Lord Tennyson, and Tasha couldn't help but wonder if perhaps the poet had once crossed paths with a dragon.

Vasili reached for Tasha's hand. The second their palms linked, the world fell away into gold light, and only dragon-song remained, the words echoing in Tasha's heart.

> *Without sorrow, there is no joy,*
> *Without darkness, there is no light,*
> *For what you love, you must always fight.*

VASILI'S HEAD THROBBED AS HE BECAME AWARE OF HIS surroundings. He lay in an awkward sprawl on the uneven stone floor of an underground atrium. People moved around him, illuminated by torchlight, slowly wiping ash from their clothing. Vampire ashes. The spell had worked.

He croaked out his mate's name, his voice hoarse. "Tasha."

"I'm here." She knelt on the floor, staring at everyone around her. One of her hands gripped his tightly in her lap. Her eyes flew to his as he remembered what had happened in the dragon realm. The wounds were back on his skin, the smell of his blood a sharp tang in the air around them. He could hear Tasha's thoughts running wild through her head and coming into his. She was aware that her senses seemed a thousand times stronger and her mind felt full of something else . . . a dragon was there inside her head. Her dragon.

Vasili? She spoke to him inside his mind.

Yes, little one, she's your dragon now.

Tasha threw herself at him, shaking hard as he wrapped his arms around her. "I'm sorry that Marina couldn't—"

"Don't," he whispered. "Please don't cry. I can bear anything but your tears." As he held her, he realized that he would always love Marina, the part of her soul that had stayed behind, but she was right. This part of her, Tasha, was the part of her soul that deserved to live now. A new life, a new her, but she was still his mate, and he would still always love her, every part of her.

He gently lifted Tasha's face up to his and smiled. "I love you. I love you more than I can say. Believe this, if nothing else." He brushed the tears away from her cheeks with the tips of his fingers.

"You don't wish that she—?"

"No." He offered her a sad smile. "You are Marina, and she is you. You are the life Marina never had the chance to live. Now is your time, and we won't waste a moment of it."

Everett limped toward them, an exhausted Tamsin by his side. "Are you all right?"

"Yes, we're fine." Vasili touched his stomach gingerly around a freshly healed wound. "And you?" Vasili examined his friend and the way he protectively held Tamsin's hand. He wondered if Everett would risk a relationship with the young woman when it was clear her grandmother had other plans for her. He could only imagine the struggle his friend faced, trying to deny himself a chance to be with his true mate.

"Uncle!" A familiar voice broke through Vasili's thoughts, and he saw his three nephews heading toward him. They'd changed only slightly in the centuries that had passed, and they were all warriors just like their father. He helped Tasha stand and put an arm around her waist.

"Grigori," Vasili greeted his eldest nephew, still marveling at how much the man looked like Ivan. The others, Rurik and Mikhail, favored their mother's dark looks. The shock of losing Ivan was still fresh, but seeing his sons healthy and happy was a balm to the wound.

"Rurik, Mikhail, it's good to see you both as well."

The three brothers exchanged a significant look. "We didn't know what happened all those centuries ago. We feared you were lost."

"I was," Vasili admitted. More than he had ever known. But Tasha had been his North Star, guiding him home.

"And now you're found." Grigori smiled softly. "My son, Jackson, is only four years old. He predicted you were back."

Vasili's brows rose. "He's a seer? I haven't heard of one of those since long before I went into the ice."

"It's been some time," Everett agreed. "They often do not live as long as the rest of us, such is the toll of their gifts. Grigori, you'll need to be careful with him—the visions can be taxing. The last known seer was driven mad by his power."

"Thank you for the warning." Grigori nodded to Everett. "But we must return to the witch house right away. I need to check on my family."

"Jeremy should have opened the portal back up by now," Tamsin murmured, her face turning pale. "Maybe I can open it." She closed her eyes and whispered a spell. A thin beam of light appeared in the air, expanding barely big enough to allow a single person through the opening at a time. On the other side, they could see the library back at the witch house in Cornwall. Everything in front of them was in tatters, as though the library had also seen a battle.

Tamsin squinted her eyes shut. "Go quickly. I'll hold it open as long as I can."

Vasili hustled everyone through the portal and waited for Tamsin, who had to be the last one through. They were back in the library, which had been utterly devastated. Shelves were toppled over, spell books scattered, reading tables smashed over, and chairs broken.

Dead vampires, almost a dozen, littered the floor. Three women stood in a defensive huddle, ready for another wave of attack. A boy stood near behind one of the still upright bookshelves, watching Vasili with wide eyes.

Grigori rushed toward one of the women and scooped her up into his arms. It had to be his mate. "What happened?"

Vasili sniffed the air and caught the scent of a thunderbird. Grigori had truly mated with one? He never thought such a thing was possible. Perhaps in this modern age natural enemies had formed unexpected alliances? He hoped so. He was not a dragon meant for war, not against his kind or others.

"Someone reversed the portal on us, and we were attacked. We're okay, though. Jeremy and Lady Superior are resting upstairs."

Grigori's gaze searched the room for his son. "Where's Jack?"

"Here!" The little boy hugged his father's legs, but after a moment he looked toward Vasili again. He waved at Vasili and Tasha shyly.

This must be my grandnephew . . .

Vasili marveled at the world he now found himself in. He was alive, his mate was alive, and he was back among his family and friends, and yet everything had changed. It would take some getting used to.

The young Jackson came up to him and Tasha.

"Jackson?" Vasili knelt to be eye level with the little boy.

The boy's face reddened. "That's me."

"I'm your great-uncle Vasili, and this is my mate, Tasha. But then, you know that already, don't you?"

Tasha crouched down beside Vasili and held out a hand to Jackson. He shook it eagerly, grinning as if they were old friends.

"You're a butterfly now, Aunt Tasha," he announced proudly. "I told the nice witch lady to make you one."

Tasha's lips parted in shock. "You did? Well, thank you, Jackson. I believe you saved all of our lives tonight. You're a hero."

The little boy shook his head and rubbed a spot on the floor bashfully with the tip of his shoe. "I'm just a boy," he admitted. "You guys fought vampires."

Vasili ruffled a hand through Jackson's hair. "Heroics aren't measured by fights but by actions. You're a hero if Tasha says you are. My mate is never wrong." Vasili pulled Tasha to his side and kissed her until she melted against him. They still had much to talk about, but for now, he could ask nothing more of life than what he had in this room.

Life could be harsh, but it could also be the loveliest thing one would ever see.

SEVERAL HOURS LATER, TASHA FOLLOWED VASILI TO AN upstairs bedroom in the witches' manor house. A hearty meal had been prepared and the library set to rights with a few cleverly cast spells to mend damaged furniture and spell books. The feast allowed everyone to rest after the fight and become better acquainted. Wounds were healed and spells cast for extra safety.

Then Tamsin's grandmother announced it was time for everyone to retire for the evening. She had graciously provided rooms for everyone. Tomorrow morning, they would all leave for London and life would resume. The London Blood Society had agreed to sweep the London tunnels and make sure nothing had survived or escaped.

For the first time since discovering Vasili frozen in the mountains, Tasha felt like she could finally relax.

She clung to Vasili's fingertips as he led her to their room. He opened the door, and they slid into the darkness as he closed it behind them.

For a moment they simply stared at each other before Vasili reached for her at the same time she reached for him. He pulled her into his arms, and Tasha closed her eyes as she breathed in his scent. They danced in the dark slowly, clinging to each other.

When Tasha lifted her head, the moonlight from the nearby window illuminated Vasili's face and made his eyes glow.

"Vasili, when we were in the tunnels . . . I never had the chance to tell you how much I love you, more than I ever realized." She tried to tell him all the things that lay in her heart, but she had trouble finding the right words.

He smiled, the expression full of a love that mirrored her own. "We promised we would always find each other, no matter what, in this life or the next. That even death could not separate us."

It was so strange to think of those first few moments when she'd stumbled upon him in his dragon form, frozen in the Alps. She remembered that moment before she'd fallen through the ice, when she'd glimpsed the figure of a man through the veil of snow, calling her, leading her toward him. But it hadn't been Vasili; she thought she'd seen a man with bright blue eyes and fair hair. She hadn't remembered that fully until she'd seen Grigori tonight and realized that the man looked eerily like him. Perhaps Marina was not the only ghost from the past who'd been helping her?

"Death cannot separate us," she agreed.

She'd thought him a complete stranger then. Now she knew him for what he was—the mate she'd loved for thousands of years. To love and be loved so greatly that nothing could keep them apart was something to make her shiver in awe. It was a wondrous and yet frightening thing.

Unable to deny herself any longer, she stood on her tiptoes to brush her lips over his. With a possessive growl, he dropped his hands to her bottom and jerked her up against his body as he deepened the kiss. His mouth moved over hers as though he was afraid something would stop them, but soon he gentled, his kiss turning slow and seductive. She clenched her legs together as a rush of wet heat followed her sudden excitement. The man was practically fucking her mouth with his tongue, and she couldn't get enough.

It was a long while before they finally broke apart for breath. Heat flushed her skin. She lowered her lashes and bit her lip to hide a smile.

"Want to remind me who I belong to?" she asked in a husky whisper.

"More than anything." His growl was so deep she heard the dragon's voice alongside his own as it rumbled from his chest. "You're mine, Tasha. For the rest of our lives."

"And you're mine." She tugged his shirt and they moved toward the bed until her legs bumped up against it. His blue eyes swirled with gold. She savored the feeling of being caged between Vasili and the tall four-poster bed.

So much had changed between them in so short a time that she was filled with a desperate longing to cement herself to him, to reaffirm her love for him in a thousand ways . . . starting with this.

She had always feared that to find happiness, to find her place in the world, she might lose herself, but it was just the opposite. To find joy and discover where she belonged in the world, she had only to *find* herself. Vasili had convinced her not to be afraid to learn the truth of who she was, both the light and the dark.

She had been so terrified of Marina's ghost and had never stopped to think that she shouldn't be afraid of the past. She *was* the past, but she was also her own future. It was an endless cycle of death and rebirth, loss and discovery, a journey far older than even the stars themselves, for they too died and could be reborn. Death was not a thing to fear, but something to accept with the faith that one would have a chance to live again, in some form.

Vasili cupped her face and peered into her eyes. "What are you thinking about?"

She blinked away sudden tears. "I was thinking about how lucky we are . . . to have found each other again."

He nuzzled her neck and pressed a kiss to her throat. "When it comes to love, there is no such thing as luck—there is only faith." Her body trembled as it became all too aware of his. She let out a soft sigh at the comfort of his body and hers fitting together so perfectly. Her dragon, the one she had unknowingly had inside of her for so long, curled up in contentment in her head.

"Make love to me," she whispered to him.

Vasili's answer was to claim her mouth in a long, languid kiss as though he had centuries to savor her taste. She, however, was far more desperate and tugged at his clothes.

"So impatient, little one." He chuckled against her lips before he stepped back to undress.

"You have no idea." She frantically kicked off her boots and socks before tugging down her jeans and removing her sweater. She wondered if, after all that had happened between them, she would ever not be so desperate for him.

Once he was fully bare, he came toward her. Vasili was her own dark god of perfection, carved out of her deepest fantasies. The dragon tattoo on his chest slowly moved over the surface of his skin as if in flight. It looked free.

"I've always loved this," she confessed as she stroked the outline of the dragon on his skin.

He chuckled and traced his fingers over her left arm. "You have one too." She glanced down and gasped at the golden shimmering shape of a dragon flying on her skin. Her dragon.

Vasili lifted her up on the bed and she fell back,

welcoming him over her. He entered her body slowly, teasing her with every inch of his hard shaft as their eyes locked. Vasili braced his arms on either side of her head, caging her beneath him. She reached up and ran her fingers through his hair as he moved on top of her. Their bodies spoke without the need for words, their mouths learning each other as though for the first time.

The sharp need for him settled into a bone-deep ache within her. He thrust into her, filling her with an intense pleasure that made stars dot the back of her closed eyelids. Fused like this, she felt completely one with him, as though neither of them had a beginning or end. His breath fanned her face as he surged inside her, and the fierce desire in his actions left her no doubt that she belonged to him. She dug her heels into his lower back, holding on as he rode her, claiming him back for herself as their lovemaking became more intense.

Tasha clawed at his back and he nipped her shoulder, both straining for more, always for more of each other, until something inside them both burst apart like a super-nova exploding to life. Her climax drew a cry from her lips, but Vasili silenced it with his mouth, kissing her until she could think of nothing but him. He rocked against her, drawing out little aftershocks of pleasure, then nuzzled her nose with his before pressing a soft kiss to her cheek.

He rolled to the side and withdrew from her body, tucking her against his side, their heartbeats perfectly in tune. They lay there in silence, her head on his chest and his arm curled around her back as she watched the sun clear the horizon as a new day dawned.

"Vasili?"

"Hmm?" His drowsy response made her smile. He toyed with the strands of her hair, the action so natural and intimate that her heart expanded with immeasurable joy.

"Will you take me flying as the sun rises?" She lifted her face, and he gazed at her.

"Do you know how to let your dragon rise to the surface?"

"I think so." She was certain she could remember if she tried. Ever since she'd come back to life in the tunnels, she'd felt her dragon inside of her, quiet, contemplative, but still there. Now the dragon wanted to fly, and her eagerness for it was undeniable.

"Come then, little one. Let's fly."

They quickly dressed and hurried down the stairs, taking the door to the gardens that would lead to the meadow, hopefully without waking anyone else in the house.

They sprinted across the gold-colored grass, and her dragon came to the surface as easily as breathing. Everything around her seemed to shrink as she grew, and then she was flying. Vasili was just ahead of her, his dark form a stunning match to the gold-scaled beast she had become. As Tasha chased Vasili, the dawn made the light on their shimmering wings seem to catch fire.

She remembered the chrysalis spell Tamsin had performed the previous night, and how she'd had to change in order to survive. How strange and yet true it was to realize she'd been like a caterpillar who'd thought her world was about to end . . . only to transform into a butterfly.

EPILOGUE

xcerpt from Barrow's Journal – My Year with Dragons

Men often speak of ages that come and go. The Iron Age, the Bronze Age, the Age of Enlightenment. These periods of time define us and set the course of history. I wonder, as I sit here now in a golden grass-covered meadow and watch the Barinov dragons take flight, if we might be on the cusp of a new age . . . the Age of Wonders.

ONE MONTH LATER

"Are you ready for this?" Vasili asked. He and Tasha stood outside the door to the home she had shared with her mother.

"Not really, but we can't wait any longer." She rang the doorbell, feeling like a stranger at her own home for the first time. She could have used her keys, but she didn't want to scare her mother by bringing Vasili inside right away. Vasili gave her hand a reassuring squeeze as the door opened.

"Tasha?" Naomi Bellamy smiled, but she was clearly confused. When her gaze slid to the man at Tasha's side, her mother's lips parted in surprise.

"Mom, this is my mate, Vasili." She had almost said he was her boyfriend, but that word was inadequate. Besides, it was better to rip the Band-Aid off faster.

"Mate? Tasha, how—?"

"Can we come inside?" Tasha asked.

"Er . . . yes, of course." Her mother let them enter, and she followed them into the sitting room. "When you called me last week, you said you were back in London?"

"I was," Tasha agreed. "Mom, I have something to tell you." Tasha waited for her mother to sit down in her favorite armchair, where she faced them on the couch. Outside, a light rain began to fall.

"You've found your dragon," her mother said.

"Yes, I—wait, how did you know?" Tasha turned to Vasili, but he was facing the window along with her mother, watching the raindrops plink against the windowpanes.

Her mother's gaze drifted back to Tasha. "Because of that." She pointed toward the window and the rain. "And your eyes . . . Your father's eyes would change color too when he experienced strong emotions."

Tasha glanced at Vasili. "Are my eyes gold?"

He nodded and brushed his fingertips along her cheek

to soothe her. She hadn't realized her emotions were running so high. She was about to tell her mother everything, everything about her father and about who she once had been in another life.

Her mother sighed softly. "If you are now a dragon, it means your father was right."

Tasha gripped Vasili's hand tight. "You mean he knew that some part of me was a dragon shifter?"

"He had his suspicions. It would always rain or snow whenever he left, regardless of what the forecast had been. He sensed there was something not altogether human about you."

She thought back to the day she had learned her father was dead, how her father's attorney had an umbrella when no rain had been predicted, yet as he left, it had been storming. Even then, it seemed she'd had that non-dragon magic, the elemental part of herself trying to get out. Had she caused the very avalanche that had led her to Vasili? She'd felt such strong emotions on the mountainside that day . . . it was possible she had.

Naomi twisted her fingers in her lap anxiously. Her light-brown eyes, so like Tasha's, darted about the room, unable to settle on any one thing.

"Your father kept bringing small dragon heart stones home for you, hoping that you would somehow find a way to bond with a dragon. But he feared it too. He knew how dangerous that world was, and part of him wanted to keep you from it."

"Dragon heart stones?" Tasha's hand went to her bare throat. "You mean the necklaces he gave me?" She wore no necklace at the moment, but before she'd left for her travels, she'd always worn one of the necklaces he'd given her. It made her feel calm, close to him.

Tasha let go of Vasili's hand and raced to her room to retrieve the small wooden jewelry box that held the gifts her father had given her. She carried it back to the living room and sat down, placing the box on her lap. When she lifted the lid this time, she felt a strange hum in the air, a whisper of ancient power that she had never noticed before. Vasili tensed beside her, his eyes glowing gold like hers as he focused on the stones.

"Your mother is right. These are dragon heart stones." As a questing dragon, he would know better than anyone what the stones were.

"But changing the weather," Tasha said. "That's not a dragon power."

"No, it isn't." Her mother's gaze grew distant. "Your father said he had known only one other dragon with such a power and that he had killed her in battle. He spoke of it only once, but I could tell it left a scar on his soul."

Her mother's smile grew bittersweet. "I know he wasn't a good man. I know that. His world required him to be hard and cruel, but he wasn't like that with us. We were something he believed he could never have: a true family. He never wanted us to pay for his sins, which is why he had to hide us away."

Tears glistened in Naomi's eyes as she continued. "I loved him, even knowing what he was. Maybe that was wrong, but when you came along, you were this perfect gift for both of us. I believe he saw you as his way of making something right in the world. But that's love, isn't it? Love is trusting that the pain and hard work will all be worth it. When I was pregnant with you, I was afraid. I didn't want our lives to change or to face the danger of being the secret wife of Dimitri Drakor and mother to his only female child. He used to laugh and say, 'Without change, there would be no butterflies.'"

Butterflies . . .

Tasha's heart gave a painful jolt. "He was right about me being different," Tasha began, her hand trembling in Vasili's hold. "Mom, I *was* the female dragon shifter he killed seven hundred years ago. I used to be a dragon shifter named Marina. When she was dying from her wounds, she cast a spell to tie her soul to Dimitri's. He carried me inside him until the time was right, never knowing that he did."

It was still odd to her that she had memories of her father as the dragon who had ended her life so brutally, and then to spend all of her life as Tasha, knowing him as a kind and caring father.

"You were . . . reincarnated?" Her mother's eyes widened, and she turned to Vasili, silently asking them both for answers.

"It's a long story, and I want to tell you everything— everything that I've learned and how I met my mate, Vasili . . . for the second time."

It took Tasha an hour to tell her tale. There were moments where her mother sat very still and other times where she twisted at her skirts until her fingers were red from abrading her skin against the cloth.

When Tasha finished, Naomi was quiet a long time, but Tasha was grateful that her mother had listened. Vasili's warm thigh pressed against her, lending her silent support.

"So this man, Vasili, was your mate as Marina and is now your mate again?"

Tasha bit her lip. "I know that Dad's death hurt you so much, like it hurt me. But I don't blame the Barinovs. What he did to them was wrong, and he paid for that." She paused, sharing a glance with Vasili, who kept quiet. "What I'm hoping for now is reconciliation. If you want, my mate's family is ready to meet you. They want to welcome you into their lives."

Her mother sniffed and wiped at her eyes. She looked far older than Tasha remembered since she'd last seen her. "They killed your father, Tasha. I was robbed of so much time with him. I don't know if I could . . ."

"I know, but you know what he was like—you said it yourself. There was a dark side to him. Perhaps he was a victim of circumstance, or perhaps it was entirely his own choice, but either way, it cost him his life. But it doesn't need to cost us our happiness." Tasha feared her mother wasn't ready to let go of her father's ghost. "Please, Mom. You've hidden from the world in fear for so long. It can't be good for you, you know that. But if you don't like it, we can bring you right back."

Her mother sighed. "Okay. Are they staying close in town?"

"No, they're in London."

"London? But how will we get there? Have you booked flights? I don't have a passport . . ."

Vasili stood and offered her mother a hand to help her rise from her armchair. Ever the gentleman. It made her heart race with an insane burst of joy.

"Just wait and see." Tasha pulled out her cell phone and sent a text message to Tamsin that they were ready. A moment later, a portal to Everett's London home opened up in the middle of the living room. They could see Tamsin standing in the foyer, Everett at her side. Behind him stood the Barinov family.

Tasha's mother gaped at the magical portal.

"Please allow me to escort you through, Mrs. Bellamy." Vasili offered his arm to Tasha's mother.

"Thank you." Her mother's face reddened at the courtly gesture, and Tasha watched her mate guide her mother through a magical portal.

She knew, just knew somehow, that everything would be all right.

JACKSON HELD HIS FATHER'S HAND AS AUNT TASHA AND Uncle Vasili led Naomi to her new family. With a wave of her hand and a whispered spell, the nice witch Tamsin closed the magical portal.

Naomi's fearful gaze swept the room. She only briefly touched on Jackson before moving on to the next person nearby, but it was enough for Jackson to see. The woman's future unfolded before him like a map of beautifully illustrated moments.

Tasha's mother would be happy, and that happiness

would grow with the arrival of grandchildren. In the distant future, her life would end surrounded by the faces of those she loved, with Tasha's hand holding hers until the breeze carried her soul to places far and away.

Breaking free of his father's hold, Jackson rushed toward Tasha's mother, startling her as he reached out and grasped her hand.

"Don't be afraid," Jackson said. "Do you see?" He concentrated on the images of her long and beautiful life and pushed them toward her. It was a trick he'd only managed to master in the last few days. Tasha's mother gasped, and her eyes glistened with tears.

"I . . . Oh my." The woman covered her mout and choked down a sob. "Is that . . . ?"

"Your life," Jackson said with a smile. "It's nice, isn't it?" At least, he thought so. He knew he was just a little boy, but the things he'd seen lately had made him far more grown-up than even his parents could imagine.

Tasha's mother managed a smile. "Thank you."

Aunt Tasha looked between him and her mother with concern. Jackson held out his other hand to Tasha and let her see the future painted so clearly in his mind. Sometimes the future was set, like this future, which was brilliant and bright. Many in his family were the same. He knew they were going to happen as he saw them, that these particular futures were going to happen, whereas some things he saw didn't always come to pass.

He had seen Aunt Piper and Uncle Mikhail were going to live on the coast of Cornwall, where they would fly over the windswept moors as mist drifted up off the sea. Their twins, Jackson's future cousins, would be coming very soon.

He had also glimpsed the adventures of Uncle Rurik and Aunt Charlotte and how they would be exploring the heart of the African jungles when they learned that they were also having children. Two boys and two girls in total would be born to them.

But it was his parents who held his focus the most. Someday, they would be in South America, hunting for news of thunderbirds. That was where his little sister would be born, and her birth would bring the news that his mother wasn't alone after all.

Jackson turned his focus to Everett Belishaw and the nice witch lady, Tamsin, but there his smile faded. There was no certain future here for them. Only questions and possibilities that could undo the fates of so many others.

As the adults all gathered around each other, making introductions, Jackson tugged on Everett's hand. The ancient English drake glanced down at him in surprise. Jackson waved for him to bend down so he could speak without the others hearing.

"You gotta take her away, Mr. Belishaw. Things will be bad if she marries him . . . that warlock. But you can't let anyone stop you, okay? And they're gonna try. Especially her grandma."

"What?" Everett asked.

"You gotta take Tamsin away," Jackson repeated. "Like my dad did with my mom. He said sometimes a dragon has to take his mate away and woo her. I don't know what *woo* means, but it sounds important."

Everett looked to Tamsin, and he became lost in thought. Good, maybe that small nudge would be enough. There were a lot of ways things could go wrong, and sometimes trying to help could actually make things worse.

Jackson saw his great-uncle Vasili watching him. Something in the man's blue eyes, eyes so like Jackson's father's, told him that Vasili knew that Jackson could see into his head. Vasili smiled and gave him a small nod of understanding, which made Jackson stand a little taller.

The world was full of wonder, of love and loss, of sorrow and joy. There were caterpillars and there were butterflies. Everything changed. Everything died at some point and something new grew in its place.

That was the beauty of life, the beauty of change. It lay in the mortality of all things yet never died itself because, with every change, there was always another butterfly waiting to take wing and soar toward the dawn like a dragon.

What a wondrous thing it was to be alive in such an age. And even when someone moved on from the world of the living, there would always be dragons who would remember them. They were the memory keepers of the universe. Nothing was forgotten, so long as dragons were there to sing.

Thank you so much for reading *The Lost Barinov Dragon*! Be sure to stay tuned for new releases from me so you don't miss Everett and

Tamsin's story which will be part of a new series called A Witch's Guide to Love and Magic.

Visit my website at www.laurensmithbooks.com to sign up for my newsletter and follow me for new release alerts!

TURN THE PAGE TO READ THE FIRST CHAPTER OF MY steamy vampire romance *The Bite of Winter*!

THE BITE OF WINTER

CHAPTER 1

So hungry. God, I'd kill to eat.

Zoey Blake gazed longingly through the diner window. Families were nestled in red leather booths, plates of burgers and fries spread out like a feast. The light from the diner beckoned to her, promising warmth and comfort. It was everything she wanted, and everything she couldn't have.

The harsh December wind cut through her thin flannel shirt and whipped her hair hard enough to sting her face. Hunger swelled up inside her like an empty balloon. A moan escaped her lips as she tried and failed to ignore the pain.

A little boy in one of the booths reached with chubby hands to grab his mother's milkshake. He sucked for a long moment on the straw before pulling back, a grin of delight on his face. Zoey could imagine the thick creamy ice cream and the sweet tangy taste of a maraschino cherry.

One of the cooks left the grill and walked toward the entrance, wiping his hands on his greasy apron. When the door swung open, Christmas music exploded into the street. The happy sounds reminded Zoey that Christmas was only a few weeks away. She used to love Christmas: the songs, the presents, the food...her family. She shuddered and buried the painful memories deep inside her.

The cook glanced down the empty street outside the diner and caught sight of her.

"You coming in?" His gruff voice momentarily distracted her from the greasy smell of food.

Zoey gulped and took an instinctive step back, her hands clutching the only real possession she had left in the world. A black leather portfolio. She'd tucked it safely against her chest, the leather barely holding warmth to her body.

"Sorry, I...I can't..." She couldn't say the words. *Can't afford it.*

Even after a year of living on the streets, shame still heated her cheeks. This time, she welcomed it. She was cold all the time, even in the summer. Her jacket had been stolen the winter before, leaving her painfully exposed.

The cook's eyes hardened.

"Then get going. You're scaring off paying customers."

Of course she had to leave. Heaven forbid he toss her some of the burnt burgers or even some moldy buns. She'd have gladly taken them. Far worse food had ended up in her stomach when she'd been desperate.

With a shaky nod, Zoey backed away from the diner and eased into the shadows where the restaurant's light couldn't penetrate. She just wanted to disappear. No one would miss her. No one would care. Everyone she had a connection with was gone. And it was all her fault.

Unshed tears formed at the corners of her eyes, and a shiver from the cold rattled her spine so hard it hurt. Self-pity was not something she could indulge in. But it was hard to ignore her circumstances when she'd spent the last month calling a ragged sleeping bag under a highway overpass home. Food was harder to come by than a decent place to sleep. The homeless shelter was half a mile away and always filled up so fast they had to turn away most of the people who showed up. They served only two meals a day with small portions since their food bank supplies remained low.

Her stomach rumbled a protest. She had to stop thinking about food.

"Damn it." She put her fist in her mouth, stumbling back into the alleyway next to the diner. The ache inside bent her over, and she wrapped her arms around her waist, hugging herself as she prayed the pain would begin to dull. Finally, it abated, briefly, and she leaned back against the brick wall of the alley, breathing slowly.

A soft scuffling was her only warning.

Zoey's eyes flew open. A man in rags and a heavy over-coat lurched toward her. A knife glinted in one hand, the blade flashing when it caught the glow from the diner.

"Hands up!" The man's rotten teeth barely showed behind his thick brown beard.

Terror seized Zoey, squeezing her lungs until she couldn't breathe. Her hands shot into the air.

"Wha…what do you want?"

"Your purse. Hand it over!" he rasped, taking one step closer.

Fear hammered against her ribs until she felt nausea and bile push their way up her throat. "I—I don't have one." She still clutched her portfolio in one hand, her fingers stinging in the cold air.

"Give me your fucking money!" His black eyes gleamed in the dim light. He could have been any of the men she'd seen at the shelter earlier today, only they were sad and broken. This man was something else. Something evil lurked in his gaze and mirrored the spark of his blade inches from her face.

"I don't have any. I have nothing…I'm sorry." Her hands shook as she took a tiny step to the side, inching away from him. Her stomach, once so desperate for food, now clenched as she struggled to control her terror.

"Don't *lie* to me! Give me what you're holding!" Flecks of spittle shot from his chapped lips as he lunged for her portfolio.

"No!" She stepped back, dropping her hands to use the portfolio as a shield.

The man held his blade with one hand and snatched at the black leather book with the other. With a cry of panic, Zoey lost her grip and the portfolio fell to the ground. Pages and photographs scattered across the snow.

"You stupid bitch!" The man snarled and dived at her.

Zoey tried to shut her eyes, but instinct kept her lids wide open. Everything slowed down. The knife slipped between her ribs inch by painful inch. He pulled the blade back out, the cold metal sharp against her flesh as he thrust it in again. Her strangled scream was drowned out by a passing bus.

Her soul seemed to coil up tight before shooting out like a firecracker, leaving her body behind. All the work, the pain, the loss of the last two years was over. Every second she'd cried, every second she'd picked herself back up, none of it mattered anymore. Her attacker pulled the blade back out and cursed before he fled into the street.

Zoey crumpled to the ground, one hand over her side. All around her the pieces of her life, the bits she'd held on to were soaking into the soil along with her blood. Hot liquid oozed through her fingers, warming them. Pain lanced through her chest with every breath. The world spun as she slid onto her back. The night sky above was lit with a smattering of faint stars, like a handful of diamonds strewn over black velvet. Her eyes burned with tears. Blood continued to pump between her loosening fingertips as she grew too weak to keep any pressure on her wounds. A tear welled up, thick and heavy, and eased down the side of her face. The trail of moisture chilled beneath the passing breeze.

Ice dug into her shoulder blades, cold and unforgiving. Invisible rocks dropped onto her chest, and a rattling noise escaped her as she fought to breathe. Her toes were numb and her arms too heavy to move. Muted laughter from people passing on the street seemed so far away. Would they see her? Did they hear her scream? Would they save her? The chill stealing over her warned her it was too late.

Too late for everything she'd never had a chance to do. A life unlived, a heart unloved, a soul alone.

Suddenly, the world around her darkened as a shape blotted out the winking stars. Glowing eyes, the color a wintery green, met her own. They pulled at her with the power of a sorcerer's spell. The sound of her favorite winter song, the "Carol of the Bells", began to echo in the air around them.

"Damn." His voice was rich and dark, a luscious baritone that made even her dying body tingle with lethargic awareness. He held one of her sketches, the white paper looked so sharp against the black sky. His eyes moved from her to the paper, some strange emotion she couldn't read flashing in his gaze.

The man looking down at her had the face of an angel, all angles and lines. His strong jaw, proud nose and bewitching eyes were framed with a halo of black hair from his head as he bent over more to look at her. The epitome of beauty. So handsome that she shivered. She truly was dying, and an angel had come for her soul.

He knelt down next to her. "I can save you. I only need you to trust me. Can you trust me?"

She tried to speak, and although her lips moved, no sound came out. Finally, she managed a jerky nod. Something deep inside her responded to his eyes. They emanated with warmth and the promise of safety shone from their depths. She trusted him.

Her angel did something unexpected. He raised his wrist to his mouth, bit into it and then put it against her mouth. She tasted blood and jerked away from his bleeding skin. A heavy scowl pulled his dark brows down.

"Poor sweetheart, just drink." The Irish lilt to his voice made her feel warm, despite the pain and the chill that threatened to consume her. Something about him, being so close...everything inside her seemed to stir to life in a way she hadn't realized she could.

A hand cupped the back of her head and held her captive while his wrist pressed deeper between her parted lips. Zoey gasped as the blood poured into her mouth and she was forced to swallow. The hand behind her head lightly massaged her scalp, the sensation wonderful and soothing. She relaxed into his gentle touch.

The tang of blood still coated the insides of her mouth when he pulled his wrist away.

"Easy, love, easy. You'll be okay now. I won't let any harm come to you." He cupped her face with his hands, his eyes fixed on hers, capturing her attention. "You will have no memory of tasting my blood. Only that you are safe, you are protected."

"Safe," she whispered. She had no memory to explain the oddly metallic taste in her mouth.

The man stroked her cheeks and nodded to himself before speaking again. "Would you let me take you home and care for you?" His earnest expression was so sharp that Zoey believed it. He wanted to help her.

"Y—yes." It was the only word she got out before she lost control of her body. Her lashes started to fan up and down and then fresh pain hit her like a freight train. She was barely aware of the man picking her up in his arms.

The sky above whirled, and the lights from the stars formed silver circles, like a cosmic Spirograph. She clamped her eyes shut as the man who held her leapt forward. The wind rushed around them, and her long hair whipped around her face but Zoey was lost in the aches surging through her body in tidal waves.

A second, an hour, a month, she wasn't sure when they stopped until she felt them grind to a halt. The pain faded, leaving her sore and bruised. She surrendered to exhaustion, hearing the man speak one last time as she let go.

"I want to keep you, little one. Keep you and never let you go."

IAN KENNEDY STARED DOWN AT THE LITTLE WOMAN IN his arms as he reached his home. She was so light and he knew she should weigh more than she did. A wee waif of a body in ragged clothes. Pity stirred in his chest like a feeble bird with injured wings.

The night was quiet in the small neighborhood where he lived. No one was watching as he slipped the key into the lock of his home and entered. A gray tabby cat lounged on the couch, watching him with silver eyes.

"Lizzy," he greeted softly. The cat let out a soft purr, her tail twitching. She was one of three strays he'd rescued in recent years, much to the frustration of his friend Connor O'Shea.

Carrying the unconscious woman into his bedroom, he eased her down onto the comforter and placed a pillow beneath her head. He grit his teeth when he leaned too close to her and the irresistible scent of blood filled his senses.

But there was more than that. Even dirty and unwashed, the scent of living on the streets didn't repel his senses as they usually did when he crossed paths with the homeless while he searched for hosts to feed from at night. A tingling ache filled his mouth, and with a low curse, he tried to stop the inevitable from happening. But he failed. Twin canine teeth extended down, ready to sink into the flesh of his prey. The flesh of the woman he'd just rescued.

Ian took a reluctant step back. Space, he needed some space or else he might give into his temptation to feed on her. She'd be out for a few hours still. He'd used his innate ability to affect her body's responses to him and gently put her to sleep. It was one of the few benefits of being a vampire.

Vampire. The word still made him cringe, but there was no point in denying what he was. He'd been alive for a hundred and ninety-five years and the older he got, the stronger his abilities seemed to become. Not only could he sway the will of most humans, he also possessed a potent ability to draw his prey to him.

This seemed to be common to all his kind. The glamour, as he liked to call it, was something every vampire possessed to some degree. Something like a pheromone, it drew human prey to them, made their victims susceptible to suggestion, to desire. And with him, it created a false sense of adoration in women. Ian rarely left the house until much later in the night to avoid being around crowds. The glamour often resulted in chaos and strange behavior.

The hollow pit in his stomach reminded him he'd been on the hunt when he'd encountered the young woman being attacked. Feeding was a priority if he was to be around her without succumbing to temptation.

It was obvious she was malnourished and needed care. And more than anything, he wanted to care for her. Too many years had passed since he'd looked upon mortals as something other than...

Shutting his eyes a brief moment, he saw flashing dark eyes, heard a woman's laugh. He'd known great love for a mortal once. Lara. His body had never felt so...human since he'd been turned. But when she'd been taken from him, he'd lost that sense of life and turned back into the predator he was.

Which is why it was so puzzling that in only an instant of seeing that woman attacked tonight, he'd needed to protect her. It was as though in her moments of terror and her dying breaths, she'd called to him—much as Lara had when he'd first met her.

With a regretful sigh at leaving the woman alone, Ian headed back outside, taking only one normal step before his body leapt into motion. The high speed of his travel, yet another one of his abilities, moved almost too fast for human sight to track. Within a minute he was in an alleyway across town, outside the diner where the woman had been wounded. The alley was empty but littered with papers. The papers from a leather portfolio lay inches from a pool of blood.

Ian knelt and began to gather the papers. Each was either a sketch or a photograph, each was captivating. He stood as he collected the binder and the last sketch. It was one of an old man, his face wrinkled, his hands gnarled as old oak tree roots clutching at a blanket as he sat on a park bench. Sadness, regret, loss of memory, all of these were locked deep into the old man's eyes. Whoever had drawn this had captured that, emotions Ian had felt every day since he'd been turned into a monster.

Something inside his chest stung and he gasped. That was odd. He'd never needed to breath before, still didn't, but his body had reacted as though it had. And the little prick of pain in his chest felt familiar, but he couldn't be sure what it was. He thumbed through the other sketches and photographs before he tucked them safely into the black binder.

"We never intervene except to feed," Connor's voice from years ago came back to him. *"The mortals must live out their lives and we cannot intercede."*

But Ian had done just that. Saved the woman from certain death. Why? He'd been moved before in the many years he'd existed like this, but there was something about her, the way she'd protected these pieces of paper as though they were her very life. The way she saw things, the details she evoked, had been a shock to his system. Jerking him out of the seemingly endless night and forcing him beneath a sun, one that didn't burn. There was only warmth here, a craving for something he lost over a hundred years ago.

A woman that made him feel like that? After so long?

That was a woman he had to save, even if only to understand why she affected him like this.

"Connor will bloody kill me when he finds out," Ian muttered to himself. He glanced around. A skinny blonde-haired waitress suddenly exited the diner's backdoor in the alley to throw a large black trash bag into the dumpster. She stilled when she saw him, her eyes first widening, then slowly turning almost slumberous.

The damnable glamour was already at work. He might as well feed while the opportunity presented itself.

"Hello," she said, wiping her hands on her apron and taking a few steps toward him.

Ian tucked the portfolio into his coat and zipped it up to keep the book in place before he started toward the woman.

"Hey there, lassie," he chuckled, hiding the hint of his fangs as they slid out. A wee bite was all he needed.

THE RIVER RAN BLACK, LIKE WATER OVER OBSIDIAN, rushing away endlessly. Connor O'Shea leaned against the bridge railing watching the water. His fingertips clung to the stone, digging in hard enough that it would have ripped his skin apart if he'd been mortal. But he wasn't mortal, hadn't been for almost two centuries. Hunger beat at his insides, hunger for blood. It never ended, the urge to track and feed, to prey on humans, a constant reminder of what he no longer was.

Inside the pocket of his coat, his cell phone buzzed. He

let out a low growl. It was probably Ian. The man never seemed to know when to leave him alone. Once, long ago, they'd been inseparable, as close as brothers. But they hadn't been that way for many years. Something was missing. He knew it. Ever since they'd lost their beloved Lara more than eighty years ago, he'd felt his body, his cursed soul, reverting to its monster state. He was on that slippery slope toward darker urges and he dreaded to contemplate what would happen to him, or worse what he'd do, once he stopped caring about life entirely. The words of Nietzsche regarding staring into the abyss came to mind.

If only I could jump, let the water consume me and swallow me in its depths.

But it wouldn't end things; he'd only wash up on shore somewhere and be that much hungrier.

He shook his head, trying to rid himself of the dark thoughts. In the distance, the city lights twinkled, heightened by a hint of merriness he sensed even from the many miles he was from home. Christmas time. A season he used to love. Now it filled him only with regret, with sorrow and longing...so much longing for a life he'd been robbed of. Being immortal was a curse. Time was frozen, like an old broken clock on a mantelpiece. The tiny metal arms never moved, never let time pass another second forward, and always reminded you that you did not work as you should. You did not belong.

I only want to move forward. So simple a wish, yet he knew it would not be a Christmas wish he'd ever be granted.

Santa doesn't visit vampires. He chuckled, but it was a far from merry sound. *If I saw Santa Claus, I'd likely take a bite out of the jolly old man.*

His phone vibrated again and he pulled it out. Voice-mail. He hated cell phones. The damn things were such a nuisance. All the chiming, the alerts, the notifications. He hit play and put it to his ear. The message was from Ian, garbled and cut out, but the main part of the message was clear. Ian had brought home a woman for Connor to feed on, but for some reason, Ian said the woman liked to be frightened as part of the excitement. Role-play. Bah. It didn't sit well with Connor, but if the woman needed it to enjoy being fed on, well, he'd oblige her.

He stepped away from the bridge and turned his attention toward the city. Time to feed.

www.ingramcontent.com/pod-product-compliance
Lightning Source LLC
Chambersburg PA
CBHW021244190726
48289CB00005B/1481